"MY NAME IS YEN. ON BEHALF OF THE NATIONALISTS, I WELCOME YOU TO MANCHURIA."

Yen told us that we were in the mountains near the town of Hunchun. Our objective, he said, was the Sungari Reservoir north of Hautien, where the Chinese Communists were using several huge caves for experimental work on atomic weapons. The reservoir, he told us, was about 175 miles away.

"We're going to fly there?" I asked.

Lieutenant Damon answered. "No," he said. "We're going to walk."

"Walk?" I was almost shouting. "And what are we supposed to do when we get there? And how do we get away again?"

The reply was silence.

CHINA MAZE

LAWRENCE GARDELLA

WORLDWIDE

TORONTO · NEW YORK · LONDON · PARIS
AMSTERDAM · STOCKHOLM · HAMBURG
ATHENS · MILAN · TOKYO · SYDNEY

CHINA MAZE

A Gold Eagle Book/May 1987

First published as *Sing a Song to Jenny Next*
by E. P. Dutton, October 1981

ISBN 0-373-62104-3

Printed in Canada

Dedication

To my wife, Marie, for the love she has given me throughout our marriage and for the understanding and support she has granted me during the making of this book.

And to the rest of my family: my mother, Muriel; my two daughters, Susan and Janet; my twin sons, whom I have never seen; my grandson, Robbie; my brother, Michael; and my late father, Edmund.

I pray that none of you will be bitter over what you are about to read. I am not and never will be. What happened, I chose freely. May we enjoy the miracle. I love you all.

Acknowledgments

There are many people who put their lives on the line so that I might survive the events described in this book. Scotty, Audy, Charlie, Nancy and Sally, and my numerous Chinese and Mongolian friends; I will never forget you. Gunny, my Marine Corps father and steadfast friend; someday I know we will meet again. And how can anyone ever forget the Dragon Lady, who took so very much upon herself for her cause and for me. Or Kim, the Dragon Lady's sister, whom I can picture today as clearly as when she was a little girl. And those five Americans, friends, who endured with me so many years ago—the promise has finally been kept.

And those others who have given of themselves in recent years so that I might tell my story. Dr. Mortimer Greenberg, who has added years to my life. The staff of Mt. Auburn Hospital, Cambridge, Massachusetts, whose compassionate care has sustained me. Maurice and Alma Woodman, friends who showed me how to begin. Asa Cole, a journalist who believed. Chuck Corn, my editor, who worked so hard in fashioning the final book; you have my lasting gratitude. And Jacques de Spoelberch, my literary agent, a person Marie and I can truly call friend; a man of his word, a man for all seasons.

CHINA MAZE

1

On Friday the thirteenth of July 1979, I was working at a construction job in Cambridge, Massachusetts, right next to Harvard Stadium. I ate my lunch alone, sitting in my car, then went for a little walk in the empty stadium, as I'd been doing every day. It had gotten to be a routine. On this day, when I came out of the stadium, three men were standing directly in my way. They were well dressed, in business suits and shirts with ties, and they looked so young that I had to smile. It wasn't hard for me to guess that they were here to see me about something that had happened twenty-seven years earlier, when they would have been playing in the sandbox.

I walked right up to them, close enough that we could have reached out and touched.

"Forget about trying to have your story published," one of them said, "and we'll pay you twenty-five thousand dollars."

I don't know why I thought that was funny. Anyhow, I started to laugh. "You can take your money," I said, "and stick it…" I started walking, and when they didn't give ground, I put my arms up and brushed them out of the way. I kept on walking, and never once looked back.

The story they didn't want me to tell is the one I'm telling now.

I do not get frightened easily, especially now that I have leukemia, and don't know how long I can expect to live. That is the most important reason I decided to tell my story after waiting nearly thirty years. Until I made that decision I had told the story to one person, a priest. I hadn't told anyone else—not even my wife or my daughters or my parents.

For one thing, I was sworn to secrecy. For another, it's a very strange story. Suppose I told you that in the space of three weeks back in 1952, I traveled a thousand miles through China while our troops were fighting the Chinese in Korea? That I attacked a couple of Chinese Communist bases, one of them manned by Soviets? That I crossed the Great Wall, walked into Peking dressed like a Chinese—in 1952? That I met a cast of characters straight out of "Terry and the Pirates"—a Mongol chief six and a half feet tall, who could hit bull's eyes on a target over two hundred yards off with a bow and arrow— and a Chinese noblewoman who led a band of mountain fighters with no allegiance to either the Communists or the Nationalists?

Suppose I told you that I killed scores, maybe hundreds of people, some with a machine gun, some with grenades, some with a flamethrower, some by slitting their throats with a knife?

Suppose I told you that I made love to the noblewoman and now have twin sons, twenty-seven years old, living in China, that I've never seen?

Suppose I told you that I believe I may have contracted leukemia blowing up an experimental atomic laboratory built by the Chinese in caves deep under a reservoir in Manchuria?

Would you believe me?

Frankly, if I heard such a story I might not believe it either. All I can say is that as God is my witness, it happened, all of it, and it happened to me.

For twenty-five years, from May 1952, to May 1977, I had no reason to tell the story. But in May of 1977, everything started to change. I was working as a foreman on a construction job in Danbury, Connecticut, when I got sick. Three times in two weeks I went to the hospital emergency room, and they couldn't find anything. The third week, feeling worse than ever, I went back to the hospital, and they took some tests. This time they told me I had acute leukemia. They wanted to put me in the hospital right there, but I said no. I called my wife, Marie, and told her I was on my way home. I was so weak that a couple of times I almost drove off the road, but I made it. The Danbury hospital had called my doctor, and when I got home, Marie had us driven straight to Mt. Auburn Hospital in Cambridge. Dr. Mortimer Greenberg, who took over the case, came straight to the point: "If we don't start you on massive chemotherapy, I give you three, perhaps four months."

I asked him, "Will that stuff work?"

He laid out the risks and the side effects. What hit me was that I might have a heart attack or go into a coma. I didn't know what to do. Marie and I talked it over, and she persuaded me it was better to try something than just wait. I stayed in the hospital forty-five days, getting blood transfusions and chemotherapy. For three weeks of that time, I was in a semicoma. Marie tells me that one arm and one leg swelled up so that they were hideous. I don't remember any of that, and there's a lot besides that I don't remember from that time, but that Marie and other people told me about afterward.

They said that when I was in a delirium, I kept talking about tunnels, blood and monsoons—that I kept calling a Chinese woman doctor Dragon Lady.

Marie was mystified. She knew I had been in the Marine Corps, but that's all she knew. In the nearly twenty-four years of our marriage, I had never told her about my experience in the service and now she was upset as well as curious. When I got out of the hospital on July 1, 1977, I was feeling better, but Marie was feeling worse—angry, confused, on the verge of a nervous breakdown.

We've been married since 1953. It's been a wonderful marriage. And here was Marie, who means everything to me, wondering and feeling hurt about a whole chapter in my life that she knew nothing about. I decided I owed it to her to tell what had happened. Once she had heard it, she felt I should put the whole story down on paper.

I still didn't know what to do. Telling Marie was one thing, but having others know was another. I decided to get help, and went to Father Chambers at St. Mary's Church in Franklin, Massachusetts, to ask his advice. He told me to have faith, to be strong—and to tell my story.

So I decided to try. I decided that the American people ought to know what we did there. For one thing, I now have a grandson, and I want him to know. For another, though I'm happy to say that I'm in a state of remission now, who knows how long that can last? The doctor doesn't. Whatever happens to me, I want it all on the record—for Marie's sake, for my daughters' sake and for my sons'—the sons I've never seen.

I had reason to believe that once word got out about this book, there were people who'd want to stop me, and that I'd hear from them. I did—and not only on that day in Harvard Stadium but a few other times that were a lot less pleasant. I'll come to those later on.

But I ought to explain right away that there are some questions I don't know the answers to and maybe never will, and some about which I can't even explain why I've got to remain silent. As a reader, your main question will be: Is this story true? Did it really happen? I can only repeat what I've said before: I believe in God, and as God is my witness, it happened, all of it, and it happened to me.

2

The adventure started on a day in April 1952. I'd been sent to the Marine Barracks at Annapolis, Maryland, full of piss and vinegar as any marine who's only seventeen years old and just out of boot camp. While I waited for a permanent assignment, I was doing routine guard duty and training exercises.

That day, I remember, I'd just come in from a two-day field exercise. After I'd put away my gear, the next step would have been a shower. Before I got that far, a captain and two MPs came into the barracks and ordered me to go with them.

I asked if I should take my gear.

No, they said, no gear.

They led me to the orderly room and from there to a van that was parked outside.

I asked myself what could be going on. I'd been in the Corps only since February and hadn't done anything to screw up that I could think of. Anyhow, I had no choice but to get into the van for what turned out to be an eight-hour ride—where, to this day I still don't know.

When the van finally stopped, I was led into a room in a one-story building. There stood a marine colonel, a major and two men in civilian clothes. Why I rated the attention of so much brass I had no idea, but in a minute I would find out.

It seemed, according to one of the officers, that I'd falsified my enlistment papers. When I asked what he meant, he said I had fraudulently concealed an item in my medical history, that as a kid I'd had asthma. Now that they had found out, I was going to be discharged.

I just sat there in angry silence, wondering how in hell they could have found out, and at the same time realizing that it didn't matter. All that mattered was that I wasn't going to be a marine anymore.

Then one of the civilians said, "Ricky, there's a way we might be able to keep you in."

I was startled to hear him use my nickname. Somebody had obviously done some checking up with people who knew me.

"You haven't shown any signs of asthma lately. We might be able to get around it—if you'll agree to something we have in mind."

"Sir," I told him, "I'll agree to anything."

It might be hard now for some people to believe I honestly said that. But at the time we were fighting in Korea. I was young and I believed in my country—I still do—and as far back as I could remember, I'd wanted to be a fighting man. So I didn't ask any questions. I just listened while the civilian talked about needing a small group of men for a mission they couldn't even discuss. "This mission is important to your country," the civilian said. "And if you go through with it, the chances are very good that you'll be allowed to make the corps your lifetime career."

Thinking about it later, I realized that what the civilian actually meant was not "If you go through with it" but "If you get through it at all."

Well, I never saw things happen so fast. Within minutes after I'd agreed, I was taking off with the two civilians in a small plane. I had no idea then where we were headed and still haven't, other than that we landed in about an hour in a terrain that was barren and mountainous. All I could see was a low building, a kind of adobe hut. Inside it was another marine colonel, along with the same major we'd left an hour before—how he got there I don't know, but he wasn't on our plane—and seven other marines. I spotted one set of lieutenant's bars; the rest were all enlisted men. It soon became clear that they were "volunteers" like me.

One of the civilians told us to sit on the floor. This was where we would sleep that night. There was to be no liberty, no passes—in fact, we wouldn't even be able to walk out of the building until told to—and what went on here was all top secret. No one else spoke. We were given mats and blankets, and told to sack out.

Sleeping was one thing they couldn't order you to do, and I didn't do much of it that night. At one point I thought I'd get up for a breath of fresh air. When I tried the door, it didn't budge until suddenly someone opened it from the outside. There stood three armed marine guards.

One of them spoke: "Nobody goes outside."

I said okay—what else was there to say?—went back to my mat, sat down and lit a cigarette.

One of the guards stuck his head in: "Put that butt out. No smoking."

"Suppose I have to go to the head?" I asked.

"You'll have to hold it till morning," was his answer.

Before long the door opened again, and in walked the major and the two civilians. It was still dark outside. One civilian switched on a bare light bulb. The civilian who'd given us the instructions the night before now told us to strip, to take everything off, including rings, watches, bracelets, even dog tags. We each got a bag to put our stuff in, and then we stood there naked, wondering what kind of mission this could possibly be. Then we each got a pile of clothes and were told to put them on. They looked just like the pajamas you saw Chinese and Korean peasants wearing in news stories about the Korean War.

The civilian who seemed to do all the talking asked if any of us had ever used a parachute. Two men said yes: the one I'd get to know as Lieutenant Damon, and a gunnery sergeant who would become one of the closest friends I ever had. His name was Robert Masters but he was known to us as "Gunny." For the rest of us, the answer was No.

The civilian said, smiling, "Well, you're all going to use one today." It began to look as though there would be no instructions, no chow and nothing to drink. My mouth was already parched—maybe because of the dryness, the heat, or maybe just the thought of my first parachute jump. We were soon fitted out with chutes and loaded into a transport plane. As it climbed, we were given three pieces of advice: first, as you were about to hit, keep your feet together, the knees slightly bent; second, don't let yourself start swinging (you might land on your back or stomach that way, and get hurt); and third, when you hit, roll to the side.

Half an hour after being told about jumping, we were ready to do it. At a thousand feet we were hooked up and literally kicked out the door. I felt the chute open with a jerk, then I seemed to be floating—until I hit the ground. Even though I tried to do everything the way they told me, I came down hard.

We were picked up and the civilian asked if everyone was all right. I didn't say a word and neither did anyone else. Then we were put back on the plane for another jump, this one at just six hundred feet. My chute barely opened before I was on the ground.

This time we were marched back to the hut and given some cold rations. Almost before we had time to finish those, we were told we were going up again, with a special harness because we were going to jump from between three hundred and three hundred fifty feet. After a little rest we were airborne again, and had hardly fallen free of the plane when the chutes opened. It was a much harder landing than the first two, but everybody made it.

Back we went to the hut for a little longer rest and, at last, some hot chow. While we were eating we were informed that we were going to participate in a night maneuver. We would be divided into two groups of four and dropped, in the dark, from about five hundred feet. Each group was to try to capture the other but there was to be no physical contact. Just how far apart we were to be dropped we had no way of knowing. After one group had captured the other, we were to make our way back to the hut. We weren't to know how far from it we were, or in which direction. A lot was never explained. But after all, we were marines.

I was in Group Two, headed by Gunnery Sergeant Masters. Lieutenant Damon was in charge of Group One. It was getting dark as we boarded and took off. After twenty minutes the order came: "Group One out!"—and down they went, one right after the other. The plane circled and my group was ordered out. Gunny ordered us to hide our chutes behind some bushes and then split us into two pairs. Corporal J. F. White was with him, and I was with PFC Jake Craig. The two of us headed up the mountain. After we'd gone about a hundred yards I said, "Let's hold it, sit down and see what's going on." Craig agreed there was no sense in just rushing around. So we stayed quiet, getting our eyes used to the dark—it wasn't really pitch-dark—for about half an hour. Then we heard some movement and I could see two figures silhouetted against the skyline to the west. Those were Gunny and White but we didn't know it yet. To the east we spotted two more figures coming over a ridge. "Shh," I said to Craig. "Don't move." We'd lost sight of the first pair, but I could see the second making their way toward us. I told Craig to stay where he was and keep a lookout while I moved forward cautiously, making my way down into a dry river bed. When I'd gone about thirty yards, there was a tremendous explosion on the mountain. I just lay there frozen, not moving. After an instant I saw two figures racing at me down the mountain. When they were almost on top of me I could see that they were Lieutenant Damon and his partner, a sergeant whose name was Mike Holden.

I shouted, "You're mine!"—and for them the game was over. Lieutenant Damon lit a flare, the signal for the entire party to regroup. Craig came up first, then Gunny and Corporal White. The six of us waited for the other two, but they didn't appear. I never saw them again.

Lieutenant Damon ordered Gunny to go with him and the rest of us to stay put. They were gone for an hour; then they came back, just the two of them, and Damon led us back to the hut. There was no way I could ever have found it, but he seemed to know which way to go. Altogether it must have taken us two hours to get there. When we did, the civilian who did the talking was waiting for us.

He asked coldly if we had any questions.

Of course we did. We wanted to know about the explosion, first of all, and then what had become of the other two men.

He ignored the first question, and to the second all he said was, "We're fighting a war. There's no cheap way out." I never learned anything more about the two men, not even their names. The names I've given for the others are their real ones.

Gunnery Sergeant Masters, whom I would always call Gunny, was the one I would get to know best. He had had nineteen years in the Corps after joining up at seventeen, which would have made him thirty-six at the time. He was everyone's idea of what a marine should look like—rugged, about six feet tall, weighing over two hundred pounds, with a jutting jaw and a dark look on his face. He'd grown up in the streets of New York City, where I'd lived the first eight years of my life. That was one thing that brought us close—a lowly "snuff" and a senior NCO.

Lieutenant Kenneth Francis Damon was slender, about five feet ten, the shortest man in the group, brown-haired, brown-eyed, and in his mid twenties. He never pulled any chickenshit about rank, but he always seemed to have something on his mind. I had the feeling, when I thought about it later, that he must have been an insider on this mission, not a last-minute "volunteer" like the rest of us.

Sergeant Mike Holden was also in his mid twenties, with brown hair and brown eyes, but he was more heavily built and a more outgoing sort than the lieutenant.

Finally there were the three of us who were still in our teens. We looked so much alike that we could have been brothers. J. F. White was a corporal, Jake "Slade" Craig and I were PFCs. We were all over six feet tall, weighing about two hundred pounds, and we were all blond and blue-eyed. The other two were less excitable than I was, and didn't ask as many questions.

One thing all six of us had in common was that we were in great physical shape. Otherwise we couldn't have taken the twelve grueling days that lay ahead.

I had another night without much sleep—and then the ordeal began. There was nothing orthodox about it, none of the usual calisthenics. And no rest. We were pushed continually, we never knew what was coming next, and we never walked.

Each morning Lieutenant Damon had a new set of maps showing the area we'd be jumping into, and the routes we'd have to cover in our allotted time. It might look easy on the map, but on the ground it was something else. We made three jumps every day: in the morning, again in the afternoon and once again at night. And then there was the running. You don't know what exhaustion is until you've run and run and run up and downhill, over rough, broken terrain. The amount of time it takes to cover a mile of that comes as a shock.

Our first day of this workout kept us at it for nearly twenty hours, with short breaks for rations. I had never in my life been as tired as I was then. I hardly had time to wonder where I was, but I did wonder a lot.

The next morning, we'd no sooner hit the ground than live rounds of ammunition were being fired over our heads. I knew they were live because I could hear them whistling and hitting. The firing did not stop—and neither did we. By this time we'd learned not to ask questions. We just took off, sprinting, while the firing over our heads continued—not too high over our heads either—until we were out of range.

From then on, after every jump the firing of live rounds was standard operating procedure. What was good about it was that it made us move even faster and keep our heads down. What was bad about it was that we were terrified. But none of us asked the civilians a single question. We knew they were trying to psych us, but it made no difference: they kept on shooting and we kept on running. Sometimes even at night, after we'd staggered back to the hut and collapsed onto our mats, one of the civilians would wake us and run us again for an hour.

After a few days, *I'm not sure just how many*, we were told we would now begin working with weapons. The three daily jumps and the running went on as before. We looked forward to the break in our routine, but it was a shock to be handed Soviet M43-PPS-43 machine guns. Of course we'd learned not to ask what they could mean.

The weapon had a folding metal stock and a circular magazine holding thirty-five rounds, and it didn't take us long to learn to handle it. From then on we carried it on all our jumps, and used it on the targets that we found along our routes—human shapes that popped up at us as we moved. We'd fire away at them and cut them to pieces. At least it was a great way of taking out our frustrations.

Besides targets—which didn't fight back—there was hand-to-hand combat training. This was with knives, and our instructors were Orientals—Koreans, I assumed, but never knew for sure. Though we were all a lot bigger and stronger than any of them, at the beginning we were pretty awkward, and they never made it easy for us. I got whacked on the head with the dull side of a knife a few times, the lieutenant had a dagger put to his throat, and even Gunny, who was saltier than the rest of us, had a hard time. But with our greater size and strength we learned almost to hold our own against them.

Days went by and we hadn't bathed once. We were filthy. The two civilians, who wore denims, were just as filthy as we were. One day they told us that from now on we would bathe every day in a lake that was nearby. The route after our next jump took us right to it. When we got there, the two civilians were waiting in a rowboat. We all piled in, and when we'd been rowed to the middle of the lake, we were told to jump in and enjoy ourselves for a while. Then we were to swim to shore.

While we were splashing around, we saw that one of the men in the boat was aiming a machine gun at us. By this time nothing really surprised us. We swam around frantically, submerging and then coming up again. Sure enough, in a minute or so the son of a bitch began firing! I suppose he wasn't shooting to kill, but it's something of a miracle that no one was even hurt.

Now our "bath," complete with machine-gun fire, became a part of the daily routine, along with jumping, running and hand-to-hand combat training. The two civilians seemed to enjoy putting us through it all, especially firing the machine gun at us. As a group we began to feel a bond, and there was no doubt that the training was sharpening our reactions and fine-tuning all our senses.

As to why we were there, the mystery remained. The pilots stayed out of sight. The marine guards and the colonel and major had disappeared after the second day. We saw only the two civilians and the Orientals—no one else but each other. We were completely out of touch with the world—except for a curious thing that happened just before our training ended, when one of the civilians gave me some sheets of lined yellow paper and told me to write three routine, undated letters to my parents, saying that I was well and everything was going all right. I suppose the others did the same thing, but we never talked about it. There was very little talking of any kind among the six of us.

On what I guessed was about the thirteenth day, the civilian who generally did the talking told us that the next day our training would end and that the day after, our mission would take place. Now we learned for the first time what it was. We were to jump, using the quick-jump chute, from about three hundred feet, armed only with knives. When we landed we'd be supplied with Russian or Chinese weapons. We would be leaving the next day.

We were in fact to be a special force like the Marine Raiders in World War II. But then came the stunner. "If you are caught," the civilian told us, "there will be no acknowledgment by the United States government of your existence, where you were or what you were doing."

The Oriental clothing had told us something about where we were going. Scared as we all were, I figured that whatever was ahead of us couldn't be any tougher than our training. But then I still had a lot to learn.

After the civilians left, we sharpened our knives, checked and rechecked our chutes and got ourselves ready.

The next morning we were up before dawn, ate and climbed aboard the plane for a flight that never seemed to end. One reason it seemed endless was that the windows were blackened so that we couldn't see anything at all. When we finally set down, the six of us were still kept aboard until finally the hatch was opened and we stepped into a huge crate on a truck that had been backed up to the plane. In this way we were transported to another plane, again with blackened windows, for a flight of six or seven hours—something like that. None of us had watches. When that flight ended, we were once again loaded into a crate. This time, after riding for an hour or maybe a little longer, we were led out of our box into a building that looked like a Quonset hut. Before us stood a marine colonel with rows of ribbons on his chest. He launched into a pep talk about the job we had ahead of us and about what it means to be a marine. I must admit that talk got to me.

Then we had our first really good meal in days. The colonel said we'd be getting four hours' sleep. I showered and walked out into the warm sunlight. It felt good. As soon as I sat down, I began to feel groggy. The next thing I knew, I was being awakened. Possibly I'd been drugged to make sure I slept; anyway, those four hours left me feeling a hell of a lot better.

Then it was back into the crate for a ride to a landing strip and still another flight, this one maybe three or four hours long. Waiting for us at our destination were the two civilians from the adobe hut and a marine colonel we'd never seen before. We all boarded a truck, which we were told would be taking us to our mission plane.

The civilian who'd done the talking said, "Boys, may the good Lord take a liking to you, and may we see you back. Good luck."

The other civilian had never said much. He said only one thing now but that one thing came as a shock: "Your pilots are Chinese."

The plane we boarded was stripped bare inside and we sat on the floor. Holden broke the silence by asking, "Would you say we're going to China, fellas?"

"Nah," I said. "They fired MacArthur for wanting to go to China!"

Lieutenant Damon broke in, "Let's cut the chatter. We're only getting ourselves excited. We'll find out soon enough."

In less than half an hour, the order came to stand up. We stood, hooked up for the jump, and moved toward the hatch, which had been unbolted and slid back. Through the opening I could see mountains—so close it was as though I could reach out and touch them. I don't know how the pilot kept from crashing. But then the word sounded: "Go!" And out we went, headed God knows where.

3

I was born in New York City on November 22, 1934. My father, Edmund Gardella, worked as a laborer and a hospital guard; my mother, Muriel, was a nurse's aide. They named me Lawrence Frederick Gardella, but my grandmother, who thought that was too long a name for a little baby, started calling me Rick and the nickname stuck.

About the first important thing—important to me and to a lot of other people—that I can remember is the start of World War II. At the time we lived at 170th Street and Amsterdam Avenue in Manhattan, and after the U.S. got into the war, there was a military camp—tents, soldiers, all—in a park right near us.

I couldn't stay away from that place; I spent so much time hanging around that the soldiers got to know me and treated me like a mascot. It got so that when my mother wanted me she always knew she could find me hanging around the camp. I remember one year bringing eight or ten soldiers home for Christmas dinner. In those days we didn't have all that much for dinner ourselves. But my mother and father, God bless them, managed to feed everybody.

That was my first encounter with the army, with men in uniform, and from then on I was hooked. I knew what I wanted to be: a soldier, a fighting man. That feeling never changed. It hasn't to this day. That I couldn't stay in the Marine Corps after 1952 is one of the few major regrets in my life.

During the war, we moved to Englewood, New Jersey. Our old neighborhood was getting bad, gangs were starting up, and my parents wanted to get out. But often on a Sunday my mother would bring my brother Michael and me into New York. Those were the days when big movie houses like the Paramount and the Strand had stage shows along with the movies, and we loved to go to those.

One Sunday, while we were walking in Times Square, I spotted a group of marines in dress uniform. I was so hypnotized that I kept following them, and got separated from my mother and brother. My poor mother finally went to the police; and three or four hours later they found me with the marines in a bar. I was maybe nine at the time. My mother was furious, but I wasn't really bothered. I knew then that being a soldier wasn't enough. I was going to be a marine.

In 1947, after the war, we moved to Allston, a suburb of Boston, where my grandparents lived. My grandfather had spent nineteen years in the army and was now the chief armorer at the Commonwealth Armory in Boston, which was the headquarters for the Massachusetts National Guard. He used to take me there all the time, and naturally I loved it. I got to know the men, I read all the manuals, I got to know weapons. Some guard officers who were close friends of my grandfather would let me field-strip the weapons at the firing range after the men were finished, and my grandfather would let me fire. Before I was sixteen I knew how to handle the M-1, the Springfield bolt action, the carbine, the four-point-one rocket launcher, the flamethrower. And I don't mean just take them apart and put them together. I mean fire them, hit targets with them—hit *bull's eyes* with them. I took to those weapons, my hands seemed made for them—even as a kid I had big hands. When I joined the Corps at seventeen, I was six feet and weighed 190. I am not boastful by nature and don't pretend to be anything I'm not. Ask me how many books I've read in the past ten years, and I'll tell you: I've read two. Ask me how I handle an M-1 or a machine gun, I'll tell you. I'm the best.

In 1951, when I was sixteen, I decided I couldn't wait any longer, and I got my grandfather to talk my parents into letting me join the National Guard. Of course I was underage, so I did something I'm not exactly proud of. I fixed up my birth certificate so it would make me old enough. I was a big kid, and had no trouble joining the Guard. By this time, I had finished two years of high school. I was no student. Now I was at the armory every day. I never missed a practice at the firing range. Some days I'd be the only one there, but that just gave me more firing time.

In the summer of '51, our unit went to Camp Drum in upstate New York, where I got some field experience. I was a private, E-2, serial number 21261628, with

Battery C, 180th Field Artillery Battalion of the Massachusetts National Guard. I loved it.

But I was still not a marine, and I became one by getting myself into trouble. In December, someone in the Guard asked me if I could drive a truck. I had no license, and I had never driven any vehicle, let alone a truck, but I didn't want to admit that I couldn't.

I drove that truck right through a garage wall—and was brought up on charges. The brass found out I'd falsified my birth certificate and was underage when I enlisted, even though by that time I was of age. My grandfather did what he could to help me. Finally I was told the charges against me would be dropped if I joined the regular army. "How about the Marine Corps?" I asked, and they said okay.

All of this may sound as though I had only one thing on my mind as a kid. But before then I had been a normal enough teenager. I played sandlot football—I was a tackle—and baseball, where I was a catcher. I got into my share of fights, won a lot but lost some, too. I did about everything the average kid does. But ever since that Sunday in Times Square, when I followed those marines, my one overwhelming ambition had been to be a marine.

When I filled out my medical form I did not mention that I had a history of asthma because I was afraid they might not take me, even though I'd been practically cured by treatments at Massachusetts General Hospital. I hadn't had an attack in a long time, and I wasn't allergic to grasses, trees, dust or pollen anymore—just animals. My father had to sign for me because I was under eighteen, and it may be that he hoped the Corps wouldn't accept me because of the asthma—not knowing that I wasn't telling them about it.

Anyhow, January 31, 1952, I was honorably discharged from the Massachusetts National Guard, and on February 1, 1952, I was inducted into the USMC. I remember asking the recruiting officer if I could get into a paratroop unit—I didn't even know whether the marines had one—and hearing him say he'd put it down on my papers. And I remember boarding a train at South Station along with a bunch of other guys for the long ride, twelve or fifteen hours, down to South Carolina. Then came the bus to Parris Island. As we got near the gate, and I saw the statue of Iron Mike, I felt like shouting, I was so proud and happy just to be there.

My feelings today are the same as they were then. I'm honored to have been a marine. The story of what happened to me I do not blame on the Marine Corps.

Saying it felt great to be there is not to say boot camp was easy. Its whole purpose was to get the civilian cockiness out of you. The DIs, the drill instructors, knew how to do that. You could get thumped for blinking an eye or for scratching a flea you thought had landed on your nose. You were kept from going to the head for hours at a time. And there were other punishments, too, such as having to stand with your arms straight out in front of you, supporting your M-1 on the backs of your hands. But the favorite of the DIs was a fist to the stomach, which knocked the wind right out of you and left no marks. I wasn't a troublemaker—never have been— but I got my share of all those punishments.

Also, there were pushups, chins, and other calisthenics, and there was the time on the firing ranges. There, for the reasons I've already mentioned, I had a head start on the others. I fired sharpshooter on the M-1, qualified with the carbine and the .45 caliber pistol. I was proud to be a marine, and proud of what I could do.

When boot camp was over, I requested combat duty overseas, which in the spring of 1952 meant Korea. I had been told then that I was too young. But now here I was, somewhere over Asia. . . .

4

We were in the air, and this time it wasn't a training exercise. We hit the ground hard—but no harder than we had been doing three times a day for nearly two weeks. We'd landed in what turned out to be a mountain meadow, not a moment too soon either. In the distance we saw the dinky little transport plane being attacked by a couple of fighters. It fell apart in front of our eyes, before the pilot had a chance to maneuver.

And someone already knew we were there. As we were getting our chutes together, a band of about twenty-five Orientals came toward us. I expected the worst. But they seemed cautious rather than menacing. One of them said what sounded like "Quick," and then I heard Lieutenant Damon answer, "Sand." The Oriental seemed satisfied. So *quicksand* was a password and countersign. Where the lieutenant had gotten it, I don't know and didn't ask, though I wondered again whether he knew more about this mission than the rest of us.

The Orientals led us quickly over several miles of this rough, hilly country. Once again I had to be grateful for the training we'd gone through. They brought us to what turned out to be a cave. We kept going deeper and deeper, for maybe three hundred yards, with no light but the flicker of torches, until we got to a blazing fire.

Here, finally, I got a good look at our hosts. They were not in uniform, but all wore pajamalike outfits of light brown or gray. Their pants and collarless shirts were like the ones we wore, but they had twine wrapped around their legs from ankle to mid thigh, so that the loose-fitting pants wouldn't catch on brush or rocks. Some wore black caps and others had cloth bands tied around their straight, silky, jet-black hair. They wore low-cut shoes, a sort of cross between a sneaker and a sandal, similar to the ones we'd been issued.

The big difference, of course, was in their looks and build. The biggest of them was no more than five feet six inches tall, and weighed no more than 125 or 130 pounds. Some were a lot smaller, and when I looked more carefully I realized that six were women—none of them much over five feet tall and weighing no more than a hundred pounds! But every one of them looked strong and lean and fit.

In a moment or so the one who seemed to be their leader spoke in English with a fluency that surprised me.

"My name is Yen. On behalf of the Nationalists, I welcome you to Manchuria. Please sit."

Manchuria! We were all stunned. The lieutenant had turned pale. He might have known more than the rest of us, but I could see now that he hadn't known everything. We were deep behind enemy lines!

Yen told us that we were in the mountains near the town of Hunchun. Our objective, he said, was the Sungari Reservoir north of Hautien, where the Chinese

Communists were using several huge caves for experimental work on atomic weapons. The reservoir, he told us, was about 175 miles away.

"We're going to fly there?" I asked.

Lieutenant Damon answered. "No," he said. "We're going to walk."

"Walk?" I was almost shouting. "And what are we supposed to do when we get there? And how do we get away again?"

Before anyone could reply, a figure came striding out of the darkness and into the circle of the fire. Yen said, "It's all right. He is with us."

We were even more startled when the newcomer spoke. In his "Good morning, lads," we could hear the burr of a Scotsman, and when he got close to the fire I could see that though he was dressed like the others, he was indeed a Caucasian. He was perhaps five feet nine or ten and weighed 170 or maybe less. There was gray in his reddish-brown hair and I could see that he was in his mid forties, but lean, hard and fit like the others.

He told us to call him Scotty, and we were soon to find out that he was the leader of one of the pockets of resistance that were left after the Communists took the mainland from the Nationalists. He explained that he'd come to China in 1935, had worked for Chiang Kai-shek and gone through the Japanese occupation and then the Civil War.

Now he sat down with us and outlined his plan.

We'd be divided into three main groups, each made up of two Americans and three Nationalists who knew the terrain. I didn't like the idea of being split from the other marines, but I could see why we had to do it. These three groups would travel the valleys leading to the reservoir. Two units of Nationalists would be guarding our flanks on the ridges alongside us. The movement of our three groups would be in the form of a spearhead, with Gunny and me on the point, Lieutenant Damon and Sergeant Holden behind us to the left, and White and Craig behind us to the right. The remainder of the Nationalists would travel behind me and Gunny and between the other units. Our communications were to be with lights that could be seen at night only if you wore special glasses. There was a code. For example, one flash would mean ''Danger, stop''; two meant ''Come quickly, we need help''; and the meaning of three flashes was ''Get the hell away as fast as you can.''

Next the Nationalists had a little argument among themselves, through which I could hear Scotty speaking rapidly and easily in Chinese. When that was over, Scotty told us the six women would be divided two to a marine group, increasing the size of each group to seven. I was worried that the women might slow us down. I'd learn later how wrong I was about that.

We were each issued two grenades, two bandoliers of ammunition, and a Soviet machine gun, along with dry food and animal skins full of water. The gun was not the M43-PPS-43 we had trained with, but one with a clip instead of a circular magazine, and it fired a 7.62 mm round. But it did its job perfectly well.

Now that we had our weapons, Scotty made a point of warning us to avoid contact or confrontation with the Communists wherever possible. If we did make contact, we were to break it off as soon as we could, and there was to be no signaling for help except as a last resort. Which meant that we were pretty much on our own.

Scotty's usually genial face turned grim as he reached into his pocket for a bottle, out of which he gave each of us a little pill in a plastic case.

"This is in case you get captured," he said. "You just take it quickly and it's over with. For I tell you, lads, no one can bear up under what they'd put you through if you got caught."

I looked at the thing for a second before finding the pocket in my pants. This was no training exercise. And nobody who fired at us would be doing it just to scare us.

"All right," Scotty said, "we're ready to go. We'll give the groups who are going up to the ridges a start of an hour and a half."

The two groups of three men each got to their feet at once and were off. While the rest of us waited we began getting to know each other. Two of the three men who were going with Gunny and me couldn't speak English. They were brothers, both in their mid thirties, solidly built and missing several front teeth. They looked so much alike that the only way I could tell them apart was by a long scar that one had running from his left ear down the side of his face and neck. We called him Sam One and his brother Sam Two. The English-speaking Chinese in our party was called Charlie. He was smaller and a bit older than the two Sams—maybe in his late thirties. Right away I noticed a special warmth in his smile. Later the thing I'd remember about him most was his great courage.

The two girls with us—and girls is what they both were, teenagers—were called Nancy and Sally. They were cute and tiny, Nancy about five feet tall and weighing less than a hundred pounds, Sally perhaps two inches taller and a little heavier. I couldn't believe the way they kept the pace under the same gear the rest of us carried.

Of course Sam One and Sam Two, Charlie, Nancy and Sally, weren't their real names. What their real ones were we didn't know and didn't want to know: as Scotty had pointed out, if you were captured, the less you knew the less you had to reveal. Though I know their real names now, I still wouldn't want to take any chance of endangering those who are still alive or any of their families.

I tried talking to Nancy and Sally, who had gone to mission schools and could get by with the English they'd learned there, though it wasn't always easy to understand them. I think they said that for a year they'd been moving around with this group, and had had much more fighting than schooling.

We were making our way through the conversation when Scotty approached us. "It's your turn, lads. God bless you. Success to your mission."

Gunny and I and the five "friendlies" took off. Charlie, who knew the area, led the way. We were traveling in the dark, at a trot or faster, the whole time. These people didn't seem to know what walking was, and again I had to think back to the training we'd been given by the two civilians, whoever they were.

After a few miles I said to Gunny, "You're the sergeant here and I'm only the PFC, but don't you think we should separate? Let me stay here with Charlie on the point, you fall back with the girls and the two Sams, so no one can catch us both together."

He took it the right way. "You got something there. Sounds good." Gunny dropped back, leaving me and Charlie up front. Without seeming to make any special effort, Charlie speeded up the pace, and we kept it through the night. Just before sunup, we signaled the ridges that we were stopping, and pulled in behind some rocks. My legs were aching and I was so happy to stop that I didn't even mind the cold dried rice that was all we had to eat.

Soon Gunny, Sams One and Two, and Nancy and Sally were up with us. We couldn't move toward our objective during the day—there were supposed to be as many Communists as there were rocks in this area—and so we chatted again, always with one of us out on guard.

Though Sally wouldn't talk about her background, Nancy told us that her parents and two brothers had been killed by the Communists, and she thought of Scotty as her father. Pointing to Gunny, she asked, "Is he your father?"

I said, "He could be, he has more time in the Corps than I am years old." We laughed at that.

After a while I had a few minutes alone. I stretched out and put my head back to look at the beauty of this strange country, the distances all bluish-green in the morning sun. Before I could think about it, I was asleep, and the next thing I knew, Charlie was waking me for my turn at guard. As soon as I was relieved I went to sleep again, and when I woke up it was late afternoon. I checked my weapon and ate some more rice.

When it was dark we started out again. We had traveled for three hours when we spotted a signal—one flash from the ridge to our left. Danger. We stopped, moved off the trail and squeezed in behind some rocks, where we spent several tense minutes before we got an all-clear and could move on again. All through the night we kept going at the same fast pace. I found it hard to imagine how the people on the ridges could keep up with us in the terrain they were covering.

When it got light we stopped and rested again through the day, hidden away in those mountains that seemed to go on forever.

After it got dark, we hadn't been traveling long when from the left ridge we got two flashes, the signal to come quick. Charlie and I hooked up with Gunny and the rest of our seven, and Charlie led us to the left into a pass, where we were intercepted by someone from the left ridge. The man explained to Charlie that there was a fight going on at our left rear, which was the spot assigned to Lieutenant Damon and Sergeant Holden. We climbed rapidly onto a ridge where we could look down into the valley. Damon and Holden and four friendlies were firing, fighting their way toward us. We added our firing to theirs while the six of them came toward us, and suddenly everything was quiet.

But now we learned that one of the girls in the lieutenant's group had been caught.

We crept along the ridge until we could see the fires of a camp up ahead. When we got within four hundred yards, we could see the girl, strung out naked on a barricade. They were torturing her. What they had in mind to do, I guessed, was to bring us into the open. Her screams made my gut crawl, and I started to get to my feet; I saw Craig look at me and begin to get up too. None of the seasoned people, marines or friendlies, had moved a muscle—but when we started forward, the friendlies grabbed the two of us, knocked us both down, and literally sat on us. I lay there powerless, listening to that poor girl scream all through the night; I didn't see how I could take it, but at the same time I knew it wouldn't do anyone any good to try to go in and save her.

At daybreak we sent out scouts, who came back with a report that the girl was the only one left in the camp. Craig and I were the first ones to the barricade. What I saw was too terrible to describe, even if I'd been able to do it. Blood was everywhere, and pieces of skin. The worst thing was hearing a moan, and knowing she was still alive.

That was more than I could stand. I turned away and was sick. Charlie came up alongside me, touched me on the shoulder, and said he would take care of it. I was walking away as I heard the shot he fired. I didn't dare look back. This was certainly no training exercise, and I had stopped being able to imagine what might come next.

We resumed our journey, which by now took us into canyons so deep that it was safe to travel during the day. After we'd gone for a long time without saying anything, I asked Charlie, finally, who the torturers had been.

"Probably bandits," he said. "With no loyalty to anybody but themselves. If they had been Communist soldiers they would not have gone away."

For another night we just kept going, and with the first light of morning we signaled the people on the ridge that we were stopping for a rest. God knows I needed it by then. But after a while I got edgy. I turned to Gunny, who'd caught up when we stopped, and asked, "Why not let Charlie and me go out on recon, to see what's around?"

Gunny thought for a moment, then said okay, but that we'd be taking off in two hours. "So be back by then. We've got a lot of traveling to do."

Charlie agreed: "Tomorrow we shall be at the reservoir."

I shouted, "What? Have we gone that far?"

"We are getting close."

Why it should have given me a lift to be that close to our objective I don't know, but that is the way I felt when I started out with Charlie.

"We'll be back in time," I told Gunny, "but just in case we're delayed, why don't you start forward and let Sam One lead you? We'll meet up with you one way or the other."

We headed northwest, and after more than an hour Charlie put his hand on my shoulder to stop me. While we ducked behind some rocks, he whispered that there were troops ahead. He'd heard the footsteps. Then I heard them too, and from behind a huge boulder we could see at least six soldiers. They stopped about two hundred yards from us and sent out two flankers.

"They are setting a camp for a stationary patrol. We're close to the reservoir, we shall see many of these," Charlie told me.

"How long will they stay?" I asked.

"Possibly for an hour, possibly for a week."

I asked, "Can we get around them?"

He replied, "With some of the men out patrolling in these mountains, it would take too long. We must go through them."

I realized now that we'd never get back in time and that Gunny and the others would be coming. "I'm heading back," I told Charlie, "to let the others know about these guys. You stay put and watch them. If they move, drop back and we'll meet you."

He agreed and I started back, keeping low. I'd traveled about two miles when I ran into Gunny and told him the situation: that it was either wipe out the patrol or make a long detour.

"Christ," he said. "That's lousy. We can't use guns, we're too close to the reservoir. The place is probably crawling with Commies."

"If you give me and Charlie two more people, and we can catch them asleep, we can take them without guns," I said. I may have sounded like a pro, but my palms were wet and my pulse was racing. I'd never killed anyone.

Gunny thought for a moment and then said, "Okay, you got the two girls."

"What?" I said. Girls? To kill soldiers? I thought he was kidding.

"They tell me they can do anything the men can do," Gunny said. "And Charlie told me the same thing yesterday."

I still didn't care for the idea, but he looked determined, and reluctantly I said Okay.

Nancy and Sally came up and the three of us headed back for Charlie. He didn't bat an eye at the idea of attacking the patrol with a force that was half female, and that reassured me a little. The four of us sat behind boulders waiting for dark, keeping an eye out for the two sentries, and listening to the noises from the camp—loud voices, laughter, a bottle breaking on the rocks. We had four hours until dark, and no water. I cursed myself for not bringing an extra skin of it from Gunny's position.

Waiting, we talked about a plan. We'd have two teams; Nancy and I would be one, Charlie and Sally the other. One on each team would be the throat man, the other the leg man. First we'd go for the two sentries. The idea was to get close and wait for the guard to change before we attacked. As for the others in the camp, we'd wait to catch them asleep or drunk.

When it got dark Nancy and I moved to within fifty yards of our sentry. We waited two hours for the change of the guard. I had plenty of time to think, more of it than I wanted. This was the real thing: I was about to kill somebody. I began to sweat, and soon my clothes were soaked. My heart was thudding and my stomach was jumping. I had to make myself calm down. Nancy must have noticed; anyhow, she came closer to me and put a hand on my shoulder. Then I really had to calm down;

I couldn't let her feel me shaking. I began to feel a bit better, and actually smiled at her.

Finally we saw the new sentry arrive. We took advantage of the change to come within twenty yards, edging closer while the new sentry sat on a rock. The signal we'd agreed on was one, two, then go. When finally we were close enough, I put up one finger, then two, and we made our move.

While Nancy tackled his legs, I put my left hand over his mouth, and with the knife in my right hand I did what I had to do, slashing the blade from left to right, straight through his throat. He didn't make a sound.

We began moving toward the main camp, counting on Charlie and Sally to have gotten their sentry too. The soldiers had a small fire going; some of them were asleep, and the others were sitting on the rocks. One was drinking, and occasionally he would say something to the man next to him. Hoping no one would suddenly go out to trade places with a sentry now, we moved closer and closer until we were just outside the ring of firelight. We watched as the last two men lay down, not sure whether they were drunk or asleep. We didn't dare wait too long.

Wondering again about Charlie and Sally, I signaled to Nancy and we started forward, into the light of the fire, and as soon as we did that I saw movement on the far side of the camp. It was Charlie and Sally, there waiting for us.

I pointed to the nearest man. We went for him, and I'd cut his throat almost before Nancy could get his legs. He never moved. I was shocked by the amount of blood that poured from his neck, but I knew I couldn't stop to be sick. We went for the second soldier, then the third. Charlie and Sally had gotten to the fourth before we could. It was over. Four bodies lay there, besides the two sentries—each one with his throat cut.

Standing at the fire, I realized that I had blood all over me. I think if Charlie hadn't come over and started talking I would have thrown up right there.

"You did very well," he said. "Was this the first time?"

"Yeah. And I didn't think I'd make it past the first one. Is it always this hard?"

"Not this hard. Not easy either."

"We'd better get away from here," I said. "Because when they find the bodies . . ."

"We fix that," Charlie said. "We make it look like bandits." He and the girls went to work stripping the bodies and collecting weapons. I was glad they didn't ask me to help.

I went back to tell Gunny it was all clear, and we started moving again, faster than before, to make up for the time we'd lost. I was grateful when Charlie finally held up his hand to signal a rest. I was gasping as I fell back to tell Gunny so he could signal to the ridges. The ten-minute break had never seemed more welcome—or shorter. Before I knew it we were moving again, at the same agonizing pace.

We'd gone another couple of miles when Charlie signaled a stop. "I can smell water," he said.

I was amazed at how sharp his senses were, and delighted to be so close. This meant we'd be at the reservoir before sunup—which was crucial, now that we'd gotten back into territory where daytime travel was dangerous. We'd covered another four or five miles when Charlie motioned for me to stop, and pointed to two figures on a ridge, outlined against the sky. We crawled toward them, saw that they were soldiers and decided to take them ourselves. Later I thought this was probably stupid, because if there had been more we would have been in trouble. As it happened, we were lucky. This time my knife must have gone straight into an artery, judging from the blood that spurted onto my shoulder and ran down my arm. I stood there frozen until Charlie gave me a slap to get me moving again. An instant later we saw that the two men had been guarding an approach road to the reservoir.

"One mile to go," Charlie told me. "We must hurry."

He didn't have to say why. There was already a touch of light in the east. We broke into a dead run and from the last ridge we saw open land below us, sloping down to the reservoir.

Soon Gunny came up and signaled to the groups on the ridges. Damon's group came in first, followed by White's. Then, to my amazement, Scotty appeared.

"What the hell?" I said. "I thought you'd stayed behind at the caves."

"I was just a few miles behind you all the way, lads," he answered. "I wasn't going to miss this. It's too big a job. And we have to do it quickly, while we can still surprise them."

"I see a road and a reservoir," Damon said. "I don't see any caves."

"The road leads to a tunnel and the tunnel leads to the caves. They are under the reservoir," Scotty said. "The laboratories were built for the Japanese by Chinese prisoners, about ten years ago."

"Is there any other way in?" the lieutenant asked.

"No," Scotty said. "Just that one."

I couldn't help wondering if there would be any way out for us.

5

I stood there with the blood of half a dozen men hardly dry on my shirt, but ready to go on with the mission. Looking back, I don't know how I got over the shock of what I'd done. Part of it was that I was just seventeen, and when you're that young you can bounce back more easily. Part of it, too, was being in a kill-or-be-killed situation. Anyhow, it was lucky that I had no idea what was waiting for me in those caves.

"Twelve of us will go in," Scotty said. Although Charlie argued that Scotty was too important to be one of the twelve, he insisted. "This is too big for me not to go in," he said. "Besides I am the only one who knows the way at all."

The other eleven would be made up of eight friendlies along with Lieutenant Damon and two others of his choosing. He pointed to me and Holden. Of the Chinese, Charlie, Yen, Sam One, Sam Two, Nancy and Sally would be going in, with two others whose names I was never sure of.

"We won't be able to just walk in," Scotty said. "We'll have to get hold of a truck that's on its way in, and take it over."

I pictured the twelve of us, all in one place—and all dead. But there was nothing I could say. And before I could even think any further, we had started moving. We had to back-track a couple of miles to a winding path that led down along the canyon walls. It must have been eight or nine in the morning when we started down.

When we'd gotten to the bottom, we stayed hidden but close to the road. Several vehicles passed, none of them big enough to hold us all. After half an hour we saw a covered truck. Sams One and Two had put on the uniforms of two of the guards we'd killed. Now they stepped out onto the road and signaled to the driver to stop. While they approached him, the two girls slipped up on the other side and leaped for the passenger. In a minute or two the bloody work was done, and the driver and passenger lay dead. The rest of us jumped onto the back of the truck, which turned out to be empty under the canvas except for a few crates.

As we drove toward the reservoir we began to see more and more soldiers, dressed in uniforms of brown or gray—loose, floppy trousers, long jackets with wide black or brown belts and fatigue caps. They paid no attention to us. I found a part of me wondering why we didn't just turn the truck around and get the hell out while we could.

After a few minutes we arrived at a gate and the Sams spoke to the guard. I don't know what they said—or whether it was because the guard was especially stupid or because the Sams were especially smart that they let us through. As we drove on, we passed barracks, several small buildings, and dozens, maybe even hundreds of soldiers. I could see a radio tower, and near the reservoir there were storage tanks—whether for fuel or water there was no telling.

Then we reached another gate. Peering from underneath the canvas cover, I guessed that we'd reached the entrance to the caves. We slowed and then stopped. We'd done so well up to now that I wondered how long our luck would hold out. I could see a soldier who looked like an officer staring at the side of the truck. He spoke to Sam One, and then waved us through. At least we seemed to have picked the right truck!

The road began to dip so sharply that we pitched forward. Then we entered the mouth of the cave, and the road was suddenly steeper than ever—something like a thirty-degree incline. There was plenty of artificial light. I could feel the sweat running down my neck and back, and my mouth had gotten very dry.

I saw that Scotty was fiddling around with the explosives he was carrying. They were light—they had to be—but he'd said they were powerful enough to do the job. I could only hope he was right.

Deeper inside the cave, the road turned left. I guessed that it must be taking us underneath the reservoir. Then it leveled off. Along the side walls we now saw concrete bunkers with steel doors.

The truck suddenly screeched to a halt in front of a gigantic steel door. As we sat there, it began rising. When it got up to about ten feet, four armed guards came out, two on either side of us. One of them started talking to Sam One, who said something back. Their voices grew harsh, and I could see Charlie getting his machine gun ready. I picked up mine too, while the arguing went on, and we peered through the canvas to watch. Suddenly Sam Two fired a burst at the two guards on his side. Charlie poked his weapon through the canvas and opened up on the other two. He almost blew their heads off. The truck lurched forward, then came to a stop directly underneath another huge door. On Scotty's orders we all jumped out and rushed forward. We heard shouts and then we could see men running, lots of them, many in white laboratory coats, the rest in military uniform. At first I saw no weapons and heard no shots. Then Scotty began firing, and I did the same. Masses of men were coming at me and falling as I blasted away. Still they kept coming and falling. Then there were shots from the other side. I could see the lieutenant moving off to the left; I took off to the right. Standing there in the open was Holden, with Nancy and Sally. I screamed to them to take cover, and they raced toward the wall. I could hear the bullets hitting the walls and feel the showers of rock fragments that followed.

Men were charging at us from the front and from a second corridor off to the right. I changed the clip in my gun and resumed firing; we must have knocked over fifty of them in those first few minutes, while we still had the advantage of surprise.

We moved forward, and since I could see that the weapons had been dropped, I slung my machine gun over my shoulder. Many of the dropped weapons were Soviet M43-PPS-43s, the very guns we'd trained with. I'd fire one until it was empty, then drop it and pick up another. There was no shortage of them, and none had been fired very many times.

But now the firing was heavier. Charlie and Yen came scurrying over to me, and the three of us made it to a large metal door with Chinese lettering on it. When I leaned my weight against it, the door opened. Inside was what appeared to be a laboratory with tables, test tubes and other apparatus—now deserted.

From the rear I could hear someone screaming at me. The voice sounded like Scotty's but I couldn't make out what he was saying. I grabbed one of my grenades and pulled the pin. Now I could hear Scotty yelling, "Close the door! Get the hell out of there!"

I tossed the grenade, and a blast of flame came at me as it exploded, knocking me off my feet and leaving me dazed. I felt pain in my legs. Looking down, I saw that my trousers were in tatters and that there was blood on them too, but I didn't think I could be badly hurt.

I got to my feet and started forward. The noise of gunfire was so loud that I felt deafened. About twenty yards ahead of me and to my left, I spotted Lieutenant Damon sprawled on the ground. I started running, then fell onto my belly and crawled toward him. I managed to drag him to an angle in the wall, which gave a little cover. He had been hit in the shoulder and was bleeding. As I lay there and wondered what I could do for him, Sally came over and pointed to herself, apparently meaning that she'd look after him. As I started to move off, I saw her looking at my legs, and waved my hand to tell her I was okay; I guess I looked worse than I felt.

I made my way to Holden, who also looked at my legs. "I just slid into the plate too hard," I told him, not sure whether I was reassuring him or myself.

With us now were Charlie and the two Sams. That made five in all. I assumed the others were along the opposite wall, though I couldn't see them. I must have been on my third enemy gun by then. Half the time I couldn't see anyone because of the gloom and smoke, but in that corridor, with those men coming at us, it would have been hard not to hit someone every time I fired. Still they kept coming. I wondered then, as I did afterward, whether they might have been drugged. Whatever it was that kept us alive, I thank God for it.

I came to another door, like the one I'd gone through, opened it, and tossed a grenade—only this time I got out of the way at once. Again there was a blast, and a fire that filled the place with such thick smoke that it was hard to see anyone. I was on top of Scotty and Nancy almost before I recognized them. Scotty was leaning over trying to fix an explosive onto a big boiler. Yen was at the far end of the boiler, firing like hell. To the right I saw another door, opened it, and went in. I reached for a grenade and was getting ready to pull the pin when something made me stop. It was a pile of crates. Going closer, I saw that my first quick glance hadn't been mistaken. Stenciled on them were the words MADE IN U.S.A.

I stared for a moment longer, then headed for the door. I lobbed the grenade on my way out, then slammed the door and made my way back to Scotty. By this time he had fixed the charges with a timing device. He looked up at me and said, ''The time has come for us to make our exit.''

The piles of bodies in that murky tunnel would be almost impossible to describe. And still people kept coming at us. We backed our way to the lieutenant, who by this time was only semiconscious. For his sake and ours we had to get out of there. I said to Scotty, ''Why don't you and the others take the lieutenant and start moving out? Yen and I will come right behind and cover you.''

He started to say No; but he knew I was right, that we couldn't all stick together. So he got the others moving, half carrying, half dragging the lieutenant with them. While they retreated, Yen and I stood still and kept firing as fast as we could. The others had piled a few enemy guns near us to make things easier. We began to back off, still firing; and just as I was thinking there was some kind of miracle about our not being hit, Yen groaned, twisted sideways, and fell on his back. He lay there motionless, and I saw that he was dead, killed by a shot in the middle of the forehead. I went on backing off and firing, in a scene as near to hell as I hope I ever get—the bodies, the smoke, the flames from fires started by the explosions, the new blasts as the fires spread.

I would fall back, stop and fire, fall back again, until finally, turning around, I caught sight of the truck where we'd left it parked, directly underneath the doorway. Sam One had been clever; the Communists had tried to close that door to trap us, but the truck had kept it from dropping all the way. As I backed up under the door, the shooting seemed to have eased off—maybe because of the fires and explosions. I lobbed a grenade under the truck and took off up the ramp, hearing the truck blow, and looking behind me as the steel door dropped down the rest of the way. After about fifty yards, I caught up with Scotty and the others. "How come you haven't gotten any further?" I yelled. "Yen is dead. That place is an inferno. Let's go!"

I could see from Scotty's face that he thought I was getting hysterical. Maybe he was right. While he was telling me to calm down, a tremendous blast sent us all toppling. "There goes the boiler!" Scotty shouted. He seemed almost cheerful.

As we started up the ramp again, I noticed a locked wooden door. I fired at the lock, breaking it open, and went in. The place was an arsenal, with countless stacks of weapons. In one corner stood case after case of .30 caliber ammunition, each one stamped WATER-TOWN ARSENAL, WATERTOWN, MASSACHU-SETTS, U.S.A. For a couple of seconds we just stared. But we knew we weren't safe there.

When we stepped out of the bunker, streams of soldiers were coming at us. This time they were moving down the ramp. We dropped to the ground, set up our weapons and started firing. Again, I couldn't understand what must be going through the minds of those Chinese, pouring in and letting us knock them off as though they were ducks in a shooting gallery.

I yelled to Scotty, "Don't you think we should get back into the bunker?"

"We'd be trapped. We'd never get out!"

"Yeah, but they're going to run over us here!"

The stench from the smoke was worse than ever. Many of the lights had been knocked out, and visibility was down to almost nothing. The less they could see, the better; but still, if they fired enough, they'd hit something. All we could do, meanwhile, was fire up the ramp.

Next I heard small arms fire hitting near where we'd left Lieutenant Damon. I crawled over to him and saw that he'd been hit again, this time in the neck, and that his left ear had been shot off. Nancy and Sally were trying to stop the bleeding, but they didn't have any medical supplies. Damon was in bad shape, but since there was nothing I could do to help him, I moved back and went on firing up the ramp. Thanks to the Watertown Arsenal, Watertown, Massachusetts, one thing we had plenty of was ammunition.

Suddenly the firing at us stopped. We stopped firing too. The quiet was terrifying. We all stared up the ramp, and then Holden said, "There's another bunker up there. Let's go and have a look at it."

Scotty opposed this. "Some of those bodies on the ramp might not be dead ones."

"Yeah," I said. "But all the same, there might be something in there that we could use. It's a chance. If we just stay here, we've got no chance at all."

Scotty thought for a moment. "Well, at any rate it's thirty yards closer to the top. Try it, but be careful."

Holden, Charlie and I started moving up in the semi-darkness, around and over the bodies. The quiet made it even scarier. There was a lock on the bunker door. Holden shot it off, and the sound of his gun in that stillness was awful. Going in, we found another arsenal, but with heavier stuff—bazookas, grenade launchers, rockets—along with more ammunition, all of it made in the U.S.A.!

We emptied a crate, loaded it with an assortment of weapons, and pulled it out of the bunker. We'd intended to drag it down the ramp, but Scotty was already moving the group up to us. We got down quickly, and I looked at the lieutenant. He was unconscious, but the girls seemed to have stopped his bleeding. I asked how they'd done it.

"With earth, wrapped in cloth," Scotty said.

"But that'll infect the wounds, won't it?"

Scotty shook his head. "It works. I don't know why, but it does."

The stillness was broken by the rumble of something that sounded like heavy machinery. I asked what. "Sounds to me like tanks," Scotty said.

Holden picked up a couple of bazookas from the box we'd filled and handed one to me. He gave Charlie some rockets and motioned for us to go with him to the opposite wall of the tunnel. When we got there, Holden asked, "Did you ever fire one of these?"

"Oh sure," I said. And I had, actually—three times in training. Looking across the tunnel, we saw Scotty standing with another bazooka. Nancy was behind him, ready to supply him with rockets. He called out, "If we can get one or two as they come around the bend, they'll block the tunnel."

Holden waved back; the noise was getting closer. I wondered whether the tanks would be carrying napalm. If they did, they could fry us right where we were.

All we could hope was to knock out the first couple and hold back the rest with them.

"Here they come," Charlie shouted, and as the first tank appeared, we all let go. That first round tore the turret off. We reloaded as fast as we could. The second tank got past the first before we could aim. I fired at the tread, Holden at the turret, Scotty at I'm not sure what. Anyhow, we stopped that one too, and set it afire. No more tanks could make it through now. But then men started coming down on foot. I fired one rocket at them with the bazooka. When I saw Holden drop his and reach for his machine gun, I did the same. We started firing, and some of the men fell, while the rest backed out of sight behind the shattered tanks.

Another lull—for how long we had no way of knowing. We used it to get back to the others near the bunker and resupply ourselves with ammunition—and it was a good thing we did, for almost at once we heard something bouncing down the ramp at us—something that might have been a rock, until it exploded. So they were just going to lob grenades down at us. We heard more of those come clattering down, and Scotty yelled, "Back into the bunker!"

We made it somehow, dragging the lieutenant with us, and slammed that heavy wooden door behind us. Then we just sat and listened to the grenades going off on the other side. I thought, Now we're trapped. They can come for us whenever they want. The barrage of grenades went on for what felt like ten or fifteen minutes, though it may have been a lot less than that. Then everything was quiet. I looked around, began counting, and realized that two of Scotty's Nationalists were missing. Dead or captured. Counting Yen and the lieutenant, that left four casualties and eight of us still able to fight. I wondered if the other side knew how few of us there were.

Breaking the lull Scotty said, "Let's go!" and threw open the door, firing as he stepped out, with three of us just behind him. We surprised a couple of dozen soldiers at point-blank range, wiping them out almost before they could fire.

More lights seemed to be going back on, as though there had been a switch to emergency power. The longer we stayed here, the smaller our chances of getting out would be.

"Let's head up to the tanks," Scotty said, and we started out, moving as many weapons and as much ammunition as we could, while the two girls dragged the lieutenant. All the way, we were having to step over the bodies of the men we'd killed. The idea that twelve of us had been able to do all this was stupefying. Even though there was more light now, the air was thick with smoke, which cut down the visibility. We could still hear an occasional explosion somewhere in the tunnel behind us. As I remembered, the bend in the tunnel was about half-way up. That would be a good point to defend. I kept fearing that sooner or later one of those explosions would bring the reservoir down on our heads, which may have been nonsense, but the higher we went the safer I felt.

We reached the burning tanks and looked around the bend at a sight I hadn't believed I'd ever see again—

daylight. But we weren't out into it yet. Two more tanks were approaching, followed by men on foot. While Scotty prepared to aim a bazooka, I remembered something I'd seen back in that last weapons bunker—a flamethrower. I started back for it. When Scotty screamed, "Where are you going?" I yelled, "Be right back" and kept on going. Inside the bunker, it took me a while to locate the flamethrower. Just as I was thinking I must have been mistaken, I saw it—another item marked MADE IN U.S.A. I picked the weapon up and mounted it on my back.

When I got back to the others, the second group of tanks had already stopped. The Chinese soldiers were now ahead of them, firing and moving down at us. Our people lay on the ground, trying to use the two burning tanks near us for cover and firing back as hard as they could.

Wondering if the flamethrower would even work, I dropped to one knee, ignited the spark, and opened up. A stream of fire came shooting out that all but scared the hell out of me. What it must have looked like to those poor guys while I waved it back and forth from wall to wall like somebody watering a lawn, I can't even imagine.

Demoralized, the poor bastards turned and ran. Scotty immediately signaled us to move up the ramp. We were firing as we went, to keep them moving. After a few yards we came to the bodies that had been scorched. Even through the smoke, you couldn't miss the nauseating stench of burnt flesh. I tried not to breathe or to look, but to keep moving.

The return fire had quieted, but now it started up again. I heard a woman scream. Nancy had been hit. As she went down, Sam One fell too. He and his brother had been carrying the lieutenant. I hesitated, and then Holden yelled, "Let's go, Ricky! Spray 'em! Give 'em a hot shower!" His yelling seemed to touch something off. Scotty started screaming, and all the rest of us did too. I turned on the flamethrower as we advanced, shouting and firing, hoping they'd think it was a regiment. We could see more and more daylight as we went forward and it was a beautiful sight, even through all the smoke.

The two tanks had stopped just inside the tunnel. When we passed them, we were at the very entrance. Though we saw no one, and there was no firing, we didn't dare walk out into the daylight. Thinking I should save as much fuel as I could, I took the canisters off my back and handed the flamethrower to Holden, telling him I was going down to see how Sam One and Nancy were. Sam Two went with me, while the others stayed put. Sam Two stopped at his brother's side, and I kept going until I found Nancy. Lying there, she tried to smile at me, but I saw that she was badly wounded in the hip. I leaned down and picked her up; she was so light that carrying her was no trouble.

"I be fine," she said, adding my name, only it came out "Licky." I smiled down at her, kissed her on the forehead, and started uphill toward the brothers. Sam One had been hit in the legs, but with some help he could walk. Sam Two had picked up a piece of lumber to use as a crutch, and he headed up the ramp on his own feet.

Then we heard Scotty yell, "Get back! Quick!" while he and the others started running toward us. "Planes!" Holden shouted. I heard the sound, and looking back, I saw that two incendiary bombs, possibly napalm, had landed at the entrance to the cave. The angle was such that the flame didn't reach us, and having nothing but concrete to feed on, it didn't last long. A second and then a third plane made passes at the entrance, trying to drop bombs down the ramp, but with no more success. Then each of the planes made a second pass, dropping conventional bombs. The concussion was terrific but the tunnel held and we were far enough down into it to be safe.

When everything was quiet again, the six of us who were still in shape to walk—Scotty, Charlie, Holden, Sam Two, Sally and I—left the lieutenant, Nancy and Sam One where they were, and made our way to the entrance. Smoke was thick around us, but everything was quiet.

"Some of this may be radioactive," Scotty said. I asked what he meant.

"The stuff that's used to make atomic bombs. I think it was in the labs you blew up," he told me. "It said so on the doors. At least I think so. I didn't get to read it very carefully."

"Can you read Chinese?" I asked.

"Oh yes, lad. I've been here seventeen years, you know," he said.

Not having much idea about the danger of radioactivity, I said, "Well, anyhow I got away with it."

He looked at me in a strange way. I don't know whether the material I blew up was radioactive, even now. But ever since I found I had leukemia, I've thought about it a lot.

Right then, I was more worried about getting through the next few days, or even the next few hours. I kept thinking about how, here in Manchuria, I'd been using guns and ammunition from Watertown, Massachusetts, maybe fifteen minutes from my hometown—stuff that had also been used on me!

Holden broke in on my thoughts. "Listen, kid, you did a hell of a job."

"I'm not such a kid," I told him. "I'm nearly eighteen."

He laughed. "How'd an old guy like you get into this assignment?"

When I told him about my asthma, and how I'd volunteered so as not to get thrown out of the Corps, he laughed again. "You got shanghaied, just like I did," he said. "Except that I got caught stealing food in Korea. The army was getting hot chow, but our old man, the bastard, decided marines were too rough for that, and fed us nothing but cold K rations. So we decided to get some good food from the army. We drew straws, and I was the one that got the short straw. I got caught, and then they gave me the same kind of choice as you. Volunteer or else. So here we both are. Maybe we should call our congressmen."

Holden told me that Gunny had gotten here the same way. "Punched an officer in Korea because the guy wanted to get his squad wiped out. They put it to him, too, and he had nineteen years in!''

"Those bastards," I said. "I wish we'd get some word from Gunny. I wonder what he's doing."

"What I hope he's doing, lads," Scotty said, "is rounding up friendlies in the countryside to come and get us."

There came the drone of planes again. We backed down the tunnel as fast as we could, dragging the wounded, and hid behind the disabled tanks. We heard the explosion and felt the concussion of more conventional bombs. This round tore up some concrete. There was a silence and Holden and I ran up the ramp to see what was happening. When we saw no sign of anyone, we signaled to the others to move up.

Of the twelve in our group, three were dead; the lieutenant was unconscious, Nancy disabled, Sam One wounded but able to fire, the other six of us in good shape. I wondered again if *they* had any idea how few of us there were. Then I heard Scotty call out, "Hey!" Looking up, I saw a convoy of trucks rolling toward us. Almost at once we heard the report of mortars, and saw the shells exploding. But the trucks were still coming at us.

Scotty shouted, "Let's go for them before they get out of mortar range!" The others of us who could walk began moving forward, firing toward the Communists as they got out of the trucks and advanced toward us, also firing. We dropped to the ground and kept at it. It was soon clear that the Communists were under small-arms fire from our rescue party. The question now was whether we could link up with them in time.

We began edging in the direction of the friendlies, hoping to make it easier, though we didn't know whether we could get to them. I could now see them advancing on the Communist troops in a skirmish line. They were taking heavy casualties, exposing themselves to save us. Realizing I wasn't far from where I'd left the flame-thrower, I turned and ran back for it.

Lifting the canisters, I felt totally exhausted. I also knew that if one of those canisters got hit by a bullet it would be the end of me. When I was a little closer, I dropped to the ground and opened up with the flame-thrower. It burned everything on the ground in front of the troops, and they broke and ran. By now I must have been really hysterical. I got to my feet and went on fir-ing the thing until it was out of fuel. Once I'd put it down, I picked up a machine gun and started using it—blazing away even when there was no longer any return fire, until the clip was empty.

When we finally reached the boulders where the main body of the friendlies were, Holden really lit into me: "You watch yourself, kid, or you're going to flip. Only a crazy man would run out in the open the way you did!" But if my nerves were shot, I guess probably his were too.

Then I saw Gunny, ran over and put my arms around him in a bear hug. I don't think I was ever so glad to see anyone.

Things looked a little better now, even though we were in the midst of enemy territory, and God knows how many hundreds or thousands of miles from any escape at all.

6

Gunny said they'd heard the explosions and seen the smoke, and that when the soldiers headed down that tunnel, "We figured you'd had it."

"Yeah," I told him. "I guess we thought pretty much the same ourselves."

White and Craig joined up with us as we were walking. Glad as I was to see them, the feeling didn't last long, because I immediately saw some men carrying Lieutenant Damon, who was still unconscious most of the time. He was in bad shape and I wondered how long he could hold on. Nancy, though weak and in pain, was able to smile. She reached out to me and I closed my hands around her tiny ones.

"It's a nice day," she said.

"It's a beautiful day." I knew what she meant—that it was good just to be alive.

I asked Scotty what would happen next.

"We head for another cave about twenty-five miles from here; we've used it often."

"But with Nancy and Sam One and the lieutenant all needing medical attention?"

"When we get there," he said.

"Well then, why don't we move?" I said. "It's going to be dark soon."

It was our fifth day in China. Gunny heard the tension in my voice.

"You been through a lot, kid," he said. Hearing this from a man practically old enough to be my father helped to calm me down.

They'd made stretchers for the three wounded out of branches, rags, vines and I don't know what else. I kept being amazed at the resourcefulness of these people, and began almost to believe they could do anything—these tiny people, some of whom weighed only half what I did, and who carried loads of gear as big as I could manage without ever appearing to get tired.

Right then I was certainly tired. We were moving through rough country, along small paths or no path at all. When at last we got to the cave, its many turns and twists all lit by torches, it was a relief to see the wounded being cared for by people who seemed to know what they were doing.

We hadn't been there long before a group of friendlies came in with what appeared to be prisoners. Some were in the dress of Communist soldiers, but there was one in denims who was much bigger than the others. As he moved closer, it became clear that he was not Chinese. Then Gunny, Holden, White, Craig and I all stared in amazement. He was the same civilian who had put us through our training for this mission, seeming all the while to enjoy watching us suffer!

Scotty hadn't missed our stares. "You lads look like you've seen a ghost. Either that, or you know this man."

''We know him all right,'' Gunny said with a scowl. At a signal from Scotty, the civilian was led away from the group. Gunny and I followed him and stood by as Scotty asked, ''What are you doing here? With them?''

The civilian looked at him with the same kind of smirk we'd gotten from him while we trained, but he never opened his mouth.

Scotty now explained that when his men had captured one vehicle far behind the convoy that had attacked us, they had found him on board. He hadn't been tied up and hadn't seemed to be a prisoner.

''Somebody should strip him and search him,'' Gunny said. At an order from Scotty his men undressed him. In his pockets, along with several scraps of paper with notes on them, they found some shipping bills from Lushun—the Chinese name for Port Arthur—and a small blue card that read UNITED STATES OF AMERICA, CENTRAL INTELLIGENCE AGENCY, with the seal of the United States, the man's photo and the name Joseph Roberts.

Would a real CIA man be carrying around an ID card like that? The question occurred to me, too, and to this day I do not know the answer. Could he have been a double agent of some kind? I don't know that either. But anyone who has read about the activities of the CIA during that period will know that some very strange things were being done in 1952.

''What are you doing here?'' Scotty asked him once again.

And again Roberts stood there like a sphinx, not saying a word.

Scotty asked Gunny, the ranking American in our party now that the lieutenant was out of action, "Do you want us to try to get some information out of him?"

We all knew what Scotty meant. Gunny said No, and Scotty went off to his men, taking along Roberts's papers. Everybody had questions and no one had any answers. After a while, Scotty came over to tell us he hadn't been able to learn anything new, either from talking to his men or through the radio transmitter he carried.

"I know you lads are tired," he said. "Better get some sleep now. I don't think it will be safe to stay here much longer."

"Where are we going?" I asked.

"A place where we'll be safe," was all he would say.

We'd all learned not to argue, but to grab whatever rest we could. I don't know how long I slept—only that I was groggy when they awakened me. I was still groggy when we got under way. The Chinese people in our party didn't take long to get started—which I suppose was one reason they were still alive.

As we moved out into the night, Holden came up alongside me and Gunny. "I'm worried about the lieutenant," he said.

"Yeah," Gunny said. "But I'm worried more about Scotty. He's nervous, and I haven't seen him that way before. Something must be wrong."

Altogether there were about thirty in the group and Scotty was up front. But this time I decided not to keep my questions to myself. I worked my way forward to ask, "What is happening? Where are we going?"

"To another cave in the mountains, about fifteen miles away." He wouldn't say any more.

I'd been walking in silence for a few minutes more when I heard the sound of planes.

"Probably looking for us," Scotty said before I could say anything. "We're safe in the dark. But we've got to get to the cave before light. They're not going to give up looking."

I began to drift back to the others, passing Roberts and the five Chinese prisoners, all with their hands bound. They were being moved along quickly by their guards, who carried automatic weapons. Though I hadn't got much out of Scotty, I also knew that we owed our lives to him and his men. Clearly our mission had been important to them; but now that it was done, they were protecting us, doing their best to help us get away, simply out of generosity. As for Roberts, how was anyone to know what side he was on? He hadn't given the least sign that he even knew us!

It took us many hours to reach the cave, and once again, while I wanted to do nothing but rest, Scotty and his men were arranging with incredible speed for guards and patrols, and had the transmitter in place. Scotty could work his radio only for very brief intervals, for fear of being picked up by the Communists. After he'd tried for a while and gotten nothing, he came over and said, "Let's talk to Roberts again."

Roberts had now been tied separately from the rest of the prisoners, who had their feet bound and were roped together by the neck at four-foot intervals. Their faces showed no expression, as if they expected nothing but the worst.

We took Roberts deeper into the cave, where Scotty tried a new set of questions, with no more success than before. Once in a while he'd manage that unpleasant smirk, or he'd lick his lips. Though I can't say that I felt sorry for him, I did have a certain respect for the way he clammed up. After a while, at a word from Scotty, one of the guards half led, half dragged Roberts away by the rope around his neck. Then the five of us marines walked over to the fire and sat down, all of us a little stunned at what we'd gotten into. We started talking as a way of comforting ourselves.

Holden said, "Rick and I were shanghaied. And I told Rick about you, Gunny. So that makes three of us."

I looked curiously over toward White and Craig, and White smiled.

"I went over the hill," he said, using marine slang AWOL. "For a girl. I thought I was going to marry her, until one morning I woke up and found the girl and my money gone and the MPs standing there. That's when I got my choice of this or a court-martial."

I looked at Craig. "How about you, Slade?" We'd taken to calling him that, I don't really know why.

"I was a little different," he told us. "I was on the boat to Korea when they offered me this. I took it. I guess I must have been out of my mind."

"Christ, no," I said. "Could you have had as good a time as this in Korea?" For the first time since we'd all been together, we had a good laugh.

I knew that Nancy's parents had been killed by the Communists. Now I asked Sally about hers.

"They are alive," she answered. "They are fine, I hope. I have not seen them in four years." She paused, dropping her head as if she were ashamed. "They are Communists. My brother, too. But I do not believe in Communism."

I really felt for her—a youngster like that, having made such a decision. "How old are you?" I asked.

"Seventeen. Like you." When I looked at her questioningly, she added, "Seventeen, *almost*."

I grinned at her and put a hand on her shoulder. The two of us were standing there like that when Scotty came back. He'd been looking at the papers Roberts had with him and that had given him an idea. "I want to talk about it with him here, to see the expression on his face."

The guards brought Roberts to the fire and sat him down. After asking him once again if he had anything to say, Scotty held up the papers. "I have something here I want you all to listen to," he said. While he read we all watched Roberts.

"Six ships sunk. Will not return. They feel the same as most of us. But hung his name on anyway. Sing a song to Jenny next."

At these words Roberts reacted for the first time with an interested, wary look.

"Does that mean anything to you, lads?" Scotty asked.

No one said anything.

"I'll read it again. Listen: *Six ships sunk. Will not return. They feel the same as most of us. But hung his name on anyway. Sing a song to Jenny next.*"

"Who the hell is Jenny?" Holden asked. Instead of answering, Scotty began to talk. "Here is what this *might* mean. The message could be in two parts. The first, *Six ships sunk. Will not return,* could refer to the six of you. As for the second part, I don't know about *They feel the same as most of us,* but the *hung his name* could refer to Hungnam and the *song to Jenny* could be Songjen. They're both in North Korea. They could be talking about real ships sunk at those places or they could be talking about other groups of operatives like you, who will not return."

Watching Roberts, I could see that for the first time he was shaken. He had turned pale and it was costing him some effort to go on looking unconcerned. The message had shaken me a little, too. What did it mean: *Will not return?* That they hadn't made any plan for us to get back? That they didn't *want* us back?

Just then two friendlies came running in and spoke heatedly to Scotty.

He turned to us. "Communist troops are two hours off and headed this way."

"Jesus," Gunny said. "What do we do now?"

Scotty didn't answer immediately, but turned and spoke again to his two men. As they ran off, he said to us, "We have to split into two groups."

"Oh no," Craig said. "Not again!"

"If they catch us together, we're all gone," Scotty reminded him. "If we split up, the pursuit has to divide, and that gives us both a better chance. And if they did catch one group…'' He shrugged, then went on quickly, ''We join up again after we've gone through the mountains.''

I asked, ''What about the wounded? They're not going to be left?''

''I don't know the answer to that,'' Scotty replied. ''They'll hold us up. It's a decision we've got to make.''

''I'm staying with the wounded,'' I said, and the rest of the marines agreed.

''You can't all stay,'' Scotty told us.

''I haven't asked anybody for anything yet,'' I said, ''and I won't ask for anything except this. I'm staying with them.''

''Okay,'' Scotty said. ''One more can stay. We'll draw lots on it. You know that whoever goes with the wounded travels slowly and has the least chance of getting away.''

While we all stood there, he picked up five empty machine-gun shells and a pebble, and handed them to a friendly to whom he spoke in Chinese. ''One of the shells has the pebble. The one who gets it goes with Rick and the wounded. Gunny, Holden, White, Craig—and I— will draw.''

White was the one who got the shell with the pebble in it. ''First time I ever won anything,'' he said with a grin.

Then Scotty was urging us on. ''We don't have much time. Ten men will go with Rick and White and the three stretchers. You have to try to make it over that mountain before dawn. It's going to be a terrible climb in the dark. We'll take the prisoners, try to draw the Com-

munists away from you and then regroup at the fork in
the next valley, on the far side of the mountain.''

"Do any of the men you're giving us speak English?'' I asked Scotty.

"Harry and Joe do. They also know the way over the
mountain.''

As Gunny, Holden and Craig came up to White and
me and reached out to shake our hands, I realized how
close we'd all become. Holden said, ''Watch it, you guys.
Be careful.'' And Gunny added, ''We want to see both
of you at the fork.''

"We'll be there,'' White said, and we all shook hands
again.

We were getting ready when I noticed Sally and the
three other girls standing off to one side, looking tear-
ful. I walked over and put my arms around the four of
them—they were tiny enough for that. ''Nothing is
going to happen,'' I said. ''We'll be together again
soon.'' Then I turned quickly and walked away. I was no
better at handling sentiment than they were.

White gave Scotty a wave as our group picked up the
stretchers. ''See you at the fork,'' he said.

"Aye, lads.'' With that we were on our way.

Outside the cave we encountered a strong wind, which
made the going over rocks and the steep terrain all the
rougher. Nancy and the lieutenant were strapped into
their stretchers. Sam One decided he wanted to walk,
with the help of his brother. The wind blew still harder
and finally it began to rain. In the darkness, the trail became narrower and the rain made the rocks slippery—in

places where we knew a slip would have sent you a long way down the mountain.

All at once while Harry and I were carrying Nancy's stretcher, my right leg slid out from under me. I managed not to let go my hold on the stretcher, and Harry immediately lowered his end of it so that Nancy wasn't hurt. But my leg had taken a deep gash as I went down.

"I fix!" Harry had to shout to make himself heard in the wind.

Familiar by now with Chinese home remedies, I yelled back. "Reach into Nancy's pocket. She has some earth in there." Harry found it, wrapped it in a strip of cloth ripped from his own clothes and tied it around my leg. Then we picked up the stretcher and were on our way.

Six hours later, the rain and wind still raged and we were still struggling up the mountain. An hour after that, Joe, who'd gone out in front as point man, came slipping and sliding down to tell us we were only half a mile from the top. I looked at the sky; the rain had slackened, and there was a hint of light overhead.

I asked, "Are we going to make it before daylight?"

Joe shrugged. "We try." Then he turned and started back up again, pulling ahead of us effortlessly. I was exhausted and I could see that White was also gasping for breath. But somehow we plodded on. Encouraged by knowing we were near the top, we could ignore the bruises, the scrapes, and the fatigue. By the time we got there, it was near enough daylight so that we could see into the valley. There was no sign of any human being.

In this light the valley below us looked brown, with a thin mist rising.

After that moment's look, we were scrambling downhill, which was at least faster going. But it was also slippery, and all the more dangerous because we were so tired.

I asked Harry whether we could stop for a rest. "No time," he answered. We kept going until all at once we heard the sound of planes. We raced for the shelter of rocks as four fighters came over so low we could have been throwing rocks at them. In the valley they made a U-turn and headed back toward us. I was sure they'd spotted us, but they went right by, up the mountain and over. In a moment or two I could hear the sound of bombs and machine-gun fire, and realized that they were going after Scotty's group. I muttered "Damn it, they're after Scotty," and Harry said, "Lots of caves."

"But if the planes pin them down, troops can catch them."

Harry said nothing. We both sat in silence until the barrage stopped. As soon as the planes were gone, Harry stood up and said, "We must go, we have no time." Once again we picked up the stretcher and were heading down the mountain.

Later we heard the planes again and dove for cover. Apparently we weren't what they were after, since they went for what looked like the same spot as before. It made us feel helpless, not knowing how Scotty's group was making out. But there was nothing to do but go on as soon as the last barrage died away. This time we made it to the bottom. What had looked from above like an open valley was really a series of narrow canyons—just the sort of place to invite an ambush.

I stared at the rock wall ahead of me and asked Harry, trying not to sound nervous, "How do we get around this?"

"Opening in wall," he told me. "We go through, then we rest for minute."

It was a good thing we had someone who knew about the gap in the wall; certainly none of us would ever have spotted it. We clambered through and sat down. Our wounded were either asleep or unconscious; Nancy's color was good, and she appeared to be holding her own. Lieutenant Damon was another story: he looked terribly pale and weak.

Harry hadn't been kidding when he said we'd rest "a minute." We had hardly sat down to rest when he was saying, "We must go."

I gestured toward the lieutenant: "He can't go much further."

Harry only shook his head and said again, "We must go." I was relieved of stretcher duty now, and that made things easier for me.

But not for long. Suddenly there was a burst of machine-gun fire from somewhere near. I looked back and saw the bearers hurrying the stretchers into the protection of the canyon wall.

I yelled to Harry, "Where's it coming from?"

"Not know!" he shouted back. Down behind the rocks, we could see White waving at us, and we started crawling toward him. Our question about where the firing came from was answered as streams of men came at us from both sides of the canyon. We were trapped. And from the look of them, I feared they had more men than we had rounds of ammunition. I was wearing my usual two bandoliers, with a total of maybe a dozen clips in all, each clip holding thirty rounds. I also had one grenade.

I turned to White and asked if he had any grenades.

"No!" he yelled back. I saw sweat pouring down his face, and felt it on mine, from the heat and tension.

I looked over at Harry. "Any grenades?" He put up one finger. That made two, not enough to be worth much. I called out to White and Harry, "You two hit the rear. The friendlies and I will concentrate on the front!" They waved at me and we moved about twenty yards apart. The Communists were firing rifles, machine guns and mortars, heavily and without any direction. We were firing back more carefully, because we had fewer men and a hell of a lot less ammunition. The sound of the mortars got uncomfortably close. I looked around at White and Harry, just as a mortar round hit squarely between them, on the very spot where I'd been maybe thirty seconds before. Seeing neither of them move, I began crawling toward them. I got to Harry first and saw that the back of his head was blown off. I scrambled over to White, praying that he'd be okay. When I reached him I almost choked. Blood was seeping from his mouth, nose and ears. I put an arm under his head, trying to cradle it, but at the same time I could see that he was beyond help—even though his eyes were open and he was staring at me intently. I think he was trying to say something, but all he could do was cough up more blood. Looking down, I saw that his stomach had been blown open. As I met his eyes again, he tried to move his left hand. Then it fell back limp, his head sagged, and I knew he was dead.

Tears sprang to my eyes, and I heard myself saying "Oh God, oh God!" Then my feelings became a blank.

What happened then must happen to a lot of men in battle at those times when they seem not to care about their own lives. I certainly wasn't thinking that now I was going to risk my life, since in my own mind I had no possibility of staying alive. I was already dead; it wasn't as though I risked anything.

I remember to this day the detachment of that moment. There was no heat, no rage, but a kind of icy cold. First I reached down and grabbed White's machine gun. Then I stood up and emptied it. It was hard to fire and not hit someone, because we were in a tiny semicircle with our backs to the canyon wall, and they were all around us.

I tossed White's gun aside, picked up Harry's, stood to my full height, and emptied it. That was a dumb thing to do—except when you think you're already dead and it doesn't matter. But somehow I got away with it. I dropped Harry's gun, picked up my own, and headed toward the stretchers, where I could see Sam One, Sam Two and three other friendlies.

In that very instant, while I moved toward them, both Sams were hit by the same devastating burst of machine-gun fire and blown off their feet. No one could have survived that; I knew without looking. At least the two brothers had been killed together and probably that was what they would have preferred.

Looking down at the stretchers, I saw at once that Damon had been hit by a mortar fragment and was dead. Nancy was unconscious, but from the movement of her eyelids I knew that she was still alive.

Besides the two of us there were three friendlies, who were still firing away. I started firing again, too, as the attackers kept closing in. Their bodies were literally using up our ammunition.

Then, one right after the other, the three Chinese with me got hit. I was the only one firing back. Yet I was aware that the firing was picking up. Why the Communists were bothering at this point I didn't know. I started to grope in my right pants pocket for the little pill in its plastic case. I found it and clutched it, then reached for the knife I carried in my belt. I am about to die, I told myself.

The gunfire increased, and suddenly I realized that it was not being aimed at me! I spotted what seemed to be a squad of Communist soldiers leaving their cover—but instead of running *toward* me, they were running *away!* This new firing, which I had thought was aimed at me, had really been intended for them!

My first thought was that it must be Scotty's group, except that the source sounded like small arms, machine guns and mortars, and there was too much of it to have been coming from them. Then I spotted a whole bunch of new people. Whoever they were, they weren't in uniform: a ragtag bunch, no two dressed alike, wearing odds and ends, including what looked like old American fatigues mixed in with the more usual pajamas. None of them wore hats, but most had headbands—strips of cloth tied around their foreheads. I knew they weren't on the Communists' side, but it still wasn't clear exactly whose side they were on. They waved at me and I waved back. More and more of them kept appearing, until there were about a hundred. I saw someone moving through their ranks—a tiny person, perhaps five feet tall, but with the authority of a leader—who said "Hello."

It was a woman's voice. If I'd been less surprised, I would have said something by way of thanks for saving my life. But all I could manage to say just then was "Oh!"

7

As she came closer, I could see that she was dressed just like the others, in a mixed-up uniform and a headband. She was slender as well as short, weighing probably no more than a hundred pounds. She was also young, and—as became clear at a second glance—very good-looking, with dark eyes, dark shiny hair, and unusually prominent cheekbones. She had a gorgeous smile, and she smiled more openly than the others.

Her English was quite good—fluent, even sophisticated, though you'd never mistake it for American speech. "How are you?" she asked, and when I said "Fine," she said, "You don't look fine."

Now I knew who she looked like. You have to remember that I was just a kid and not much of a reader. But I had read the comic strip "Terry and the Pirates," and to me this amazing woman looked just like the Dragon Lady. When I blurted this out, she asked, looking amused, "Who is the Dragon Lady?"

"You know, in 'Terry and the Pirates.'"

"Who are Terry and the Pirates?"

I must have looked embarrassed, but her smile reassured me. "Oh, it's a long story," I said. "But there's a Dragon Lady in it, and she could be you."

"Dragon Lady. A good name. I like that name." Then her smile went out. I was to learn how quickly she changed from one mood to another, but this time I was startled.

"Are any more of you alive?" she asked.

"This girl is the only one," I told her. "We had two scouts out, but they haven't come back."

The woman was looking down at Nancy. "Who is she?" she asked.

"She was helping me escape from the Communists." I didn't think I should say anything just then about the other group.

"You don't like Communists?" she asked.

"No I don't."

"I don't like them either," she said sharply, making it sound both angry and businesslike. Coolly, she asked, "Where are the others?"

"Dead," I answered, still wary.

"No, I mean the *others*."

I still hesitated. "Who are *you*?" I asked. "Where do you come from?"

She smiled again. "From these mountains. They are my home. They are *my* mountains."

Since she hadn't said what her name was, I asked, "Is it all right if I call you Dragon Lady?"

She appeared to think for an instant, then nodded briskly. "All right. Dragon Lady." Looking me up and down, she noticed my leg. "Are you hurt?"

"It's all right." Actually the leg was hurting a good deal, but the bleeding seemed to have stopped.

"We'll fix it." She spoke to a couple of men, who sat me down and put a kind of cream on my leg, making it feel moist and cool, and covered it with a bandage. "It will be better," she said. "Now tell me where you are going."

Again I tried to dodge her question with another question of my own. "How did you get here?"

This time she laughed out loud. "I told you. These are my mountains."

"How did you know we were here?"

"We saw you coming over the mountain. Then we saw the Communists attack you."

I would have liked to ask why they hadn't tried to warn us, but I didn't dare. I was, I must admit, a little in awe of this woman.

Then I was distracted by the smell of meat cooking somewhere. "That smells good," I said. She shouted an order, and in a few minutes someone brought me a plateful of meat. It might have been horse, buffalo or snake for all I knew, but it was delicious. I carried the plate over to Nancy. She was lying on her stretcher with her eyes open, and she smiled.

"Want some food?" I pointed to the plate, and she nodded. I tore off a few tiny pieces, propped her head up and fed them to her. She ate slowly, but between us we had soon finished everything on the plate. After that, a man brought a kettle full of hot water, which I used to rinse the bandages on Nancy's hip, and the wound itself. It didn't look red or infected. When I'd retied the bandages, I took off my shirt, wrung it out and bathed myself. By the time I put the shirt back on, several of the

Dragon Lady's men were laying out the bodies. I went over and found Damon and White lying side by side. They both looked so terribly pale, these two fellow marines whom I'd never really gotten to know, even though I'd been with them now for something like three weeks. The lieutenant must have been in great pain during that time, but he'd never complained. Much of the time he'd been unconscious—thank God for that. I'd never found out why he'd taken on this mission, or whether he'd been hooked up in any way with Roberts and the other civilian. He'd seemed a decent guy, not a sadist like Roberts. White had been closer to my own age, and less of a riddle. We'd at least had a few laughs together.

When I bent down and went through their pockets for identification, I found nothing except the little pills in their plastic cases. They were now just two corpses, several thousand miles from home, with nothing on them to tell the history of how they'd lived and died.

"We must bury them now, soldier." The Dragon Lady's voice made me jump.

I objected. "There's nothing here but rocks."

"We shall cover them with rocks. We must do it."

I could feel tears rising, and I turned away, embarrassed to be crying in front of this tiny woman. But here were these two men about to be covered with rocks—no coffin, nothing to mark their burial places, no word to their families. I turned away, trying not to shake. But of course she knew I was upset. And now her voice sounded soft. "It's all right. We will take care of it, soldier."

Marines don't use the word *soldier*, and I wanted her to know that. "I'm not a soldier," I said.

"I watched you," she answered. "I saw how you were ready to die."

"Why did you wait the way you did, and then help us?"

"We cannot help everyone," she said. "We cannot fight all the time. There are too many Communists and not enough of us. So we are careful. But we believed we should not let you die." Someone called to her, and she answered and was gone.

I walked over to look at the other bodies: Sam One and Sam Two, both brave men, and Harry, whom I'd just met. How very easy it was to imagine my own body lying beside them!

I heard a commotion, turned and saw why the Dragon Lady had been called away. About twenty captured Communist soldiers had been led into the area, and were now being herded into a circle. The Dragon Lady walked around them and pointed to one who seemed from his uniform to be an officer. She pointed to the rock wall where I had come so near to dying, and the rest of the captives were led there and lined up against it. They all looked petrified with fear. Several dropped to their knees. Now, while I looked on in disbelief and horror, the Dragon Lady walked to one of her men, took his machine gun, and calmly opened fire on the captives. When she had emptied the clip of ammunition, she borrowed a second gun and emptied it. With a third gun, she walked up to the corpses and put a burst of fire into each one.

Her face could have been a mask. Handing the last gun to someone, she approached the officer, now the only survivor. His hands were tied and he had been pushed to his knees, where he huddled with his head bent over. One of the Dragon Lady's men handed her a thick-bladed sword like a machete. She walked up to the officer from behind, lifted the sword into the air, and brought it whistling down, severing the man's neck with one blow.

I had to turn away. When I looked back, her men had made a tripod of three captured rifles, and were putting the head on it. Others were dragging the corpses of the Communists and arranging them around the tripod as though they were spokes in a wheel. The Dragon Lady saw me flinch, and walked over. "You don't like this?"

I shrugged. "It's not up to me. I guess you have to do it."

"You are a *good* soldier."

"I told you I'm *not* a soldier." Somehow, I couldn't quite explain about being a marine.

"You don't like being called that?"

"No, I don't."

"Then I call you…" She hesitated. "I call you Khan."

"Khan? What does it mean?"

"Khan is Prince of Princes, someone who deserves respect. A leader."

"I'm not a leader."

She said, smiling, "I watched you. You *are*." Then came one of her lightning changes. "I think we may be traveling in the same direction, and you can go with us."

I didn't know what to say, because I still wasn't sure whose side she was on. I wondered whether I should lead her right to Scotty's group—if there still was any such group by now.

"Which way are you going?" she asked.

I finally concluded, what the hell, if it hadn't been for her I'd be lying over there on the ground right now. "This valley is supposed to lead to a fork, where we will meet some others."

She nodded. "I know where that is. We will take you." She motioned to two of her men, who picked up Nancy's stretcher. As we moved out, I couldn't help feeling that someone up there must be looking after me. I would have hated to be here with a wounded girl on a stretcher without the Dragon Lady. I thought of the way she'd shot all those soldiers, and of the officer she had decapitated. I supposed she had done that to remind her men of who was in charge; to kill that way took a strong stomach.

I asked, "How long will it take to get to the fork?"

"We will arrive late tonight."

"Thanks—Dragon Lady," I said. And then, "I keep wondering, Dragon Lady, how old you are."

"Very old," she said—though of course she wasn't. "Very old and wise."

"You're all so young, you—" I started to say girls, but stopped myself. "You ladies. My friend Nancy, on the stretcher there, is only sixteen."

By way of reply, she called out something in Chinese. In a few moments two Chinese girls came running up to us. "This one, Lee, is only fourteen. And this one, Sue, is fifteen." They looked no more than twelve—but they were both carrying rifles.

"They're so young to be fighting," I said.

The Dragon Lady replied, "The village they come from was wiped out by the Communists. They were almost the only ones to escape. After that, they joined us."

I started to say something about the Nationalists, and she looked at me sternly. Then she was silent for so long that I wondered what I'd said that was wrong. "The Nationalists cannot win," she said finally. "They cannot handle the country, they waste many lives."

"But you're not a Communist—" I began, and this time I was sure I had said something wrong.

"No. And I am not Nationalist." After that she said nothing for so long that I decided to drop back with Nancy and her stretcher-bearers, who had fallen behind us. The two girls, Sue and Lee, were walking alongside her.

"These my friends," Nancy said to me. I smiled to see her looking so much better.

"How is your wound?" I asked.

"Much better. They put leaves on it." She gestured toward the stretcher-bearers. I smiled at her again, reaching down to squeeze her hand, and walked beside her for a while. Then I heard the sound of planes. The Dragon Lady was about fifteen yards ahead.

"I hear them," she told me before I could say anything.

"What do we do?"

"We keep going."

"Suppose they spot us?"

"They won't see us. They are jets; they are too high and too fast. The canyons are deep and narrow."

"What do you suppose they're looking for?" I asked her.

"You. Many soldiers are looking for you too, because of what you did."

"What do you mean?"

"At the reservoir. We were near. We followed you, and we saw some of the fighting."

Again, they'd been there and had done nothing! Taking a chance, I said, "We sure could have used some help."

A fierce expression came over her face. "I have my own people to care for and we do not fight unless we have to. To try to save you there might have cost us more lives than all of you." Then her face softened. "But I saw that you Americans were good fighters."

I had not said anything about being American but had wondered if she knew that I was. Now I shrugged and changed the subject. "So you'd been with us a long time. I thought you said you picked us up when we climbed that mountain."

"We saw you at the reservoir. Then we moved away, and then we saw you again as you came over the mountain."

"And we didn't see you at all."

"Oh no, we know how to follow you so you can't see us."

I had never heard anyone more sure of herself and of what she knew. So I asked, "Are the Communist soldiers following us?"

"Oh yes, they are very close. That must be the reason why your group broke into two parts, I think."

I didn't want to agree. Instead, I asked another question: "Were those the same Communist troops who hit us just now?"

"No. The ones we destroyed were from another division. There are many troops around here. That's why we have to keep moving."

"So the ones who were following us are still following."

"Oh yes."

Again, as if it had been timed, came the drone of planes. This time I could see them, flying at perhaps four thousand feet. I took the Dragon Lady's word for it that they couldn't spot us, and kept moving.

About an hour later, she signaled a stop. "We rest here for a while," she said. "We eat, and you will get to take a real bath—a swim."

We pulled in near the canyon wall. Among the rocks I saw several pools of water. I walked over to one and put my hand in; it had been pleasantly warmed by the sun. I thought of my last "swim" in training, with machine-gun bullets whizzing overhead. What day had that been? Exactly a week had passed since we were dropped into Manchuria. For the two weeks before that we'd been in training, with that daily exercise in the water. Could it have been only three weeks ago that I'd been given the choice of "volunteering" or being discharged for not mentioning my asthma? My God, I thought: the blood, the death, since that day! Three weeks ago who could have dreamed I'd be meeting Scotty, and now this woman? With people I hadn't even known then—Damon, White, Sams One and Two—it was as though I'd already been through a lifetime, and had seen them die!

"You take off your clothes and swim," said the Dragon Lady. "Then I shall bring you clean clothes."

I stood there waiting for her to walk away. Finally I said, feeling awkward, "You must have a lot of work to do."

"First give me your clothes."

I didn't know what to do, except plunge in with my clothes on. The pool was small, maybe ten feet across and four feet deep. A couple of strokes took me to the far side, where I sat down on the edge. The Dragon Lady went on standing where she was, laughing.

"Now give me your clothes," she said.

"First bring me the new ones." I saw Nancy being helped to the pool by the two girls Lee and Sue, I turned around quickly when they began taking her clothes off, and the others started to laugh. After a few moments Nancy said, "It's all right, Ricky, you can turn around now."

I did, and saw her sitting down in the water, with only her head above it, while the other two held onto her. Taking off my shirt and pants, I threw them to the nearest rock, keeping on the underwear I'd been issued in training—something that was a cross between a loincloth and a diaper. I stayed under the water, hearing laughter from the others, until one of the Dragon Lady's men came running up, and what he said brought on another of those sudden changes of mood. The laughter stopped and she hurried off. In a moment, a man brought me some clothes and told me to hurry. When I asked him why, he said "Hurry" again as though it was the only English word he knew. I had started after him when I remembered something. Running over to where my old rags were and reaching into the pocket of the pants, I found my little pill in its tight plastic container and transferred it to the pocket of the new ones. I spotted Nancy limping along, helped by Sue and Lee, and yelled at her, "Get on your stretcher!"

"This is good," she said.

"But you may break that wound open!"

The girls propped her into a sitting position on the stretcher, and I moved on past them to find the Dragon Lady. She told me there were Communist soldiers not far ahead of us. I asked what she was going to do, and she replied, "I am thinking about it. I don't like to go around. We'll see how many there are."

People kept running up to her, shouting, and then running off again. The stretcher-bearers brought Nancy up near me. "They talk about fighting," she explained. "She tells them what to do."

Now the Dragon Lady herself came back to speak to us. "You will not come with us, this is not your fight. I shall leave some men here with you."

I had had enough fighting for the moment and wasn't inclined to argue. I asked, "How far away are the Communists?"

"You see that ridge?" She pointed. "They are just on the other side." She shouted more orders, and four men came up to join us. They nodded and smiled as, with barely a look behind, the Dragon Lady moved away toward her troops. The men began talking to Nancy, who translated for me. "They say they take us to safer place."

"Where?"

"Higher on mountain. They say we have more protection there, can see down below, where is fighting."

The men lifted the stretcher and began moving up the mountain. After a few hundred yards, they stopped among some huge boulders and one of them handed me a pair of binoculars. Nancy explained, "They are gift from the Dragon Lady to you."

I was going to have Nancy tell them to thank her. Then I thought I would thank her myself, and realized that I might never see her again. It was as though we were living in another century, in this place where killing and getting killed were everyday occurrences that everyone accepted.

Using the binoculars, I spotted the soldiers. "My God," I said to Nancy. "There must be a couple of hundred of them!"

For half an hour we waited with no new developments, until the Dragon Lady's fighters opened up. They'd gotten within fifty feet of the Communists before firing. I could see the Dragon Lady and her people moving out across open ground, with no protection, while the Communists stayed hidden among the rocks. Then, before the Dragon Lady and her force could see them, I spotted four tanks coming from a trail that ran along the canyon, all firing regularly. The Dragon Lady's people in the hills began dropping mortar shells among the Communists, but they did not have the range of the tanks. I was certain now that she would be killed.

Finally a mortar stopped one of the tanks, but there were still the other three. I couldn't stand to watch. Turning to one of our bodyguards, I barked, "Machine gun! Give me machine gun!" He didn't understand, so I turned to Nancy: "Tell him—" She was already explaining. In a moment he had handed me his weapon and I was sliding down the mountain, mostly on my butt, feeling the raspberries form on my skin as I went toward the three tanks. The men in them wouldn't be expecting anything from the rear. Near the bottom, I almost tripped over the bodies of two of the Dragon Lady's men. Seeing that one of them still had four or five hand grenades hooked to his belt, I stopped to grab them. As the last of the tanks moved slowly by, I ran toward it, climbed up the back, and pulled the pin from a grenade. I tossed it into the open turret, jumped, and headed for cover.

There was a loud boom behind me and the third tank stopped dead. I'd had the advantage of surprise, and once the grenade went off, the men inside would have been crushed like chunks of meat in a grinder. When I saw, to my amazement, that the two other tanks hadn't even paused, I went for the second one. Scrambling up onto it, I saw the turret was closed. After puzzling for an instant over what to do, I pounded on the top of the hatch. And damned if the thing didn't open! I flipped the grenade in and then headed for the lead tank. But this time I was out on open ground, and in an instant the tank commander had popped his head up and spotted me while I headed for the nearest cover, which happened to be the tank I'd just stopped. Looking back to see how far away the moving tank was, I saw two of the Dragon Lady's men already on top of it. They dropped their grenades, leaped, and then came the explosion.

Heavy gunfire was now coming from the hills above me. Diving for cover, I looked back and saw what looked like hundreds of the Dragon Lady's men swooping down on the Communist position. It was only then that I realized what her tactics were: she had brought her attack force out into the open, risking all those lives, including her own, to get the Communists to commit themselves. She now had them trapped between her attack force and the reserves in the hills.

I could see they didn't need me anymore—if they ever had!—and I made my way up to Nancy, who asked, "Are you hurt?" I'd forgotten about the raspberries on my rear and on the backs of my legs—until just then, when I tried to sit down. But I answered that I was all right.

Then the Dragon Lady came striding up and stood there looking at me. "You see, you fought like a Khan."

"You fooled me," I told her. "I didn't know you had that reserve force."

"We had to draw them out. In a battle you have to expect to lose some people. If you do not understand that, you eventually lose *very* many. But the tanks were a surprise. My scouts did not see them. We took care of them—with your help, Khan."

I was embarrassed, but before I could begin to blush the Dragon Lady said, with one of her sudden shifts of mood, "We have much to do," and began issuing orders. The bodyguards picked up Nancy's stretcher and we moved toward the main body of the Dragon Lady's force. Nancy wanted to walk, but one look from the leader kept her from leaving the stretcher.

We went by the shambles left by the fight, passing more corpses. I had seen many by now, but hadn't gotten used to them. Soon we were making our way along a series of narrow passageways in the canyon walls. I was about twenty yards behind the Dragon Lady, and I kept thinking how smart, beautiful and feminine she was, as well as a warrior, leader and strategist. Tough as steel, she could march with the strongest man, she could execute prisoners in cold blood, and then sit and laugh like a girl while I tried to take a bath. And here I was, walking with that long shiny hair, those slim shoulders and boyish hips, right before my eyes.

After about an hour of walking, we came to a low valley. A sickening sight was waiting: bodies, many of them hacked to pieces, lay everywhere.

When I asked what had happened, the Dragon Lady said nothing. Then I could see for myself that these were not the bodies of soldiers. They were civilians, village people. The men had had limbs hacked off. Many of the women had been staked to the ground, spread-eagled, and obviously raped.

It was all I could do not to spill my guts. When I saw the children, I couldn't look any more. I dropped to my knees and started to vomit. They had been tied in bundles and used for target practice. When I saw the Dragon Lady, her face was expressionless. "Why?" I asked her. "Who did this?"

"Probably the Communists," she answered. "Probably it happened this morning, just before we met them."

"But why these innocent people—those children—little babies?"

The Dragon Lady touched me on the shoulder. "They were not on either side. The authorities destroy them to frighten other villages, to say, 'If you do not join *our* side, you see—this is what happens.'"

Men and women were burying the bodies and I knew they needed help, but I also knew I couldn't do anything. I saw that Nancy had been crying, and in a way I was glad. At least I wasn't the only one who was so badly shaken. I took her hand and she gave mine a squeeze. I squeezed hers back, and she started to cry again.

We stood there until the Dragon Lady came up to us and said, "We go now." We traveled for three hours and then stopped for the night on a high ridge. I hadn't eaten since morning, but I had no appetite after what I'd seen. I lay down with Nancy beside me, neither of us saying anything, and looked off through the clear night at the hills in the distance. After a while the Dragon Lady walked up and sat with us. Seeing how shaky I still was, she said, "You must get your mind under control. You must not be weak. Weakness will destroy you."

I raised my head to look at her. "I've been here for about a week," I said, "and I can hardly believe all the things I've seen and that I've done. Nobody in the world would believe me if I told them."

She said again, "You must practice controlling your thoughts."

Nancy, who'd been lying there silently, suddenly said, "Look!" and pointed to the sky. "A star, going very fast."

"We call it a shooting star," I told her. "You should make a wish."

Nancy seemed mystified until I explained, "Where I come from, people believe that if you make a wish when you see a shooting star, it will come true."

Suddenly she sounded like any little girl anywhere. "I wish—"

"You mustn't tell," I said. "Or it won't come true."

When I looked down at Nancy a little later, I saw that she had fallen asleep.

"It is good that she sleeps," the Dragon Lady said. "You should sleep also."

"But my mind keeps racing," I told her, "and I can't."

"First you should close your eyes and think of nothing. Then think of something that is good, and you will sleep."

"The only thing that's been good about all this is the people I've been with," I said.

"Then think of that. Learn to wipe the bad thoughts from your mind. Then you will be in control and you will be strong."

I put my head down on my hands, closed my eyes, and tried to follow her advice. It must have worked; at any rate, the next thing I knew, the Dragon Lady was shaking me awake. She gave me one of her smiles, and then she said, "We must go."

I shoved some dried rice into my mouth. It had been hard to take at first. Back then I guess I hadn't been hungry enough. But by now I was used to it; it's what I had for breakfast and most other meals as well.

We hit the trail, still carrying Nancy on a stretcher, though by now she was more and more eager to walk on her own. The path went uphill and downhill until I wondered once again whether these mountains would ever end. We didn't stop for a rest until three or four hours later, when there was a change of point men, and the ones who were being replaced came to report to the Dragon Lady. After talking with them, she came over to Nancy and me. "We are three hours away from the fork," she said. "We have not yet spotted your men, but we have seen a Communist force. We are watching them, but we have to be careful."

The trail here was even rockier than it had been. We had gone down into a valley when two scouts came running, and I began to hear what sounded like firecrackers in the distance. The Dragon Lady told me in a moment that the Communist advance guard had made contact with my friends, but that the main force was still two hours behind.

Soon we climbed to the top of a ridge, where it appeared to me from the location of the firing that the Communists had Scotty's group pinned down. I was ready to go, and shouted to the Dragon Lady that we had to do something.

"We wait," she said.

Here was another of those strange twists in the woman's personality. I couldn't understand her not agreeing that we had to do something. "They need help!" I all but screamed.

She said again, "We wait."

This time I was loaded with grenades and clips, and had my own machine gun slung over my shoulder. I yelled, "I'm not waiting for anything!" and went storming down the slope, as fast as I could go on that trail. I knew that by moving a bit to my left it might be possible to surprise part of that Communist force from the rear. It was a foolhardy notion, but I was in no mood to stop and weigh my chances.

The noise of firing made it possible to get within a hundred yards of the Communists without being seen. Four men had their backs toward me. I hit one of them with a burst that bowled him over, then fired at the others as they turned. Now, of course, the advantage of surprise was gone. Before I could decide on my next move, I heard firing from behind me and off to both sides. When I looked around, fearful of being surrounded, I saw the Dragon Lady and her troops. Whatever it was that had made her change her mind so quickly I can't be sure. Had she been waiting to see how brave I would be? Had she planned to be right behind me all the time? Anyhow, it was a relief to see her there; we now had a full-scale attack in progress on the enemy rear.

At the moment, I was not planning tactics. My blood was up, I was in a kind of animal rage. I remember pulling the pin on a grenade and tossing it, and at the same time charging downhill so fast that I got caught in the explosion I'd set off. In fact it knocked me off my feet and left me momentarily dazed. Then I was firing again and I went on until my clip was emptied. As I was looking for a safe spot to change clips, two Communist soldiers stepped out from behind a boulder about three yards from me. Once again I'm sure it was surprise that saved me. If they hadn't been just as startled as I was, they could have cut me down. In the second while they froze, I threw my gun at them. It hit one of them square while the other ducked a little. Then I was simply charging into them. I weighed 190 or 195 pounds, or maybe a little less just then because of my new diet, as compared to their 120 or 130; so for them it was a little like a small American boy being hit by a pro football tackle. I grabbed the knife from my belt and drove it into the neck of one man just above the collarbone, pulled it out, and went for the neck of the other. Then I was on my feet, grabbing one of their guns, firing until it was empty, and lofting it in a high arc toward where I thought the Communists were.

I felt a hand on my arm, and saw one of the Dragon Lady's men. The fighting had stopped, and I didn't even know it. My clothes were drenched with my own sweat and splashed with other people's blood. For the next few minutes I was still too dazed to be quite sure what was happening.

Gunny and Scotty had been there talking to me but I have no recollection of what anybody was saying, and I'd made no move to hug them or show any sign of welcome. I remember seeing Charlie smile at me, and I remember Gunny putting his hand on my shoulder. Then the Dragon Lady was saying, "The main force is not far. They are coming quickly. You people had better go."

Gunny was saying, "We've got a lot to thank you for," and she was answering, "Don't thank me. Thank Khan."

All at once things came together, and I was out of the fog. "Khan!" I said. "That's me, you dumb bastard!"

Gunny grinned and grabbed me, and then Scotty came over and grabbed me too. And Charlie. I looked around for Holden and Craig. "When are the others getting here?" I asked.

Scotty had stopped smiling. "I have some bad news, Rick."

"Bad news," I said, dreading what I would have to hear: Holden killed, and Craig. And Sally. Scotty ended, "And most of my people."

Now I felt myself coming apart—until I looked at the Dragon Lady and felt her staring straight into my eyes. I tried to make my mind a blank, but then Gunny asked, "What about the rest of your group?"

I told him that Nancy and I were the only ones left. "The lieutenant, White, Sam One and Two, Harry, Joe, they all got it." I looked over at the Dragon Lady. "And if it hadn't been for her, we wouldn't be here either. I had my knife at Nancy's throat and the little white pill in my hand when they came along."

Scotty was eyeing her in a very cautious way, and she was looking at him in the same manner. "Do you two know each other?" I said, jumping in as only a kid can. "Scotty, you know the Dragon Lady?"

It was Scotty's turn to be puzzled. "Where did that name come from?"

"It's the name I gave her, from 'Terry and the Pirates.'"

"I don't know who Terry and the Pirates are," he said, "but it's a good name all right."

"Are you two really on different sides?" I asked.

Each looked guardedly at the other, waiting, until finally Scotty spoke. "We follow different paths. Once we tried to get her and her people to join us, but they wouldn't do it."

The Dragon Lady said simply, "We must be leaving. We must say good-bye."

"Where are you going?" I asked, feeling still more shaken.

"Up there." She gestured toward the mountains.

I was realizing for the first time how dependent I'd become. I'd felt safe with her and her people. "Why don't you come with us?" I said.

When Scotty looked at her, the suspicion was gone from his face. "Why don't you?" he asked. "We still would like to have you with us."

She hesitated. "One moment, please," she said, and walked off to confer with three of her men.

His eyes were still on her as Scotty told me, "Lad, you could not have found a better person to help you out of trouble in these mountains."

"Her people saved my life," I said. "They're not bandits, are they?"

"No, lad. They just don't want to choose sides, the way we have chosen ours."

After a couple of minutes, the Dragon Lady beckoned to Scotty, and he sat down cross-legged on the ground next to her for what seemed a long time, but might have been five minutes. At one point I saw him look toward Gunny and me. Finally he signaled to us and to Charlie.

"She says she will go with us," he said. "But there cannot be two leaders. She says she should lead us because she knows the mountains better than I do. And—"

"Wait a minute," Gunny interrupted. "You led us all the way. We can't change that now."

But Scotty held up his hand. "As I was about to say, I agree with her. She does know the mountains better than I do."

Gunny looked toward me. Not wanting to offend Scotty, I said, "She's very smart, she seems to know her way around and I respect her."

Gunny still didn't seem crazy about the idea. "But where's she going to lead us?"

"Get ready for this, lads," Scotty said. "I have a wee surprise for you."

I told him, "I'd like to know what the hell could surprise us now."

"She and I have been going over our plans. Port Arthur is our destination, but it seems to me we cannot head toward it directly because the Communists are looking for us and will be expecting us to go that way. I haven't been able to make contact with people who would help us, so we have to go in another direction. That is why I agree with her plan. It is also why I think she should be the leader. Are there any objections?"

Clearly, any objection now would be from Gunny. We stared at him and waited. He looked unhappy, but he kept quiet.

"It is settled, then," Scotty said, turning to the Dragon Lady. "You are the leader."

She was instantly on her feet. "Excuse me, please," she said, and then whipped around and began to call out orders. In a few seconds six of her men had taken off. Her unquestioned authority still amazed me, and I turned to Scotty to ask, "What in the world did she say to them?"

"She has sent them on ahead to the Great Wall to find a place where we can cross. Once they find it, they'll backtrack and rejoin us."

Mystified by everything, I heard her explain that we would begin by going west to the Changchun. She described this as an open area of low hills and valleys, more fertile than the country we'd been traveling in. We would see trees and fields of wheat. But there would not be the same protection that the mountains had given us.

"Oh great!" Gunny broke in. "So we go off in the opposite direction from where we're heading—and lose our cover to boot."

"And if we do not go in my direction," the Dragon Lady said, with a slashing motion across her own throat, "perhaps we lose our heads."

Gunny hadn't thought she knew enough English to pick up what he'd said and answer it like that. Now, for the first time, he actually nodded and said, "Okay, she wins."

"We have to reach the Khinghan Mountains," she went on. "They are west of here, in Inner Mongolia, near the Russian border."

"The Russian border?" I said. "I don't want to go there!"

"Not *into* Russia," Scotty explained. "We'd be going west, because that is the one direction they would not expect you people to go."

"And so what do we do when we get there?"

"We cross the plain of Changchun, then the Liao River. We stay on the north side of Chihfeng and we go into the Khinghan Mountains, then we turn and head south to the Great Wall, which we cross between Kalgan and Changteh. We stay west of Peking and head toward Chengting. We stay west of that, too, pass it, turn east and go to Laichow Bay. There we try to get a boat to go to Weihai, which is about two hundred miles from Seoul, in Korea."

All this left me in something close to a state of shock, and Gunny looked to be in the same condition.

"It's going to be a long trip, lads," Scotty told us.

"It's already *been* a long trip," Gunny said.

"But not compared with what's ahead."

The Dragon Lady now said, "Across the Changchun plain is three hundred miles. The entire trip might be a thousand miles, but it is probably less."

"A thousand miles—on foot!" Gunny exclaimed.

But the Dragon Lady only shrugged.

"Well," I said finally, "maybe we'll get to see some Cossacks over there."

Scotty laughed. "No, no Cossacks, but you may be seeing Mongolians, and they live about the way they did when Marco Polo went to China."

"No kidding," I said. Gunny said nothing, but he didn't look thrilled.

"We cannot wait," the Dragon Lady told us now. "The Communists are an hour away." She turned to Gunny and me. "Do you come with us?"

"You bet we're coming!" I said.

She gave her orders, two of her men picked up Nancy's stretcher, and we were on the trail again. The rest of her people—there were about a hundred altogether, twenty-five or thirty of them women, I would guess—simply faded into the countryside. Scotty, Gunny and I hit the trail together, and it was a while before I could bring myself to ask what exactly had happened to the others in his group. He told me that they had all died in an attack by fighter planes—the ones we'd heard passing over. "The bastards!" I heard Gunny mutter.

I asked, "What happened to the prisoners?"

"We took care of the Communist soldiers as soon as we left the cave. We couldn't drag them along." Scotty's face left no doubt what he meant. "We kept Roberts with us. In the second attack, the fighters got him."

"Did he ever say anything?"

"Not much. Only something about showing the Chinese we could give them trouble behind their borders."

"But if he was some kind of agent, what was he doing carrying around a card that identified him that way? And what in hell was he doing with Communist Chinese troops?''

Nobody knew the answer then and I don't know it to this day, nearly thirty years later.

But now it was my turn to relive all the deaths I had seen—Damon, White, Sam One and Sam Two and all the others. And then it was time to prepare for what was ahead. Scotty told us that we'd be coming to mountains higher than any we'd yet had to climb, and seeing people who still used bows and arrows. But at least we'd only get into the foothills of those mountains. We wouldn't have to cross them.

Up ahead, the Dragon Lady was waiting for us. She now explained her strategy for eluding the Communist soldiers. ''Do you see that mountain?'' She pointed ahead of us. ''There is a tunnel through it, and that tunnel leads to another tunnel. They will not see us, they will not follow us. After we go through, we shall have a chance to rest.''

We arrived at the tunnel entrance while it was still daylight. Inside, we moved through pitch-darkness. For some reason the Dragon Lady said there were to be no torches; instead, we each held onto the belt or sash of the person directly ahead, and groped along in single file. Once our eyes became accustomed to the darkness, it was not as total as it had seemed at first. But it took us two hours to get through, and when we emerged the daylight was almost gone. We came to a stone bridge where the Dragon Lady was waiting. She urged us to hurry.

''It is safer in the second tunnel,'' she said.

We moved past her, once again in single file, holding onto belts and sashes as before. The Dragon Lady moved past almost at a run, still urging us on: "Move quickly, move quickly." How she could be so surefooted in such dark I had no idea, but by now I was less and less surprised by anything she did. All at once, the leaders brought the column up short. We could hear scraping sounds up ahead.

Curious about what was happening, I slipped from between Gunny and Scotty, linked the two of them up, and worked my way toward the head of the line where I began to see light. I could make out Charlie and the Dragon Lady moving a boulder away from an opening. Pretty soon we were all rushing through a narrow downhill passageway that led outside. I hung back until everyone but Charlie and the Dragon Lady had gone through, since it occurred to me that they could use some help in moving back the boulder; I weighed nearly as much as the two of them put together, after all. But they signaled for me to go ahead. How they got the boulder back into place I don't know. Maybe it had been balanced in such a way that moving it was easy, or maybe they used a chunk of timber as a lever. I'm still not sure.

We had come out into a clear night, and we seemed to be in a bowl-shaped valley, walled in by mountains on every side.

"We stay here for the night," the Dragon Lady said. "No fires."

Once we'd settled down, Gunny, who was trained in first aid, changed the dressing on Nancy's wound. It was looking a lot better, he said. After we'd been sitting for a while, talking of nothing special, Gunny said, as though he couldn't help himself:

"When the planes first attacked, and we started to run for cover, Sally fell—I don't know if she tripped or was hit. Holden ran back to help her and they were both sprayed, cut apart. Craig saw this and just jumped into the open and started firing and running toward the two of them, and the planes tore into him too."

After a pause Scotty said, "Yes indeed, and Gunny here would have done the same foolhardy thing if I hadn't held him down." Scotty was not offering praise, either. "It was stupid," he declared. "Just plain daft. You may be sure you cannot survive long doing that kind of thing."

"But those Chinese," I said, "those friendlies back at the tunnel walked into Communist fire deliberately, for our sake!"

"That was quite different. They were trading their lives for yours, for they felt what you were doing was important. Holden and Craig sacrificed their lives for *nothing*. If Sally had just lain there, she would have had a better chance than she did after Holden drew attention by running to her. The same was true of Craig. He gave his own life without helping the other two at all. If you hope to get home alive, you two had better learn never to do such a thing."

And now it was just us two, Gunny and me, out of the eight who had started training together only a little more than three weeks ago. A little more than a week ago, six of us had made the jump. Now two of us were left to tell the story—if we ever got to tell it. Whether anyone would believe it was something else again.

"Another thing we'd better all do," Scotty said now, "is get our sleep while we can. We have a long way to go."

I woke in the morning to the sounds of the Dragon Lady's people preparing to hit the trail. Sometimes I wondered if they ever slept; they were still awake when I settled down, and here they were, up before me. I felt stiff and achy, as I did nearly every morning, but I knew that after a little walking I would begin to loosen up and feel better. Dried rice was the menu again. This time we moved so fast that I was shoving it into my mouth as I started along the trail.

After we'd walked for a while I asked Scotty the question that was still puzzling me: "Why isn't the Dragon Lady a Nationalist?"

"She was once," he told me. "But finally she couldn't stand the betrayal, the corruption, everybody stabbing everybody else in the back. She believes, as I do, that the Nationalists would have won if it hadn't been for the black market, the profiteering, all the crookedness that undermined them. Do you remember the weapons we found in the tunnel?"

"With all those 'Made In U.S.A.' signs? You bet I do!"

"There is little doubt about where those weapons came from. Originally they must have been supplied by the United States to the Nationalists."

"And then captured, to be used against us," Gunny said, glowering.

"Captured—or sold," Scotty said, and Gunny's face got even darker.

"I suppose," I said, "the Dragon Lady knows who *we* are."

"You mean that you're Americans?" Scotty laughed. "It would be hard for her not to. As for your status, what branch of the service you're in or if you're in the CIA, that hardly matters. If she wanted to betray you, she could have done it easily and long before this. There's no need to worry about her. Worry about getting through the journey you have ahead of you."

I shook my head. I was worried all right, but what occupied me most right then was wondering if all the canyons were ever going to end. We'd go from one into a valley with a small river running through it, follow the river for a while, and then we'd see the valley deepen, narrow, and turn into still another canyon.

Suddenly, one more time, I heard the sound of planes. Gunny was obviously nervous, but I knew we were deep enough that we couldn't be spotted. The difference between my reaction and Gunny's wasn't really that I was an old pro and he was a rookie, but simply that he'd seen some of his close buddies destroyed by planes right before his eyes only a couple of days ago. When I told him to relax, he looked at me doubtfully, a little annoyed to be given advice by a seventeen-year-old kid, until Scotty backed me up.

"They can't see us," he said. "We've had the good luck that they didn't catch us out in that valley we just went through."

The path began to go uphill, which made it harder on the legs, and for a while we just ramped along without talking. Then Scotty began talking again about the Mongols—their bows and arrows, their huge swords—and about how there were tigers in China.

"Saber-toothed tigers?" I asked, quite seriously.

With a straight face, Scotty said, "Yes, and some dinosaurs too."

At that Gunny burst out laughing, and I said to Scotty, "Well, *you* never heard of 'Terry and the Pirates.'"

He admitted this was so, but before I could fill him in on what it was about, we heard the planes again. Then came the sound of small bombs exploding. It wasn't likely that they could see us, but they were making some very close guesses about where we were! The Dragon Lady signaled with her arms for us to pick up speed and follow her, and we broke into a run. The problem was that in this narrow canyon there was no place to go except along the path. We ran about a hundred yards and then followed the Dragon Lady as she scrambled up rocky ground to a cave in the side of the mountain, where we sat out the barrage.

I called out, "Is Nancy here?"

"Here, Ricky." She was doing a little better on the pronunciation, but it still came out closer to "Licky."

Then I yelled for Scotty and he answered. I asked whether making a light was permitted and was told to go ahead. Like most of the friendlies, I had a cache of my own. I tore a strip off my sleeve, which was too long and baggy anyway, and set it afire. In the moment while it flared, I wished I'd skipped the idea, because of what

I saw—bones everywhere, along with dozens of human skulls.

"Did you see that, Scotty?" I said.

"Lots of people in China lived in caves," he told me. "Some still do. This may have been a burial place."

The discovery snuffed out conversation for a while. It wasn't long before the sound of the explosions had stopped, and the Dragon Lady was saying one more time, "Let's go. Quickly."

Almost at once we were on our way out of the cave and scrambling back onto the path. At this point it was rocky, narrow and steep. A few hundred yards farther along, we came to the crest and started down over a stretch that was rougher and more treacherous than anything so far. One side was close against the mountain; on the other there was a steep drop-off. When the front stretcher-bearer stumbled and fell, landing on both knees, my heart all but stopped at the thought of Nancy, stretcher and stretcher-bearers all tumbling down the mountain. But the bearer at the rear dug in his heels and got his end onto the ground quickly enough to keep control of the stretcher. I pushed my way forward, which wasn't easy because the path was so narrow, and could see that Nancy was okay. The knees of the man who'd fallen were badly cut and bruised.

The Dragon Lady came back up the trail as I was helping him up. Her face had a set look, and she wasted no time or sympathy on his injury. I couldn't understand what she was saying, but from the way she gestured, it was clear that she was warning him he would have to do better, or he and the girl would end up at the bottom of the canyon. She shouted up the line, and at once another man appeared to replace the injured one, who hugged the side of the mountain and let people slip past him.

Falling in behind Scotty, I learned that the injured man had simply been sent to the rear of the column, where he could be helped if he needed it.

"It could have happened to anyone," I said.

"But those it happens to don't live very long here," was Scotty's answer. "Because she showed him no sympathy, he'll be a lot more careful from now on."

The Dragon Lady had obviously been living this way for years. I'd been here ten days and considered myself lucky to be alive.

After trudging for a long time in silence, I found that the path was beginning to be less steep. Then we crossed a low ridge, and the Dragon Lady signaled a stop. I could see people, a lot of them, lying on the ground. After an instant I knew that "people" wasn't the right word. Those were corpses.

As we got closer, I could feel my stomach going queasy, and sweat beginning to stand out on my face. There were people who had been staked to the ground. Limbs had been torn off. Women had been raped. I turned away and retched. Nancy, who was now walking part of the time, came over and put a hand on my shoulder. I heard the Dragon Lady asking, "Where are the children?"

A number of her men fanned out to begin a search, while others gathered the bodies so they could be buried. Someone came running to the Dragon Lady, and I hurried after the two of them, though Nancy was calling after me, "You wait."

On the other side of a low rise, the Dragon Lady stood with a couple of her men. Each one was holding a tiny corpse.

"You should not have come," she said.

I asked, "What happened?"

"They were buried alive. They are not alive any longer."

They'd all been thrown into one pit, maybe forty of them. Just to make sure they were dead, her men were uncovering them one by one, and then burying them again. What I couldn't understand was what made people go out of their way to be so cruel, above all to young children. Even Scotty was shaken up, and he'd been fighting here for eighteen years. Nancy was crying—that is, tears were rolling down her cheeks, though she didn't shake or utter a sound. I put an arm around her and said, "It's going to be all right"—not that I had any real reason to think so.

I told Scotty, "I can understand Communists killing Nationalists, and Nationalists killing Communists. But why these villagers?"

"The Communists think they're teaching a lesson to the countryside. Their message is: Don't dare be against us! Be with us, or else!"

"Does it work?"

"People don't want to die. They don't want their children to die. So when they see something like that"—

Scotty jerked his head toward where we'd been—"it takes a brave person to dare to fight the Communists."

I thought of *us* here, fighting the Communists, and of the little pill in my pocket. Then once again I heard the drone of planes and there was no time to think about anything.

8

There were two planes, and after one pass they must have spotted us. Now they circled and dived. The Dragon Lady yelled, "Down!"

I heard machine-gun fire. Because we were on the downhill side of their approach, they couldn't get a really good shot at us. After one pass, they had to begin a rapid climb to keep from plowing into the far side of the valley wall. As they pulled out, the Dragon Lady yelled at us to get up and move. With the planes wheeling for an approach from the opposite direction, she sent us running to the other side of the valley, so as to be on the downhill side again.

Twice more we went through the same maneuver, which was just that much more exhausting for me because I was half supporting, half carrying Nancy. Then the Dragon Lady began edging us toward an exit from the valley—a narrow, wooded gulch where we'd be safe from the planes. Once we made it, Gunny declared, "The woman is a genius."

"Now you see what I mean," I said.

Gunny looked at me smiling. "You sound like a proud papa. Or something else."

"Oh, cut it out," I told him, and pretended to take a swing at him. But his remark startled me. I hadn't admitted to thinking of the Dragon Lady in any kind of romantic way, even though she was a young and attractive woman. I'd thought of her as my general, the leader I depended on to stay alive. That was the way things were going to be. The decision I'd made wasn't a conscious one at all. It was just *there*.

She dropped back now to talk briefly with Scotty, who came over to us to report what she had said: "A few miles ahead there are inhabited caves. She knows the people and we're going to be able to stop there and get supplies. The Dragon Lady says you mustn't be surprised when you see the people."

Even though I'd about had my fill of surprises, for the hour or so it took us to reach the caves I found myself wondering what was in store for us. During a pause while the Dragon Lady talked with two of her scouts, Nancy caught up with me. She had been walking pretty well and was looking chipper. Now she took my hand and said, "We run?"

I laughed. "You feel good?"

"Yes."

"Good! All the same, we walk." I gripped her hand strongly as a kind of support and we started forward together. What stopped us before we'd gone a hundred yards was the sight of a group of people dressed in animal skins, as though we'd stepped into prehistoric times! It sounds strange even to speak of cavemen, but that is what they were. We watched while the Dragon Lady spoke with them. Then she turned to us.

"We shall rest here tonight. Inside there is food."

The series of caves we now entered were almost like rooms, a good deal smaller than the huge caverns where I'd first met Scotty. There must have been fifty or sixty people living in them. Once we'd sat down, they brought us bowls of something thick and hot—a sort of porridge. Whatever was in it, to anyone as hungry as I was it tasted delicious. The main course, as usual, was rice.

After a while the Dragon Lady told us that tomorrow we would begin crossing the plain—and that we would be doing it on horseback.

I had been on a horse once in my life—on a Sunday Boy Scout outing. And one of the things that gave me asthma was horses. When I told Scotty about this, he asked me how bad it was.

"Not so bad. I haven't had it at all lately. But that may be because I've stayed away from animals. I never thought I was enlisting in the cavalry."

Gunny and Scotty both thought this was funny. But the Dragon Lady didn't. She got up and in a few minutes she brought me a small pouch. "Tomorrow, when we ride," she said, "you must take this. Do not eat it, just put some of it under your tongue."

Inside the pouch I found what looked like sand. "I'm not going to put sand in my mouth," I said.

She laughed. "Put a little under your tongue. Just a little. Try it now."

So I stuck a very little of it under my tongue. It had no taste and after a while I forgot it was there; either it dissolved or I had swallowed it. But I was going to need another kind of magic to teach me how to ride!

"Well, how long will it take us to cross this plain?" I asked.

"A few days, perhaps. We shall have to cross the Liao River, and that is perhaps one hundred miles away," she said. At least it wasn't a thousand!

As we talked, a couple of little girls had come up to stare at Scotty and Gunny and me. We were probably the first white men they'd ever seen. While they stood there, shy and hesitant but with no intention of going away, I motioned one to come closer. Then I clapped my hands together, and after a few more motions she got the idea of a game of pattycake. The other kids watched with big eyes, and the grownups all had big grins on their faces.

After I'd played the game with the second child, and then the third, a woman came and said something in a scolding voice, and the kids ran off. Though I didn't know a word of her language, the tone was so familiar that I could almost translate: "Now don't make pests of yourselves, just run off and leave our guests alone!"

I was thinking how wonderful it was that I could play games with these kids even though we came from countries thousands of miles apart and couldn't speak a word to each other. Then all of a sudden fatigue hit me, and I was ready to sack out. We were given some skins to lie on and to cover ourselves with, and in no time I was asleep.

When Scotty woke me the next morning, every muscle ached. There was a strange smell in the air and I saw some men smoking. Though I'd been a smoker—nothing like a pack a day, but regularly—I hadn't had a cigarette since soon after I "volunteered," for the simple reason that there weren't any. I said to Gunny, ''Maybe one of those guys would give us a smoke.''

''No. You don't smoke,'' Nancy, who'd been listening, said firmly.

''Why not?''

The Dragon Lady answered. ''They smoke opium. If you want a cigarette, I shall find one for you.'' She waved at one of her men, who walked around a bit, looking for someone in her party to bum a smoke from. In a while he brought me a couple of hand-rolled cigarettes. I gave one to Gunny, and we both lit up. From the first drag I knew this was a mistake. Coughing and gasping, I finally managed to ask, ''What the hell was that—rope?''

Scotty told us, chortling, that it was made from the fibers of a plant. ''And the Mongols love it!''

The laughter had hardly died down before the Dragon Lady said, ''Now we shall go and get the horses.'' She led us to an open place where a couple of dozen of her men were holding four animals each. Altogether there must have been nearly a hundred—enough for all of us. Where she'd managed to get them, I have no idea even now. But clearly—whether because of fear or love—she was respected in this country, and there hardly seemed to be any limit to what she was capable of. By then, if someone had told me she was going to produce an aircraft carrier on this plain, I guess I would have believed it.

None of the horses had saddles, and the bridle was a single rope around the head. A second circle of rope over the back and behind the front legs served in place of stirrups. One of the Dragon Lady's men walked up to me with a horse that they must have picked for its greatness, though it looked to me like a monster. While I watched, the others began mounting with ease—even little Nancy—and I wondered again how I would ever manage.

Then I saw that Gunny was having trouble too. He'd get his body up but couldn't get a leg over, or else he'd get one leg up and the horse would move a bit and he'd lose his nerve. I laughed out loud and he glared at me. "I don't see you up there either, hot shot," he said.

That stung me. I grabbed the rope in my right hand, tried to get a handful of mane in my left, and with a leap and a pull managed to get my left leg over the horse and my weight on top of him. I was about to say something when my horse fidgeted a little. In a new fit of panic, I clutched at his mane and neck, and barely managed to stay on.

There was laughter all around, but then Gunny had gotten the hang of it too, and we were off—beginning at a slow walk that I suppose was for our benefit.

After watching the way the others hitched their feet into the ropes and used their heels to make the animal move and the way they handled the reins, I felt more secure. Scotty was staying close to make sure Gunny and I managed. "We're going to be awfully conspicuous, crossing the plain this way with so many people," I told him.

"It's a chance we've got to take. Perhaps we can do it because it's so unexpected." Scotty added that later we would break into smaller groups and begin to ride faster.

I stayed with the Dragon Lady, together with Scotty, Gunny, Nancy and eight or ten others. After a while the Dragon Lady started spurring her horse forward and all the others began to speed up, with Gunny and me doing our best to imitate them. At first I was bouncing with such a jolt that my spine seemed to be forcing itself up through the top of my head. Then Nancy pulled alongside me. "Move with horse," she said. "Like this." I watched the way she rocked, using her legs so that she went up and down along with the motion of the animal and soon—though it was certainly no featherbed up there—I began to feel more comfortable.

We'd ridden about an hour when the Dragon Lady held up her hand and called out the order, which Scotty translated for us, to walk with the horses for a while. This was a great relief to me. After we'd walked for a while, we were told to give the horses some water and then wipe their nostrils with it. For that I used another strip torn from my sleeve. Like the rest, I carried my water in an animal-skin bag, which I refilled wherever I could. The sun was up and it was beginning to be warm; I took a few swallows, but I was careful with my supply. Then I looked around at the countryside—a vast level space with trees here and there, and a few fields of grain.

Still walking our horses, we began moving into a series of low hills, all the time on the watch for planes.

Suddenly I called out to Gunny, "You know what? I've been with this horse for over an hour and my eyes aren't tearing a bit!"

"So the stuff you took must work," he said.

I caught up with the Dragon Lady to ask what the stuff in the pouch had been.

"A certain leaf, ground up. Many among us have this . . . illness that you have. The leaf prevents it. Don't people use something like that where you come from?"

"No. We just have shots." I made the motions of giving an injection to show what I meant, and she nodded to show that she understood.

I thanked her again and dropped back with Gunny and Scotty. Maybe twenty minutes later, the Dragon Lady ordered us to remount and we were off at a full gallop. I was already sore—especially my seat—but the riding was now a lot easier except that the insides of my legs were chafed. Looking around at the others—dozens of Orientals mounted on horses, wearing rags and skins, carrying machine guns and bandoliers—I wondered whether the wild Mongols I'd heard about could have looked much different.

At the top of a hill a rider appeared in the distance. As he headed toward us, I saw him hold up both hands, lower one of them, and then repeat the same signal. The Dragon Lady returned it, and sent four riders ahead to meet him. What a strange sight it was, almost as if we had been on the ocean—the rider appearing at the top of a hill, as if on the crest of a wave, and then sinking out of sight, appearing and disappearing again, until he and his four-man escort wheeled up beside us. The first of the scouts brought his horse alongside the Dragon Lady and the two of them continued at a gallop, talking as they rode. It was at least twenty minutes before she signaled Scotty, Gunny and me to come up, and told us what she had learned: "There is a river ahead and Russians are there." It was a Communist base, she explained, where the Russians were serving as advisers, teaching the Chinese to fly jet planes. When I asked, "What do we do?" she looked at me and said, "We shall see."

After we had ridden a while longer, the chafing along the insides of my legs worsened. The skin had been rubbed raw by friction. When I told Scotty, he shouted, "You should have wrapped something around them before we started."

Once again it was clear how much I had to learn about taking care of myself in these surroundings. And how lucky I was to have hooked up with these people!

It seemed like hours, though I knew it was no more than a few minutes, before, blessedly, the Dragon Lady signaled for us to dismount and walk our horses again. Soon I spotted a couple of scouts galloping in and, as I feared, our rest came to an end. The scouts rode on either side of the Dragon Lady as the three of them talked. The day had begun to be really hot, and it was a relief when I could stop again and douse my horse's head with water.

Noticing that the Dragon Lady had slowed, I hurried to catch up with her and hear her report of what the scouts had found. There were, she said, six planes, perhaps more, several hangars, several shacks with soldiers in them, a radio station and two buildings that might have trucks in them. "Those," she said, "would be useful to us."

"But how do we get them?" Gunny asked, in the voice of somebody who already half knows the answer, and doesn't like it much.

"We attack," the Dragon Lady said.

Gunny rolled his eyes, but she ignored him. Turning to Scotty, she said simply, "Tonight." The two scouts were already drawing a map in the dirt.

Scotty asked how many Russians there were.

"We do not know precisely but perhaps one hundred people in total." She looked down at the map and studied it for a while in silence. "We shall not try to attack during daylight. So now we travel more slowly and arrive after dark. We hope to strike while they are eating or sleeping. We divide into groups. One attacks radio station and building next to it. This must be done with great speed. Other groups attack planes and the second building and the shacks."

She looked around as though waiting for someone to say something. Finally I asked, "Where are we now?"

"We are north of Port Arthur. And we are going west. We shall cross the river near Tiehling."

"And once we cross the river and get by the airfield, how far is it to the mountains?"

"Two hundred miles." She smiled as she said it.

We went off at a gallop, and traveled for the rest of the afternoon, resting the horses and ourselves periodically. The ground was covered with a low growth that might have been moss. Everything looked green and peaceful, and I thought of what I'd seen in only eleven days in China—the blood, the bodies, the children buried alive. If I ever got married and had children of my

own, how could my family have anything to do with the
Rick Gardella who had been through all this? Would I
ever be able to tell them what I had seen—and what I had
done? If I never told, what would it be like to live with
that secret for the rest of my life?

I thought of what the Dragon Lady had said about
controlling your mind rather than letting it control you.
I'd work on that; I'd have to. How else could I handle
the memory of those bodies?

"Wait!"

Scotty's voice shocked me out of my trance; they'd all
slowed down for a short rest and I'd gone right on. So
much for mind control.

The Dragon Lady explained that she was ordering one
of her riders out to call together all her leaders. Then we
would go over her plans for the airbase. Within half an
hour the leaders had arrived. We all sat in one large circle, with the Dragon Lady in the center. She used stones
to plot a diagram of the base, describing each group's
assignment, going over it repeatedly until she was sure
everyone knew exactly what to do. Scotty, Gunny and I
were to join her group in attacking the radio station and
the buildings adjacent to it.

Each of the group leaders was then given twenty minutes to rejoin his unit while the rest of us mounted and
rode off, walking our horses occasionally but taking no
long rests, and eating nothing but a few handfuls of rice
while we were on the move. Later in the afternoon the
Dragon Lady called in her leaders for another briefing.
As we went back to our horses, Gunny said to me, "Kid,
when we get there . . . take it easy, will you?"

"What do you mean?"

"I mean, don't lose your head."

"What makes you think I'll do that?"

"Look, kid, all I mean is that you've been through a lot, you've been lucky—*we've* been lucky—and let's not push it."

"Gunny," I said, "let me tell you something. I'm not going to push *anything*. If we could get around that base, I'd skip it gladly."

"Okay," he said. "That's more like it."

A rider was approaching. Since there were always scouts coming and going, I didn't pay much attention to him—until he got close and I saw that it was Charlie.

"Where the hell have you been?" I yelled at him. Though he'd been gone only a short time, it seemed long the way everything did here—a day seemed like a week, a week seemed to go back a year. He grinned at me, pointing to the west. The Dragon Lady, coming up alongside us, said, "He has been to Mongolia, getting ready for our arrival there."

"What did they say when they heard we were coming?" Gunny asked, clowning.

Charlie, clowning back, hunched his shoulders and let out a growl. "They say that," he said, laughing.

"You tell them we said the same," Gunny told him.

As it was getting dark we stopped, and one by one the outlying groups came in. The Dragon Lady's orders were to proceed on horseback the moment it got dark. Fifteen minutes later, all the groups had assembled and stood waiting by their horses—more than a hundred altogether. The Dragon Lady pointed to a hill a couple of hundred yards ahead. Over it and perhaps a hundred yards down the side, she told us, we would find the base that was our objective. We now formed into a skirmish line and when the light was gone from the sky she mounted, as a signal to everyone to do the same. We set off at a gallop. I must admit that I was scared, but also exhilarated.

Once we got over the hill, we were almost on top of the base before we sighted it. We had seen no one and met with no fire when I spotted the radio station and adjoining building that were our targets. As we raced past, people were coming out of another building. My machine gun was off my shoulder almost before I dismounted, heading for the station.

I got through the main door and started up the stairs. By then I was hearing automatic fire outside. Two men stepped out of a doorway on a landing halfway up the stairs; I opened fire and knocked them both down. Stepping over them, I raced for the head of the stairs and kicked open the door I found there, revealing a man at a radio transmitter. I blasted at him and bowled him over. By this time Gunny was directly behind me. He opened fire and hit two men who had just come through a doorway to one side of the transmitter.

I took a deep breath and looked at the three bodies. All of them were Chinese.

We raced through the building, firing at anyone we saw, and finally we shot up the radio transmitter itself. Suddenly all was quiet around us though we could hear firing and explosions outside. Running out, we saw the planes ablaze. The firing stopped entirely. In a matter of ten minutes, the fight was over. We had not suffered a single casualty.

Following the Dragon Lady inside the second building, we found the bodies of ten men, all of them Russians—five officers in black uniforms, five enlisted men whose uniforms were brown. Outside my own group of marines, the only white men I'd seen since I landed in Manchuria had been Scotty, Roberts—and the ten dead Russians. These were the military advisers who had been teaching the Communist Chinese to use the weapons supplied to them by the Soviet Union.

Christ, I thought, we've killed ten Russian soldiers. If it were known, that would be enough to start a world war!

"What about the trucks?" I asked, and the Dragon Lady said, "There they are." I watched as several canvas-covered trucks were being pulled out of the garage-like building and one of the hangars. I could see people already climbing into them. They were small, holding maybe twelve or fifteen people each. The horses were to be left behind.

We lost no time in getting out of there, and were soon crossing a bridge over the Liao. Looking back, I saw the buildings we'd set afire lighting up the sky.

"They could see that all over China," I told Scotty.

"Aye, they might. But by the time they can do anything about it, let's hope we are in the mountains."

We drove without lights, over a road full of bumps and potholes. After an hour or so we stopped short with a screech of brakes, and Gunny and I landed on top of each other in the front of the truck. The reason for the stop, we soon saw, was a couple of Chinese on foot. After speaking with the driver of the lead truck, they came back and got in with us. As we continued our bone-rattling ride, they and the Dragon Lady talked, with Charlie listening and explaining what he heard. The area up ahead was full of Communist troops—and there were also Russians.

"More Russians!" I exclaimed. "Hey! We're not *in* Russia, are we?"

"We're a long way from it," Scotty insisted.

"Then what is it we've gotten into? What's going on?"

Scotty said quietly, "Take it easy, Rick."

"Take it easy, hell!" I shot back. "I'll take it easy if you'll just tell me what's happening, and why we go on running into more troops and more Russians everywhere we go!"

Nancy had come over to sit next to me. Now she put her tiny hand on top of my big paw. I looked at her, felt ashamed and mumbled something about being sorry.

"It's all right, lad," Scotty said. "Just let me tell you what I can. It appears that the Mongols are upset because of the underground testing that is being done in this area. The men who just spoke to us say those were atomic explosions. We can't be sure of that. The Mongols are saying that animals from their herds are dying and that it's because of the explosions. They are ready to fight."

"And here we are in the middle of it," I said. "It's like the tunnel all over again."

"At least we don't have to worry about being bored."
His good-natured tone somehow pacified me, and for a
while we jolted along without speaking. With no head-
lights and no moon, once again it was hard to see the
reason when we came to another halt. We got out and
people from the other trucks came together in the darkness while the Dragon Lady went into another huddle
with her men. Then she came back to tell us that up
ahead there was another base, a big one—the headquarters responsible for the underground explosions. "Russians and Communist troops are there," she said.

"So what's the plan?" Gunny wanted to know, while
Scotty asked, more diplomatically, "May I speak with
you for a moment?"

The Dragon Lady wasn't used to being interrupted.
But she went off to confer with Scotty. In a couple of
minutes they were back and she announced that we
would go around the base.

I was the last one to get back into our truck, and it was
starting to move so quickly that I almost didn't make it.
When I asked Scotty what he had said to make the
Dragon Lady change her mind about the base, he answered, "I told her we'd already attacked one of their
bases, and that they had radios and would be after us."

"I wasn't sure she would listen," I said.

"She has an open mind, lad. But you have to understand that every time she comes across a Communist, her
instinct is to destroy him. She's got good reason for
that—I'll tell you about it sometime—but she also has
good sense. She wouldn't have lasted this long if she

hadn't. Just now she saw that we'd better bypass that camp."

At that moment we struck something in the road, and Gunny and I were both thrown off-balance again. When we righted ourselves, Scotty was sitting there so coolly that I wondered whether he'd developed some kind of balance from living the way he did. "What were we talking about?" he asked.

"About *her*."

"Yes?"

"About what was wrong with her, that you two couldn't get along."

"I didn't say anything was wrong with her, lad. We just didn't see eye to eye."

Again we came to a stop, this time because one of the lead trucks had overheated. Steam was coming from under the hood and the driver was making angry noises like any driver anywhere. In a moment the Dragon Lady had ordered that the truck be left behind. "There is no time to worry about it," she said. "The passengers will be divided among the other trucks."

Her tone was so decisive that I couldn't resist saying, "Aye, aye, sir!"

"You are *sir*!" she told me cheerfully. "*I* am Dragon Lady!"

After we had been riding for a while, I saw that Gunny had somehow fallen asleep. I had actually dozed a little myself even though the road was now bumpier than ever—like driving over a bed of railroad ties. Dawn was coming. As the sky grew light, I saw huge, dark mountain peaks up ahead. I couldn't take my eyes off the scene but stared at it hypnotized until we came to a stop. We all got out and in a little while the Dragon Lady came up, walking with the same swift and erect bearing as always. I wondered if she ever slept at all. She told us that Charlie would lead us to a meeting place that had been set up while she went on ahead. At my questioning glance, she said, "I must meet some people before our group arrives. They do not like to be surprised."

"Didn't Charlie already do that?"

Scotty took hold of my arm and said to her, "We understand."

"What did I say wrong this time?" I asked him.

"Nothing, lad. You just didn't realize that Charlie didn't actually make personal contact with the Mongols. He could not have reached the mountains and returned to us on the other side of the river in two days and a half. That would have meant covering five hundred miles on horseback. Even he couldn't have done that. What he did was to reach the outskirts of Mongol territory and send word on ahead that we would be coming. But she must talk to them herself, the way any ambassador pays respects to the rulers of a nation he is about to enter. It is merely good manners."

Soon we were heading into the mountains, following Charlie in the lead truck. The Dragon Lady had gone off in a different direction. After a while we halted and everyone got out. I watched the trucks being driven off into a gully where they would not be noticeable from the road. "By the time the trucks are found," Charlie told us, "we will be up in mountains."

"And how do we get there?" I asked.

Charlie smiled. "We walk."

I really didn't mind, after all the riding. A good deal of the way I stayed beside Nancy. Her wound had looked bloodier and more dangerous than it actually was, I now realized, but her recovery was still a kind of miracle. "You know, you are a terrific girl," I told her, and she gave me a brig grin. "Let's go up and walk with Scotty and Gunny."

"All right," she answered. "I go." Letting go of the hand I'd given her to help her walk, she broke into a run and I began jogging to keep up with her.

"I thought you'd gotten enough running," Gunny said.

"Go to hell," I told him cheerfully.

From then on the four of us kept up a steady pace, though things became more difficult as the path got steeper and the altitude began to be noticeable. The mountains were completely barren, without a tree or shrub. But once I looked off to the right and saw an animal, moving fast.

"A deer!" I shouted.

"A gazelle. Faster than a deer," Scotty corrected me.

It was the first animal of any size that I'd seen roaming wild since we came to China. "Are there any other animals around here?" I asked Scotty.

"You mean besides the saber-toothed tiger?"

I told him to go to hell too.

After a couple of hours Charlie put up his hand to signal a stop. We clambered in among the rocks along the trail and sat down. I was tired yet tense, and it must have shown. When I turned over and lay on my belly, I felt hands rubbing the back of my neck, soothing me. I looked up and saw Nancy. "You sleep," she said.

The next thing I remember was wakening to a rumbling noise that felt to me like thunder. Sitting up, I saw Charlie and Scotty both staring up the mountain. From up there, about fifty horsemen were charging down toward us. My amazement grew as they came closer. They were all huge strapping men. They were armed with swords. And one of them had red hair.

9

"Are those Mongols?" I whispered to Scotty.

"Aye." He said it without moving his lips.

"Then how come the red hair?"

"There are all kinds of Mongols." If he was trying to get me to shut up, it was for some reason I didn't understand.

"All the Chinese—" I persisted.

"Mongols are not Chinese. I'll tell you about it later."

Then I saw the Dragon Lady, who said, "We go with them." Pointing to another group of big men leading extra mounts, she added, "We ride." This time, thinking ahead, I took off the loose skin jacket I'd been given at the caves and put my feet into its sleeves, as if it had been an extra pair of pants, to keep my legs from chafing. The man who came riding up to us now was even bigger than the others, with a voice like a bear growling. There was even something bearlike in the way he looked—huge, powerful and hairy. Neither he nor any of the others had the yellowish skin of a Chinese. Some, like him, were dark; others were as fair as any "white" man, though nearly all had high cheekbones. And they all wore clothing made of animal skins.

"All right, lad," Scotty said. "Move lively now."

I took the reins of an animal near me. As I climbed onto its back, I saw the huge Mongol looking at me, laughing and pointing.

"It's the way you're wearing your jacket," Scotty said. "He thinks it's funny. Easy there, lad," he added— though I knew better than to start anything just then, and anyhow there wasn't time, because we were already moving.

At first there was no trail. We were heading through rough country, over a series of ridges that gave way to gentler slopes and then narrowed into canyons. We did finally come across a trail of sorts, which took us over a slope. On the other side, nestled among the mountains, was the Mongol camp. Looking down on it, I guessed there were two or three hundred inhabitants. When we came to the center of it, a big bearlike man spoke to the Dragon Lady, who turned and motioned for us to dismount.

The Dragon Lady still sat on her horse, face to face with the Mongol leader. They dismounted simultaneously and walked toward each other until they were no more than inches apart. He must have been a foot and a half taller than she was, and probably weighed more than twice as much. What he said to her sounded ferocious. She stood her ground and responded in her high, thin voice, pointing to him, then to the sky, then in the direction we'd come from. It was as though they were carrying on a kind of duel. They went through the whole thing all over again, and then he took a step back and began to laugh, shaking his head up and down. She yelled something and as he stared at her, I could feel those black eyes burning into me. For a moment I actually caught his eye, and I glared right back. Nobody was going to stare me down!

He spoke again to the Dragon Lady in the same laughing half growl, and she pointed to Scotty, Gunny and me as she answered. Finally he motioned for her to sit down, and they went on talking in lower tones.

Looking around the camp, I asked Scotty about the huts the Mongols lived in. "What are they made of? Looks like corn husks to me."

"Aye, lad, it's something of the sort. Here they call it kaoliang, and it has many uses. They build their houses from the husks; they make wine and porridge from it, they use it for fuel, and they feed it to the animals."

"They sure don't waste anything, do they?"

"That's right, lad. There's not much out here for anyone to waste."

I spotted some children clustered together off to one side of the camp, and looked toward Charlie. "Mongol custom," he told me. "When men do business, women and children keep back."

After a while I felt secure enough to drift away from the group and head toward the children. Near them a group of women were silently huddled together. I was within a few yards of the children when I heard a screech behind me, whipped around and saw a huge form coming at me. Without thinking, as a kind of reflex, I swung and caught him right on the jaw—and as any boxer can tell you, that's the worst place to get hit. There he lay, flat on his back, looking like a fallen tree, and in another second or two I was surrounded by Mongols. Then the one I'd hit was on his feet, coming at me again and making threatening noises. It dawned on me what I'd done and how it might affect all of us. While I tried hard not to show my fear, I heard screaming and yelling from the center of the pack of Mongols. It was the Dragon Lady, making her way toward me. Her air of command must have been what got her through to the center of the circle. With the Mongol chief just behind her, she came striding up and stood beside me.

She shook her head and said, sounding almost amused, ''You hit his lieutenant! That is not good in this camp.''

''I thought he was going to attack me.''

''I understand. Still, it is not good.'' For a moment she seemed to be thinking. Then, with a look straight at the chief, she pointed to me and said, ''Khan!''

The chief seemed surprised. He looked at me and then back at her.

''Khan!'' she repeated, louder than before.

Again those menacing black eyes of his took me in. This time he strode toward me and brought down his face over mine until we were almost touching. I felt his rotten breath as he growled out something meaningless to me, except that the word *Khan* was in it.

I stood my ground. Part of it was bravado, part of it was feeling the honor of the Marine Corps at stake. The chief reached out his right hand to grab my shoulder. I brushed the hand away. While he glared at me, the Dragon Lady smiled, which made me feel a little surer of myself. When he reached out with both hands, I thought he was going for my throat, and I put my arms between his and knocked them to the side. From his puzzled look, this must not have been what he expected. Then his lieutenant came over, said a word or two, pulled out his knife, and pointed it at me. The chief turned with a growl to the Dragon Lady, looking first at me and then at his lieutenant. Then he began to walk away, with the lieutenant reluctantly following.

By this time Nancy, Gunny, Charlie and Scotty had worked their way through the circle. As the Dragon Lady looked first at them and then at me, she wasn't smiling anymore.

She said, "You have to fight the lieutenant."

I would have my choice of weapons, she went on— either a sword or a bow and arrow.

Trying to keep my voice cool, I said, "I've never used a sword or shot a bow and arrow in my life."

Scotty broke in, "Tell them you'll use a machine gun."

"No guns," the Dragon Lady said.

Then Charlie was explaining. "The Mongols love to wrestle. It is one of their favorite sports."

I looked over to Gunny, who said, "For Christ's sake, knock if off, Rick."

Scotty was looking angry too.

"Hell," I said to both of them, "all I did was go over toward the kids!"

"The Mongols have their own rules, very strict rules," the Dragon Lady said emphatically.

I said I was sorry I'd broken their rules, and asked when the fight was supposed to take place.

"When the sun is high," the Dragon Lady said. Nancy had come and taken hold of my arm. But the Dragon Lady said to her and the others, "Now I talk to the Khan alone, please."

As the four of them walked away, she looked at me straight in the eye. "These are hard people. They are part of the Tungus tribe. Most of them live in Siberia, but a few small groups stay here in Mongolia. They are the best hunters in the world."

I understood her to mean that I could never win with a bow and arrow. I said, "What if you told them no weapons, just hands?"

"I shall see what he says." She walked off toward the Mongols, who had moved to a distance of maybe a hundred yards. While I waited, trying not to think at all, I saw a little girl standing no more than ten yards from me. No telling where she had come from, or how she got there. Finally, not knowing what to do, I said "Hi." She didn't answer me, but went on staring and gnawing her knuckle. When I held out my hands to her, she started to reach out, but then drew back. I took a few steps toward her and knelt down. "What's your name?" I asked, hoping she would hear the friendly tone in my voice.

The Dragon Lady had come back. Now she said, "This is my sister."

I stood up. "Your *sister*?"

"Yes. My small sister. Her name is Kim. She is twelve years old."

I knelt down again and said, "Hi, Kim." The Dragon Lady said something in Chinese. Kim took the knuckle out of her mouth, put her hands behind her back and smiled. I put out my hands again and this time, after hesitating, she reached out to catch hold of them.

I moved a little closer to her. "Hi, Kim," I said again.

She looked up at her sister and then smiled again. But she was still too shy to speak.

"Didn't you teach her any English?" I asked the Dragon Lady, who said something to her sister. Then Kim pointed to me and said, "Hi, Khan."

Now, from the Dragon Lady's change of expression, I knew it was time to talk business.

"Soon the sun will be high," she said. "We have to make our plans. You must be careful, for the lieutenant is very strong."

"Have they agreed to hands, no weapons?" I asked.

"Yes. I made them understand that bow and arrow or sword would be unfair."

I thanked her, but her face remained dark. "Do not thank me. He says he will eat you up like a deer."

I glowered at that, and she said, "Now you must listen"—and she told me how to fight. I never doubted for a moment that she knew exactly what I had to do.

"You understand?" she said finally.

"I understand."

There was shouting, and I turned to see the lieutenant storming toward us, followed by what seemed to be everybody in the whole Mongol camp. The lieutenant halted at about thirty yards, and the crowd halted too. He yelled something that ended in a growl, and the Dragon Lady made me understand that he was challenging me. "Now you go to him."

"Okay," I said, and while she followed I walked half of the way toward him. Stopping short, I said, "Now you tell him to come the rest of the way to me. Or...or...I'll think he's a woman."

"Shall I tell him that?"

"Yeah," I said, surprised to find myself giving her an order. "Tell him that." And she must have done it, because when she had spoken the lieutenant, who'd been standing there with his arms folded, suddenly grew furious. Dropping his arms, he went into a crouch and started toward me, circling to my left. The people behind him let out a kind of gasp, and then screamed.

The lieutenant had come within ten yards and was still circling, getting no closer. As he finished one whole loop around me, the Dragon Lady shouted, "Remember the plan!"

Suddenly he lunged. Remembering, I dropped to the ground, bracing my weight on my left arm and kicking out with both feet. I caught him on the shin and kneecap, feeling the impact all the way up to my hip, and saw him fall. Jumping up, I pounced on him and put my right elbow into his throat. I could tell that he was in pain.

Then I was in pain myself for one excruciating instant before I blacked out completely.

My next memory is of waking up in a hut somewhere, with the worst headache I ever had. Once I got my eyes to focus, I recognized Nancy and then the Dragon Lady, both smiling down at me, then Gunny, Scotty—and the Mongol chief.

"My head," I said. "God, but my head hurts."

Nancy, kneeling beside me, laid her hand on my forehead. "It's all right, Ricky, you be well."

I lay there not saying anything, trying to smile, and after a few minutes things began to be a little less confusing. I discovered that my clothes had been changed, and that I was now dressed in skins, just as the Mongols were.

"Who put me into these?" I asked, and Scotty, looking toward the two women, answered, "They did."

"What?" I stared at them, and it seemed to me that they both blushed. Then I asked, "Whatever hit me?"

Gunny said, "Two buddies of that bastard! When you decked him, one of them came at you with a club."

Whether it was a coincidence or not, just then the chief said something angry to the Dragon Lady, who sounded angry too, and they both went outside. In a moment she was back. "You come," she said to me.

"But my head hurts so—"

She broke in, "Khan, you must come quickly!"

The throbbing in my head seemed to explode when I moved, and for a bit I just stood there, waiting for it to ease, before I got through the doorway.

Outside I saw that it was dark. Several fires were burning, and gathered around them were what once again seemed to be everybody in the village. In front of me stood the chief, with his lieutenant and two other men behind him. "Those are the two guys that hit you," Gunny told me. From the size of them, one would have been more than enough. But I could see now that they weren't about to start a fight. The chief spoke to them and they dropped to their knees. Next the chief spoke to the Dragon Lady and pulled the sword from the scabbard at his waist. The Dragon Lady said, ''Now you shall deal out punishment.''

''What does he want me to do,'' I asked. ''Cut off their heads?'' And I very nearly laughed.

''Yes,'' she replied. ''If you wish.''

As though to prove he wasn't kidding, the chief walked up and held out the sword with its handle toward me.

''Take it!'' the Dragon Lady said in a loud whisper, as I hesitated. ''Don't wait! Take it!''

I reached out and grabbed it in one hand. When the chief let go, I had to grab with my other hand to keep from dropping the thing. ''What do I do now?'' I asked.

''You are to deal out the punishment,'' she said again.

I turned to Scotty and Gunny, who were no help, and then glanced at the chief. His black eyes blazed as though there were fires inside them, but he stood silently waiting for what I would do.

''Holy Mother of God,'' I said softly to myself, and took another look at the Dragon Lady and then at Nancy standing near her. Neither gave me any sign. Turning back, I held the sword with both hands and slowly raised it above my head.

The lieutenant and his guards still did not move. Very slowly, I brought the sword down, point first, and drove it into the ground. Then I turned to the chief. ''No,'' I said. ''They live.''

The chief did not move. While he stood looking at me, I walked over to the three kneeling men, bent over each one and helped him to his feet. I touched each one on the shoulder in turn and then walked up to the chief. When my face was a foot from his, I said, "Friends, friends!" I touched my own chest, pointed to our group and to the three men, and repeated, "Friends, friends!"

Then the Dragon Lady was speaking to the chief, while he stared into my eyes as though he might burn holes in them. Finally he turned to his people, and growled something that ended in a shout of "Khan!" as he pointed to me.

The people all cheered and waved their arms. The chief walked over to where I had driven the sword into the ground. He drew it out with one hand, lifted it over his head, and called out, "Khan, Khan, Khan!" while the people went on cheering and waving. I saw the Dragon Lady and all the others cheering too.

Scotty came over to me and said, "Well, lad, I guess you have them on your side now." And there were a few good-natured digs from Gunny. While the cheering died down, the chief was speaking again to the Dragon Lady. Now she told us that he wanted us to sit at the fire with him and share his food.

When we'd walked over to the fire and I'd started to sit with the others, the Dragon Lady said, "No. Do not sit here." She pointed to the chief. "You are to sit there. The lieutenant sits on one side of him. He wants you to sit on the other side."

"You see, lad," Scotty said, "you're royalty now."

So I sat next to the chief, who began speaking to me. Not understanding gave me a good excuse to wave to the Dragon Lady to join me. "Tell him I need you here as interpreter."

When she explained, he nodded and said—to my surprise—"Okay." Then he growled out orders to a couple of his men, who brought some chunks of the meat that had been roasting on a spit. This was the first fresh meat I'd eaten since the Dragon Lady rescued us, and it was certainly good. I asked her what it was, and she told me it was antelope.

Once the chief finished eating, he gave another order, spitting out bits of gristle as he spoke. Promptly one of his men brought over some skin bags of the kind we carried water in—but these, the Dragon Lady explained, had wine in them, made from kaoliang. The chief held out one of the bags. I took it in both hands, tilted it back and drank. Though I'd never been much of a wine drinker, it tasted fine. Scotty and Gunny were also being taken care of. Every time I looked, it seemed, Gunny's head would be tilted back with a wineskin above it.

After we'd all gorged ourselves, the dancing began. For a beat, people were pounding the ground or the wineskins with sticks or their bare hands. Before long the Dragon Lady walked to the center of the circle. For some minutes she danced alone, as gracefully as she did everything else. Then Gunny, in his cups by now, got up and staggered toward her. The next thing I knew, she had come over to me, taken me by the arm, and pulled me to the center of the circle. I was sober enough to avoid tripping, and in a couple of minutes I was actually enjoying myself, keeping the beat along with the Dragon Lady. After Gunny fell down and sat laughing, Scotty came forward to help him back to his place. Just as I was beginning to feel winded myself, the Dragon Lady took my arm and led me back to where we'd been sitting. The chief looked at us good-naturedly and said, "Okay!" It may have been the only English word he knew.

Our places in the center were now taken by the lieutenant and his two friends. Watching their movements, which were graceful and energetic, I said to the Dragon Lady, "I've seen that kind of dance before."

"It is a Cossack dance."

"You mean they're *Russian?*"

"Many Cossacks lived in southern Russia, but some lived in Asia also."

"So the same customs just go on for thousands of years?" I said. I felt as though I'd made an amazing discovery.

She nodded. "Many things have stayed the same for longer than that. The Mongols are much the same, as fierce as they were when Genghis Khan was their leader."

"*Genghis* Khan?"

"He was the great khan who organized the Mongol tribes and trained them to be fine horse soldiers."

"Cavalry?"

"Yes. Perhaps the best cavalry that ever rode horses."

Having seen these men ride, I could easily believe that.

The dancing stopped, and the party began to quiet down. The wine had given me a glow, but my headache hadn't gone away. Now I was tired and beginning to feel cold. When I told the Dragon Lady this, she said, "You stay in my house." After she'd spoken to the chief, he gave some more orders, and at once a couple of men came running with spare clothes—jackets, pants, boots—for all of us.

Once I'd put mine on, I began feeling so drowsy that I could hardly control the urge to sleep. But the Dragon Lady put her hand on my shoulder and said, "You must wait. You must not go until I tell you." She spoke to the chief again. He reached out his greasy hand to pat my back, saying again, "Okay, okay."

"Okay," I said, and gave him a tap on the shoulder.

The Dragon Lady said, "It is all right. You may go. He hopes you sleep well."

Getting up, I waved my hand to the chief as a way of saying "Thanks for everything." Then I smiled at his lieutenant. Smiling too, he stood up and held out his right hand. As I reached for it, he grasped my arm just above the elbow, and I did the same. When I turned to the Dragon Lady, she nodded in confirmation. "It is a sign of friendship."

Then Gunny, Scotty, Nancy, Charlie and I all followed the Dragon Lady into her hut. Like the others, it was made of the husks of kaoliang, and although it didn't look large from the outside, there seemed to be plenty of room in it for all of us. I noticed Kim already sleeping off to one side. The Dragon Lady motioned us to another part of the hut, where she picked up several large skins from a pile and gave each of us one. I rolled up in mine, comfortably warm, and had hardly put my head down before I was asleep.

When I opened my eyes again it was morning. Scotty was already awake. I reached over and poked Gunny, who was still snoring. He blinked and said, "Christ, can't a guy even get any sleep around here?'' There was no sign of the others, and I wondered where they had gone. Then I smelled food cooking, and after a couple of minutes the Dragon Lady and Kim came in carrying several skins containing food. I saw something that looked like corn, and asked Scotty about it.

"Aye, lad,'' he said. "It's what we call maize. It was brought over from America and the Chinese started growing it. They use it for fuel, too, the way they do kaoliang.''

"I'm a meat and potatoes man myself,'' I said as the Dragon Lady brought me a skin filled with corn, meat and kaoliang, "and I was wondering how these Mongols could live on rice and get so big!''

"In China there are potatoes too,'' the Dragon Lady said. "But not here in the north.''

"In the south,'' Scotty explained, "they grow sweet potatoes, and also peanuts and tobacco. China has more different foods than you might suppose. It also has a huge population to feed. That is the problem.''

The Dragon Lady's face had turned serious, even sad. "China must have peace,'' she said. "When we have peace, we shall grow enough food for all the Chinese people.''

I stopped eating to look at her. All I could think of was to reach out my hand and give hers a squeeze. But in an instant her look and mood had changed again. "Today we shall have fun,'' she said brightly. "There will be games. Mongol games.'' She got to her feet and went off while we finished our breakfast. I'd been given a lot of food, but it was no more than I could handle. Feeling both well rested and well fed, I got to my feet, pushed aside the skin that covered the entrance to the hut, and peered out.

"Holy God!" I exclaimed. "Am I seeing things, or is that a camel?"

The camel wasn't the only surprise, either. The man riding it was no Mongol. He was white.

10

We stood there dumbfounded while the Dragon Lady ran to greet the new arrival. Behind him were a dozen others, all riding on camels. The leader dismounted and spoke to the Dragon Lady in a language that wasn't English. He looked excited, and so did she.

Then the Dragon Lady was pointing to us, and the two of them were walking toward us as we stood in the doorway of the hut. The stranger might have been in his middle thirties. He was not tall—perhaps five feet eight or nine inches—but broadly built, weighing maybe 180. He wore skins like the Mongols, and as he came closer I could see that he had dark brown hair and that his face was rugged but pleasant. He smiled often as he talked to the Dragon Lady.

They headed for the hut, and he said, "Well, mates, how goes it?" His accent was not American; he sounded a little like Scotty, but not quite.

Next Scotty was saying, "Glory be! Audy! It's been years!" And the two of them were embracing, while the Dragon Lady stood smiling and Gunny and I stared in bewilderment. Scotty invited the other to sit down and share our meal, and then he said, "Lads, I want you to meet Audy, who's an old friend from Australia." We

soon learned that he had been in China since World War
II.

"I was a coast watcher during the war," Audy explained. "First in Burma and then in China with two
Australian mates. Our job was to keep an eye out for
Japanese ships. Both my mates were killed by the Japs
and after the war I decided to stay. I feel the same as
Scotty does about China. Wouldn't go back home in a
million years."

When Scotty asked what he'd been up to, he said,
"I've just come from the Gobi, taking care of some
business."

Inquisitive as always, I asked, "What's the Gobi?"

"A desert," Scotty explained. "Between Russia and
Mongolia."

"I tell you, Scotty," Audy went on, "on my way back,
we heard a lot about some group been giving the Commies a hard time. They're in one bloody awful mood
down on the plains, especially Manchuria. Don't know
what these blokes have done, but the Commies are sore
about it."

Scotty grinned at him and then we were all laughing.

"It was you blokes, was it? Been having yourselves
some fun?"

The laughter went on for a while before Scotty remembered his manners and introduced Gunny and me
by name.

"Pleased to meet you," Audy said, "You chaps
American, eh?"

We both hesitated. Then Gunny said "Yup," and I
chimed in, "That's right."

Audy laughed. "I fought with you chaps during the war. I'd know a Yank a mile away in the dark."

"Used to see a lot of Audy during the war," Scotty reminisced. "But afterwards he went north into Mongolia, and I lost him."

"I've been up in Mandal," Audy told him. "Then down to Sain Shanda and across the mountains to here. Wanted to see my friends out there."

I couldn't resist saying, "They're sure some friends."

"What do you mean?" Audy asked.

"If you'd been here yesterday, you'd know," Scotty told him, "It's rather a long story. For now I'll just say that we have here with us a young khan." And he pointed to me.

To keep Scotty from going into the embarrassing details, I said, "Oh, it's just a nickname the Dragon Lady gave me."

Audy now looked more confused than ever. "And who, may I ask, is the Dragon Lady?"

"*She* is." I gestured toward her.

"Well, that's a new one on me."

"Rick—Khan, that is—gave her the name," Scotty said. "And that's another story we shan't go into now."

Audy turned to the Dragon Lady and spoke to her in what I suppose was Chinese. She answered in English, "From now on I am Dragon Lady. That is my name. And," she added, pointing to me, "his name is Khan!"

"We're all learning new things," Scotty said. "Until we got here I never knew the Dragon Lady had a sister."

With a cool look, she said, "There are many things about me that you do not know. But there is no time now to tell you everything. Now we shall watch the Mongol sport."

Gunny was up and heading for the door. "I've still got a little of that wine in my system," he said. "I could use some air." He stepped out, but after a second or two he stepped back in.

"My God, they've got *wolves* out there!" he yelled.

The others seemed mildly amused. Going to the entrance, I stuck my head out and saw, sure enough, half a dozen of the snarling animals. Wondering what they thought was funny about that, I said, "Have a look for yourselves!"

"The Mongols keep them as pets, Rick," Scotty told me.

"Wolves? As pets?"

"Aye, lad. They're tame, they're friendly."

"Bullshit!" Gunny said. And when I reached out, intending to pet one of them, he made a lunge for my hand.

"Friendly, huh?"

But the Dragon Lady said, still looking amused, "Come. I shall take you with me."

Following her out, I found there were now no less than a dozen of them, most of them bigger than German shepherds, jumping all around us. The Dragon Lady, who was carrying some of our leftover food, walked calmly up to them, with me still as close behind her as I could manage, while they jumped at her and took the morsels from her hand. The air outside was cool but I was sweating. Looking back at the hut, I saw that Audy,

Scotty and Gunny were all staying put. The Dragon Lady dropped to her knees, and the "pets" began licking her hands and face. She said, looking up, "Khan, sit next to me."

Nervous as I was, I found to my surprise that the wolves really were friendly. After they'd licked my hands and I'd begun petting them, out of the corner of my eye I spotted Gunny, moving very slowly in our direction. Several of the wolves turned and snarled at him; but the Dragon Lady spoke to them and they were quiet. She called to Gunny, "You come here, sit with us." Soon he was part of the playful group.

When Audy and Scotty finally sauntered over, I had had all the play I wanted. We strolled about the camp and saw some of the camel riders who'd come in with Audy. In answer to my questions, he told me he was the only Australian in central China—"from Inner Mongolia to the Gobi to the Russian border," as he put it.

"Just as I'm the only Scotsman in Manchuria," Scotty said.

"Do you have your own territories, or something?" I asked.

"It's just where we'd rather be, off by ourselves," Audy said.

"Aye," Scotty agreed. "But we're close, even though we're many miles apart. And we help each other whenever we can."

"Does the Dragon Lady have a territory too?" I asked.

"She's all over China," Scotty responded. "She travels from one end of the country to the other to help people she cares about, and because it is safer for her that way."

"She cares about her country, but she would like to see it without Communists," Audy added.

"Do you think that will ever happen?" I asked. "Nothing seems to go back to the way it was before."

"The Communists won't last long," Audy said. "If they last a hundred years, that is not long as the Confucians see it. What the Chinese have more of than any other people in the world is patience."

"Would you say the Dragon Lady has patience?" I asked.

"Yes, lad," Scotty told me. "A very great deal of patience."

"I wish I knew more about her—where she came from, and about her family. Do you know?"

Audy looked at Scotty, who seemed to hesitate. Then he said, "We can't tell you everything at once, lad. We've got to keep you interested." Before I could press him further, the Mongol lieutenant appeared and he and Audy gripped arms in friendship. When they sat down and began talking in what I suppose was a Mongolian language, I wandered off, found Kim, and was soon showing her and several other children how to shoot baskets, using some makeshift substitutes. In the middle of this, the Dragon Lady came by and led me to where the camels were tied, many of them resting on the ground. In a minute she was showing me how to ride one.

Like the horses, the camels had simple bridles of rope. I took hold of the rope in my left hand and threw a leg between the humps. As soon as I was mounted, the camel got to its feet as though I had given it a signal. The Dragon Lady untied another animal and mounted it gracefully. "You hold on," she said. Then she gave my camel a swat, and we were off, loping along at an easy gait. Its huge stride and deep up-and-down movement made it very different from riding a horse, and of course I was much higher off the ground. It glided through the camp and up a slight rise just outside it, at such a clip now that I didn't suppose any living creature could overtake me—until I caught a glimpse of the Dragon Lady coming up behind me. By then we were a good distance from the camp, and the Dragon Lady turned her mount, calling out that she would race me back. All along the way, I had a feeling that she was going just fast enough to keep up with me.

As we dismounted, I could see a crowd gathering in an open field on the other side of the camp. There were shouts, and as we approached it appeared that an archery contest had begun. Six bowmen were lined up and shooting at targets that seemed hardly visible; they must have been at least two hundred yards away. The Dragon Lady told me that the targets were skin bags filled with water, and that in fact they were about the size of a human head. But the archers seemed to be popping those bags with almost every shot. What astonished me even more was seeing the archers move back another seventy-five or a hundred yards and begin shooting all over again. Though they didn't have quite the same accuracy from that distance, they still hit more often than not.

While I watched, the Mongol lieutenant came up and motioned for me to go with him. When I nodded in agreement, he lifted a thick arm and laid it over my shoulder. I could hear Gunny laughing as we walked off together.

We came to the archers, who stopped shooting when they saw us. One of them handed his bow to the lieutenant, who then gave it to me, along with an arrow. Though I had never fired an arrow before, there was nothing for me to do but fit the arrow to the string and do my best to pull it. The lieutenant, from behind, put his hands over mine and helped me draw. The arrow went off at a crazy angle, and he brought another. This time I managed by myself to draw the bow a couple of inches before I let go. The arrow made a gentle arc and fell with a plop a few yards in front of me.

I said, laughing before anyone else could, "I guess I'm better with a machine gun."

"More is needed than the strength of the body for this," the Dragon Lady told me. "The strength of the mind is also needed. You must concentrate."

After a few more shots with no improvement, I handed the bow back to the lieutenant and grasped him by the arms as a way of thanking him. Then, with smiles all round, I walked back to join Gunny and the others, and we followed the Dragon Lady to a field where riding events were to take place. I was surprised to see that the horses being led out were hardly bigger than ponies. The Dragon Lady, reading my thoughts, said, "Small, but very strong."

Hearing hoofbeats, I turned and saw a new group of ponies being ridden at top speed by children—some of them no more than six or seven years old. The Dragon Lady told us that they had learned to ride almost as soon as they learned to walk.

After the horse races came camel racing. Then there were wrestling matches, and finally Scotty came to tell us that we were invited to a hunt as honored guests; the Mongols would do the actual hunting. We were scattered among twelve small parties, some going after antelope, others after deer or bear. After an hour's ride I waited along with Nancy, absolutely motionless, for what seemed an endless time, until a huge brown shape ambled over the rocks in our direction. We were downwind, so he was nearly upon us when the hunters, all at once, drew their bows, and the arrows went zinging like bees out of a hive. The bear, which must have stood five feet tall, dropped in his tracks. In moments a litter had been made, and the dead bear was being carried back to camp.

While we waited to make a meal of the game that had been killed, Audy described his adventures in China—how he'd come here as a coast watcher, how his two buddies had died, how he and Scotty had been involved in a savage battle along thirty miles of the Great Wall. When the food arrived, I ate as much as I could hold, stoking up for the days when there wouldn't be any kind of feast. Afterward the chief stood up and led our group into his hut. There, while we all sat in a circle, the chief began to speak, with Scotty translating.

He told us that all along the Khinghan Mountains his people's herds were dying, and some of their horses. They didn't know the reason, but they believed underground explosions were somehow to blame. The people who had set off the explosions had their headquarters at the same base we had gone to such pains to avoid. The Mongols were now so angry, Scotty told us, that they had decided to go to war against the people at the base.

"With bows and arrows?" I wasn't being facetious.

Scotty smiled and shook his head. "Bows and arrows are a part of their tradition, for games and for hunting. But they use more modern weapons, too."

Then I asked whether they had any experience in attacking from an open plain, and the Dragon Lady said bluntly, "No. But still they will do it."

Scotty said quietly, "I think we owe them something lads. I think we ought to help them."

Without hesitation, Gunny and I agreed.

The Dragon Lady got to her feet and addressed the chief. He smiled as she spoke, looked us over, then spoke to her again. Turning to us, the Dragon Lady said, "We go tonight, and we must go quickly. We must attack and then move south at once."

"All of us?"

"Oh yes," she answered. "The entire village will be moved deeper into the mountains, for once we attack, the Communists will be looking for us." The people of the village were nomads, she explained. "They move all the time. Ten or eleven times a year, they move on again to where the hunting and the grazing are best. Their home is not one place. It is everywhere."

Soon the lieutenant and his two men entered, and the Dragon Lady began laying out a battle plan, while Scotty translated. We would be using horses to approach and to escape afterward. The base, between Chihfeng and the mountains, had its center in one main building; a mile from it was a tunnel leading to the underground testing area. We were to concentrate our attack on the central building.

The Dragon Lady told us that she wanted to take half of our force, but that the chief would not permit this. He said it was his job, that his people would do it. "So there will be just twenty-five of us—the seven who are right here and eighteen others. With his men that will be about one hundred."

I said that was a lot of people.

"It will be a big job to do," she replied. "It will not be as easy as the other base. We had better see to our weapons."

We got our machine guns and bandoliers, and headed back to the chief's hut, where the lieutenant and his two friends were already cleaning their weapons. These were Russian-made, of the same kind as the ones we carried.

The Dragon Lady now went into more detail about the attack. We'd go in from the west, the near side of the camp; as always, she made a sketch in the dirt to show what she meant. "We shall attack from the northwest and the southwest and close them in. A third group in the center will stay back to cover our withdrawal. The Communists will think that we intend to withdraw in the same direction from which we entered, but they will be mistaken."

To attack the main building, she went on, she and
Audy would go with the chief in the northwest group;
Scotty, Gunny, Charlie, Nancy and I would go with the
southwest one. She said, looking at me, "You must keep
Charlie close, for he knows this area very well."

I nodded. I had no intention of letting Charlie get far
away.

We all walked outside to where the others were
mounting up—a motley crew in ragtag uniforms. In addition to their automatic weapons, I saw that several of
them were carrying bows and arrows. Of the two groups,
the Dragon Lady's moved out ahead of ours, with the
backup people in the rear. Riding two abreast, we had
soon left the light of the campfires behind us, and found
ourselves in total darkness. A now-familiar chill ran
through me at the thought of what lay ahead, of how far
I was from home. It was a long time before I could shake
off the mood.

We came to a stop and Scotty rode forward to learn
what was happening. He came back to tell us that this
was where the groups were to divide. We started forward again with Charlie leading us off to the right, while
the Dragon Lady's people veered off to the left. The icy
feeling went through me again as we separated.

After about half an hour, Charlie raised his hand to
signal a stop. I watched while he talked with several of
the Mongols. Then they dismounted and raced off into
the darkness, carrying guns, bows and quivers of arrows. We dismounted too, tied the horses off to one side
and sat down in a circle. A chill seemed to have settled
into the air, as though my own mood had become a per-

manent condition. But this wasn't my imagination; by now the night had grown very cold.

"Those who went ahead will open the way for us," Charlie said. "We wait for a time, then we go." He reached into his jacket and pulled out an hourglass. "When all the sand is on the bottom," he told us, "it will be time."

"Suppose the scouts aren't back by then?" I asked.

"We go anyway." Charlie did not sound cheerful when he said that.

But before long the scouts were back, with their quivers almost empty of arrows. "The way is clear," Charlie said to us. He looked at his timer. We had only a little while longer, perhaps only a few minutes.

"They killed the guards?" I asked Charlie.

"Yes."

"Suppose the bodies are found before we go in?"

Charlie did not answer. Either he wasn't worried or he was being very cool in the face of danger. In a couple of minutes he mounted his horse, the rest of us followed suit and we were off, proceeding down the trail at a walk. When we got to the bottom we fanned out onto the open plain. I took the machine gun off my shoulder, removed one of the clips from the bandolier around my waist and snapped it into the gun, which I cocked and rested on my lap, marveling at how small it was. All the same, I was very nervous and so was everyone else.

A war cry sounded, and we galloped out onto the plain. I wondered that any horse could keep its footing out there, where at first I couldn't see anything at all. Then lights began to appear, more and more of them, until I could make out buildings and people darting between them. Gunfire sounded at a distance off to the left; that, I assumed, was the Dragon Lady's group attacking. I lifted my weapon, positioned it and began firing almost the instant I leaped from my horse. Taking cover as best I could whenever I had to change clips, I headed toward the buildings.

Once again, surprise was on our side. I heard a few explosions off to the left and concluded that the other group must be going for the buildings. About forty yards off I saw two of the Mongols go down, while a group of Communists charged toward them. I sprinted that way too, with Gunny about five strides ahead of me, firing and screaming at the Mongols, "Stay down! Stay down!"—even though they couldn't understand what he was saying.

Then a grenade blast knocked the charging Communists off their feet. It knocked Gunny down as well; he'd fallen within ten yards of the Mongols. I could see, as I hit the dirt beside Gunny, that they were still alive, and I prayed that he would be too. I spoke to him, and for a moment there was no sign of life. Then he said, "Can I open my eyes now? Did you get 'em?" Old fox that he was, he'd decided his best shot at staying alive, alone and out in the open, was to play dead.

Now he yelled, "They can't kill us! We're not human!" To me he said, "I just needed the rest."

Already people were running all over the place again, roused by the explosion, while we lay beside the wounded Mongols, firing at the buildings. Then to our left we saw some of the Dragon Lady's group racing toward them. I concluded that they must be going to set explosive charges, and stopped firing in that direction.

Bodies lay everywhere and some of them were our people.

Charlie came running up with four Mongols, who carried off the wounded men. No more Communist troops were visible, though there was some firing from buildings where they'd taken cover. I saw some of our people running, and then I heard Charlie shouting, "We go! Quick! To horses!"

Sprinting to where a couple of the Mongols were already gathering the mounts, and trying all the while to stay low, I saw that a number of the horses had been hit, and were sprawled out whinnying with pain and terror. This meant that most of us had to ride double. We were a fair distance away from the buildings when the explosion came, rocking the ground under us. That would have been the main building, I knew. But I didn't look back, as we headed for the shelter of the mountains and the Mongol camp. Besides the advantage of surprise and the Dragon Lady's military genius, up to now we had also been just plain lucky. We couldn't afford to gamble on more of the same.

The Dragon Lady's group had been close to us for a long time; but it was not until some time after we linked up, and were deep into the mountains again that we could afford to stop. The Dragon Lady dismounted and walked up to me smiling. She said, "It is done."

"We got the building you wanted?"

"Yes. Now we can go back to the camp."

In another couple of minutes we mounted again, and after maybe half an hour we were at the camp. I was not prepared for what we saw. With the chief growling out orders, everyone was busy getting ready to move on— even the small children had jobs to do. What had been a village of a few hundred people now became a mounted party of the same number, riding along the trail at a slow gallop with patrols out in every direction. The next time we stopped, the chief walked over and began to speak. With the Dragon Lady interpreting, we learned that we had lost forty people in the attack plus about a dozen more wounded, only one of them seriously. The chief was thanking us for our help. He knew we Americans would now be trying to get out of China, and to assist us he was sending thirty or forty men with us on the trip south.

We thanked him but it was hardly possible to say how grateful we were. The Dragon Lady told us what we already knew—that we had to depart as soon as possible. And before we could reach the sea, we had to cross the Great Wall, which Scotty told me was about 150 miles away.

"Will they have planes out looking for us again?" I wondered.

"They will not be able to find us in these mountains," the Dragon Lady answered. And by this time I was ready to believe anything she told me—that she knew everything and could do anything.

We started out with Audy loping alongside me on his camel, which he said he would be leaving with the Mongols until he came back for it.

"What do you mean? Back from where?"

"I mean from the sea, mate," he replied. "Where you and Gunny will be safe."

I turned to him in amazement. "Are you really going all that way with us?"

"Why of course!" He sounded amazed at my supposing it could be any other way.

We stopped after about an hour to rest and water the horses. While we were walking them along the trail again, Gunny came alongside me. I told him how strange it felt to be in a place where you didn't see any other Americans. "Do you suppose we're the only ones in China? Or do you think they dropped a lot of other parties for missions like ours?"

"I wouldn't be surprised," was his answer. "What the hell, it wouldn't cost them much. Drop a few of us in, all over China. If we succeed, fine. If we don't . . ." In the gray light of early morning, I could just make out the hand he ran across his throat.

A few minutes later, we got the signal to mount and ride again. The sun would be coming up soon and I could see an occasional tree and a few patches of grass—a relief from the rocky canyons we'd traveled in so much of the time. I rode along thinking of how these Mongols, people from a world so different, were now my friends—and how a month ago the odds on my ever having met Nancy, who now rode alongside me, would have been one in a million. Now she was someone I'd miss when I was out of China—if I ever got out!

A strange bellowing broke into my thoughts and I looked up to see half a dozen riders approaching. Scotty, when I asked about them, told me they were scouts—the ones the Dragon Lady had sent ahead to the Great Wall. He went on to explain that it was essential for us to cross the wall by dawn on a certain day, which was a holiday when there would be a lot of people congregating there for festivities.

The Dragon Lady rode up now and told us that the scouts, after crossing the wall, had been into Peking which was nearby. Before we crossed it, she added, the Mongols were to leave us. "Then," she said, "we shall split into two groups. My group will go into Peking, and the other will go around it. Then we shall meet on the south side of the city. We shall be not far from the water then. And we shall go on the water to Weihai, and there we shall try to find a boat that will take you and Gunny out of China."

I asked why her group was going into Peking.

"There is someone I wish to see." From the sound of her voice and the look in her eyes as she said it, I knew there was no use asking anything more.

Now the Dragon Lady told Scotty that one of the men who had ridden with us wanted to talk with him. A young man came up and bowed to Scotty, who bowed in return. After the two of them had sat talking for a while, Scotty came over to tell Gunny and me what he had learned.

"That lad operated a radio transmitter. He was one of the three who were trying to help us get away from the tunnel, back there in Manchuria. One radio operator turned out to be a traitor, and all three of those stations were destroyed. Most of the men in them were killed. He is one of the few who escaped.'' Scotty went on, looking still more somber, ''He says that before they were attacked, he had tried to establish radio contact with a station operated by Americans, to tell them about you. He is certain they were able to receive his signal because he could hear them sending. But they wouldn't answer or even acknowledge his message.''

Gunny said, ''Those rotten sons of bitches. They're throwin' us to the wolves!''

''But Gunny,'' I said, ''suppose they didn't believe the message. Maybe the guy's wrong and they didn't even *get* the message. That's possible, isn't it, Scotty?''

''Aye, it's possible. It surely is.'' But he didn't sound very sure.

All the same, I kept telling myself it *was* possible. Otherwise I'd have to believe they didn't *want* to rescue us, and maybe wouldn't even let us rescue ourselves.

11

After my own effort to cheer up Scotty, I began to realize how perfectly lousy I felt. "Why would they *not* want to save us?" I asked aloud.

Audy said, "Politics, mate. Ever hear of politics?"

The Dragon Lady broke in, as though she had heard too much griping, "When we cross the Great Wall, Peking will be only thirty-five miles south. I must go there." She stared at me. "*You* will go to the south of it with the other group."

I said without hesitation that I was going to Peking with her, and Gunny did the same.

"No," she said. "It is not your affair."

"But if you hadn't helped us with *our* problems, where do you think we'd be today?"

Again she said No. But this time I was not to be overruled, and after some more sparring I said, "Look. I would just rather be with you than away from you. I feel safer. It's not going to be all that easy for me to leave China; I might not even leave at all." I knew I'd gotten carried away, but just then that was the way I really felt.

"Are you serious, Rick?" Gunny asked. There was a strange look on his face.

"Yeah. I've gotten to feel so much better when I'm with these people, I don't want to go anywhere without them." I wound up, looking straight at the Dragon Lady, "And I am definitely going to Peking!"

"If you feel so strongly," she replied, "I shall not stop you. But you must not go because of feeling that you are in debt to me."

Gunny and I both assured her that that wasn't the reason, and before long we were on the way, with the Dragon Lady in charge as always. The Mongols, she told us, would soon be leaving us. "They will go back toward the mountains, toward the Gobi, until things are quiet again." Since they were nomads, and continually on the move, she told us, the Communists could never be sure where they were. And besides, the Communists preferred not to fight the Mongols so long as the Mongols left them alone.

Nancy had been nearby during the entire conversation. When we were on our way, she rode up alongside me. "Ricky, you say you stay in China?"

Though I'd said it on the spur of the moment, I now found myself thinking about it. "I don't know, Nancy. There is a lot of fighting here, and it's a hard life, but I've found real friends. And I don't know how I could leave you."

"What will your mother and father, your—"

"My family?" I gave the word she had been groping for. "They'd be unhappy, and I'd miss them. I'd miss my home. But the idea of leaving you . . ." It was something I was going to have to figure out—assuming I'd be given any choice in the matter.

A few minutes later we heard bellowing again—and now I knew that was the signal the scouts gave as they came in. Almost at once, three riders came down the slope on our right. We stopped but didn't dismount while they spoke with the chief and the Dragon Lady. After a couple of minutes Audy said, ''There's something funny,'' and in another minute or two Scotty dug his heels into the flank of his horse and cantered forward to investigate. He and the Dragon Lady came back with grim faces.

''There is a large Communist force on the far side of the mountain,'' she told us. ''They are only three miles from us. They do not know we are here—not yet.''

''How many are there?'' Gunny asked.

''Perhaps a thousand.'' She went on, ''Although they do not know yet, we do not have much time before they find us. We cannot avoid them unless we go back in the direction we came from, and we do not want to do that. We must get ahead of them, to the west, before we strike. Then, when the chase begins, they will think we are headed further up, toward Mongolia. After that, there is a pass we must reach before they do.'' She would take a small force of no more than a hundred—enough to hurt and confuse them, while the rest moved ahead to get the soldiers off our trail. We would move while it was still light, so that we would have the dark to escape in.

I turned to Nancy: ''This time you stay with the main group.''

''Oh no,'' she said. ''I go with you.''

The Dragon Lady agreed with me about Nancy. ''Charlie will lead the others to safety,'' she said. ''You must stay to help him.'' She added a few words in Chinese, which made Nancy stare for a moment like a little girl who's been told it's her bedtime. But then she turned to me. ''You be careful,'' she said.

''Don't worry,'' Gunny told her. ''I'll look after him.''

Along with Gunny, Audy and Scotty, I moved up to the head of the column. The chief wouldn't be going with the raiding party but his lieutenant would. Moving out, we rode hard for an hour. Then, after pulling up in a cloud of dust, we got down and proceeded on foot. We started up a slope that looked down onto a canyon with a natural bridge over it. Before long, something like seventy-five of us were charging over the bridge, leaving the rest to cover us from behind, and making our way down the side of the mountain to where scrubby trees and rock formations gave us some cover.

When we were about five hundred yards from the bottom, the Dragon Lady signaled a stop. According to my estimate, we had less than two hours of daylight. We had good cover here, but with no weapons heavier than the machine guns we carried, once again we were depending on the element of surprise. Gunny was ten yards to my left, Scotty and Audy were on his far flank, and the Dragon Lady had posted herself about twenty-five yards farther downhill. As time passed and the light faded, I began to fear it would be dark before the soldiers arrived. Then we saw them, less than a quarter of a mile down the trail.

We were to hold our fire until we had a signal from the Dragon Lady. I watched the soldiers and her with my heart pounding as they made their way slowly up the rocky trail. Then they were directly below us. Still no signal. I looked for the end of the column, but it seemed to have none. God, there were a lot of them! They began to go under the natural bridge. Soon it would be dark.

She waved her weapon finally, and we all opened up. Completely surprised, some soldiers dove for cover, some looked up for attackers. There were so many that they got in each other's way. At last they began trying to climb toward us, firing as they came. But the terrain had been well chosen; it was steep and rocky with some virtual cliffs between them and us.

Now, as suddenly as we'd attacked, we had the signal to withdraw, and we were scrambling back up the mountain, firing as we went. By then it was really dark. As soon as we got to the level of the natural bridge, we stopped firing altogether; the muzzle flashes would have given us away. Staying low, we raced over the bridge. This was all part of the plan—a feinting action to make them think we'd kept going to the top of that mountain and were heading down the other side. And it worked. We crossed without having a shot fired at us. Dark as it was, we ran all the way back to the horses. Though my breath was coming in gasps, I managed to say to Gunny, "Can you keep up, old-timer?"—and he managed to answer, "Screw you!"

After we had leaped onto our mounts and ridden off, I lost sight of Gunny and the others. But the Dragon Lady was directly ahead of me, and I had no intention of losing her. After maybe half an hour we halted, and she rode down the length of our column and back. "We did not lose a single person," she said. "And now I must ride back to make sure the Communists did go the other way.''

I told her Gunny and I would go with her, but this time she would not be overruled. "If it is necessary for us to escape quickly," she pointed out, "we may have to separate, and you two do not know these mountains."

"Aye, she is right," Scotty told us, and there was nothing we could say. The Dragon Lady picked twelve men and divided them into two groups—one to go south, the other to ride with her back toward the bridge—while the rest of us, who made up the main group, went in still another direction. After about twenty minutes we were dismounting on a ridge, where we moved our horses in among the boulders. We waited here until two of the scouts came riding back. They raced over to talk to Scotty and Audy, and in an instant the order came to mount again—quickly. Scotty told me, when I asked what was the matter, that there were Communist soldiers twenty minutes away and headed in our direction.

"I thought we'd lost them!" Gunny said.

"We had," Audy replied. "These are others. The ones we attacked may have radioed for help."

We galloped hard for half an hour, I have no idea in what direction. After we had stopped, I asked Scotty how the Dragon Lady would know where we were.

"Don't worry, lad," Scotty told me. "She'll find us. Meanwhile get some rest. We don't know when our next chance for that may be."

I remember trying to settle down—and I must have succeeded, because the next thing I remember is being wakened out of a sound sleep by the noise of horses. Still groggy, I got to my feet and half walked, half stumbled over to where the Dragon Lady stood talking with Scotty and Audy. I wondered again when she ever slept.

The news was that the Communist troops were headed west. We had fooled them. By now they had stopped to wait for the force that put us on the run. We could not wait to see what they did next—whether they would continue west or turn back. We would have to be on our way at once.

We had been on the trail only a little while before two more scouts came in and spoke excitedly to the Dragon Lady. Suddenly we changed direction and were heading up the mountain as fast as we could ride. Five hundred yards farther uphill, we dismounted to walk our horses through a narrow pass. Then we climbed again. We paused at a relatively level spot where there were new orders: about a dozen people, among them Scotty, Audy, Gunny and me, were to follow the Dragon Lady on foot. There was now a moon. After walking awhile we came to a ledge. Looking over, we saw the reason for our change of plans. Down below us were riders, lots of them.

The Dragon Lady whispered, "They are moving toward the pass. They will probably come this way."

Audy asked the question for all of us, and she replied, "We cannot permit them to go through, or they may run into our main force. Some of us will stay and defend the pass. The rest will ride to Charlie and warn him."

Gunny and I volunteered to stay and fight with her, along with Audy and six others, while Scotty and the rest rode to find Charlie.

"Will the ten of you be enough?" Scotty asked.

"Yes," she told him. "The pass is narrow. Leave our horses back there, we shall be able to get them."

There was nothing more to say. While Scotty took off, we moved toward the pass, keeping down in a half crouch. At a point just above it, we took positions and settled down in the darkness to wait. My heart pounded so that I wondered whether the Communist soldiers could hear it, while time seemed to drag on forever. Then we heard the sound of horses below us. With the moon in and out of clouds, just now we couldn't see much, though we knew the precise location of the pass and how narrow it was. They would be able to get through only one at a time while we might be able to knock them off, almost sight unseen, by firing down into the canyon.

The signal came and we began firing. There were screams and shouts from below. Sometimes the moon would be hidden and sometimes we'd have glimpses of men scurrying like rats down there. I remember hearing the expression, "like shooting fish in a barrel." It seemed that easy.

When the signal to stop firing came, I wanted to go down and see what was happening. But the Dragon Lady said, "No, no, we want to hold them back as long as we can. Then we run."

"Righto!" Audy echoed her. "We run like hell!"

The moon popped out for a few moments, lighting up the scene as if it had been switched on from above—and in those few moments we saw that the soldiers were slipping through the pass and that some were edging up toward us. Once again we began blasting them and hearing the shouts and screams from below. As we fired, the Dragon Lady shouted something in Chinese and two of her men took off to bring the horses closer. In a few minutes we heard bellowing, the signal that the men were back, and she called out the order to move—quickly.

We scrambled up the mountain and, luckily for us, there was no longer any light from the moon. As soon as we reached the horses, two of the men went ahead as scouts, we mounted, and then we were riding, mostly downhill. Once we reached level ground, we were able to pick up speed. But just which way we were going I had no idea. In fact, the way these people got around in the dark, over rough terrain with no clearly marked roads and often not even a trail, remained a mystery. It also made me realize once again how dependent I was on them, how helpless I would have been except for their company.

I lost track of time, too—not having had a watch since our special training began—but we might have ridden fifteen minutes before the scouts came back and reported seeing more troops ahead of us. To elude them, the Dragon Lady had us veer off in a new direction, keeping the same breathless pace. We came to a hillside where there were caves, dismounted and walked our horses in. There were to be no fires. Instead, each of us was to hold onto the tail of the horse just ahead. "Or else you get lost," the Dragon Lady said. "Caves go off in many directions."

One more thing that struck me was the way these people functioned in the dark of a cave—how much better than mine their eyes seemed to be. After a while my own vision improved, and I began to pick up things where there was hardly any light at all. Right then, though, the darkness in the cave seemed total. I could literally not make out my hand in front of my face. As I walked, I sometimes used one hand to feel for walls or ceilings, but even so I sometimes bumped into one or the other.

After a while I heard the Dragon Lady speaking in Chinese, and I could feel scouts brushing past, on their way out. She said to the rest of us, "We stop here. No talking until we find out where the troops are." We stood there in the dark and silence, waiting for I don't know how long. Then came a couple of hoots, followed by a whispered conversation. The orders now were to leave the cave, mount again and ride as fast as we could go.

Once we were out in the open, the moonlight seemed absolutely glaring. We must have ridden for a couple of hours while I wondered how much longer our luck could possibly hold out, even with the Dragon Lady's genius at outwitting her enemies. I had to force myself not to think that way—to make myself believe we'd get through, that *she'd* get us through.

When we stopped for a rest, moving our horses in among the rocks once again, Audy said, "I think we lost them."

"But perhaps not for long," the Dragon Lady replied. She wasn't going to let anyone relax very much. "If they do not bother us, we should make contact with Charlie soon. But we must not lead the Communists to him."

While we sat there resting, I looked over toward the Dragon Lady and saw her looking gloomy. Moving nearer, I asked if anything was wrong.

She said No, and then I asked, "Don't you ever get tired?"

"No," she replied. "I am strong."

I said I didn't mean that; I meant tired of this kind of life, riding, fighting, moving around all the time.

"This is my country," she said. "And in my country there must be fighting—for now."

"Some day soon it will be different, won't it?" I said, not knowing what I was talking about.

She answered, "Not in my lifetime. More time must pass. Blood must be spilled."

How old was she? She might have been twenty-five, though she looked still younger. Back in the States, a woman her age would be either getting married or worried about a job—maybe expecting a first child. This young woman was a military leader, with no sign that she had ever lived any kind of life but this one.

A couple of scouts rode in and she told me with a smile, "We have lost them." Charlie's group was about an hour away; we would be with them soon after sunrise, but now we would have to go—quickly.

Had there ever been a time when it wasn't necessary to move quickly?

Soon after we started moving, Gunny pulled up beside me. "Well," he said, "I kept my word to Nancy."

"What was that?"

"That I'd look after you."

''Don't be too sure,'' I said lightly. ''We're not back yet.'' Though I meant it as a joke, the Dragon Lady, overhearing, told him, ''The Khan is right. We cannot be sure of anything until we know it is done.''

The sun was coming up by then, and though we'd been through a long, hard night, our spirits picked up when two scouts came riding in with a couple of men from Charlie's group and word that everything was all right. It wasn't long before I saw Charlie and Nancy waving at us as we moved down a gentle slope. I galloped toward them, dismounted and gave Nancy a hug.

''I told you it would be all right,'' I said. I wasn't sure she understood every word unless I spoke carefully, but I knew she knew what I meant.

We learned that the Communist troops had gone off in the wrong direction. But when Scotty spoke of needing sleep, the Dragon Lady's reply was, ''That will have to be later.'' As we moved ahead, walking our horses, Gunny came alongside me again.

''Rick,'' he said, ''were you serious back there, about staying in China?''

''Yes, I was. I feel closer to these people than to anybody I've ever known.''

''You're just a kid,'' he said. ''You still haven't given much of a chance to your own country and your own people.''

''Yeah, I know you're right,'' I told him, aware that I hadn't really thought through what I'd said, meaning it without having decided anything. For two nights and a day we'd been on the move, with only one brief rest in the mountains, and I was beginning to feel the effects of fatigue. But we went on pushing ahead, eating and drinking as we rode. Midday came and went before there was an order to halt. Soon after that, I saw the Dragon Lady coming toward us with the Mongol chief and his lieutenant. The chief held out his hands to us, and while I looked up into that fierce face, the Dragon Lady translated what he was saying. ''This is where we must part. He wishes to thank you. He hopes that he has shown respect to you for the help you have given him.''

Then he went up to Nancy, put his massive hands on her little-girl shoulders, engulfed her in a hug and finally kissed her on the cheek. With each of us, he repeated the farewell ceremony. He had a few extra words for me, the last in the line; ''Khan'' was one of them.

''He says he is proud of you, and proud to have you in his camp. You are welcome to return any time you wish; you will always be greeted as Khan.''

Touched and proud to have this warrior treat me as a brother, I asked the Dragon Lady to tell him I was happy to have his friendship and his good feelings, and grateful for his help. He gave his fierce smile, and again the Dragon Lady translated: ''He is sending the lieutenant and forty of his men with us, to protect us. They will go as far as they are needed, even to the sea. The Communists hate the Mongols and are afraid of them.''

Then the Dragon Lady brought her little sister Kim to say good-bye. I put my hands on her shoulders and said, ''Honey, I'm going to miss you.'' When Kim put her arms around me and squeezed, I felt closer to tears than I had been in a long time. She went on hugging me until I told her softly, ''You must be brave like your sister.'' But she still didn't let go until the Dragon Lady came to lead her away.

"All the women and children are going north," the Dragon Lady told us. "It will be safer for them there."

We spent some time shaking hands with the Mongols who would be leaving. When they had all mounted and thundered off, we were left once again with about a hundred people, the same number we'd had crossing the Changchun plain. About a dozen had died in combat, and altogether about thirty women and children were leaving, but the forty Mongols who were joining us made up the difference.

Our party mounted and we were on our way again, this time with the Great Wall as our destination. The pace was a little easier than before; we'd trot, walk, then trot again. There was not much talk; everyone, I guess, was busy with thoughts of his or her own. And we were all exhausted. When, around midafternoon, the order came to dismount, I simply slid off my horse.

It started to rain. The air was so cool that I felt chilled almost at once. I put on the few extra clothes I had, but they didn't help for long; the animal skins repelled water only for a while, and as soon as they were soaked they became cold and clammy. The rain had turned into a driving torrent by the time we mounted again, and I felt as though I were freezing. After a while Nancy pulled up alongside me. She must have seen how I was shivering, for she said, "I am cold also. Can I ride with you?" Though she made it sound like a request for a favor, I had a feeling that she was doing it for my benefit. Holding onto her bridle, she nimbly transferred herself to my horse and sat behind me, with her arms around my middle. Though there were so many layers of soggy clothing between us that her nearness didn't help a lot, after a few minutes I did feel a little less miserable.

As it was getting dark, we came to a hillside where there were caves. After the Dragon Lady had sent scouts ahead, she led us deep inside to a huge open cavern where fires were lit. We all sat near them, trying to warm ourselves. I was so tired that the voices of Gunny and Scotty, sitting close beside me, sounded as though they came from a far-off echo chamber. Then Nancy was leaning over me, saying, "What is wrong, Ricky?" But even with her face so near mine, I could barely hear her. Then I couldn't make out anything at all.

The next thing I remember is awakening with bodies piled over me. I was scared when I tried to move and couldn't. Then Nancy and the Dragon Lady, still pressed close against me, were asking if I was all right.

"Yeah, I think so," I stammered, still feeling confused. I discovered now that I was wearing a completely different set of clothes, all of them warm and dry. Then I noticed Scotty, who said, "You had a rough time of it, lad."

"Yeah, you were one shivering son of a bitch," Gunny said. "We were real worried about you."

"How long have I been out?"

"Maybe fifteen, sixteen hours," Gunny said.

"Christ, why did you let me sleep that long?"

"You were one sick bloke," Audy chimed in. "Trembling like a bloody leaf, sweating and screaming. You must had had some bloody awful nightmares."

"How did I get into these clothes?"

"They changed you." Scotty gestured toward Nancy and the Dragon Lady. "That's your third set. You kept sweating right through them."

When I looked at the two women and smiled, they might have been blushing—except that no one just then had time to be embarrassed.

"They had everybody lying alongside to get some heat into you," Gunny told me.

When I had thanked the Dragon Lady, I asked, "How about the wall? Are we going to get there on time?"

She smiled. "Do not worry. We shall reach it in time."

Then I asked if there was anything to eat. Nancy said, "I get food." Scotty laughed and Gunny teased, "Room service and a pretty waitress. Some guys have all the luck."

Nancy brought some soup with meat in it, which tasted wonderful. While I ate, Scotty explained that the Dragon Lady had gone out to find a certain root, which had been boiled in a soup, and which they had gotten into me somehow while I was lying there, either delirious or dead to the world. Whatever the root had been, it had worked—that and the body heat.

When I'd finished the soup, I asked the Dragon Lady when we would be at the wall.

"We shall rest here today and travel tonight; we shall cross the wall before sunrise." Then she was on her feet again. "I must go and see Charlie and take some food to him. He has been on patrol."

"What a woman!" I said to Scotty, after she left.

"Yes," he answered, "and from a very powerful and highly placed family. She could be living in comfort on Formosa, but she chose to be out here fighting."

When she returned, it was late afternoon outside the cave; the rain had stopped, she told us, and there was no sign of trouble. But she sounded somehow far away as she said it. After she'd stood silent, almost in a trance for a minute or so, she said abruptly, "I think the Communist soldiers have gone the other way." Then came yet another of her abrupt swings of mood. "We had much fun with them, didn't we?"—and her eyes flashed as though she'd been through an exciting game.

"Well, if that was fun," Gunny told her, "I bet we're going to have a lot more fun before we reach the water."

The Dragon Lady was laughing. "They must have tens of thousands of soldiers looking for us."

Gunny rolled his eyes. "I don't see what's so funny about that," he said, and suddenly we were all laughing—though the idea of being chased by an army can't have seemed any funnier to the rest of us than it did to him.

Charlie walked in and told us that it would be dark in one or two hours, and that everything was still quiet. Spotting me, he asked how I felt.

"Never felt better," I told him. And somehow it was true.

He said, smiling, "You did not look better last night."

Then, without any preliminaries except the Dragon Lady's eternal "We must go now," we began to walk our horses out of the cave, moving single file into the evening light. It was cheering to see a little piece of daylight before it faded away.

The main Mongol party had left us a supply of meat, maize and kaoliang for our trek south. Seeing the bundles tied onto the backs of some of the horses, I was reminded that with most of them gone, we were again down a hundred people—not a lot with thousands possibly searching for us. Everyone was silent, probably thinking about the odds just as I was. I began wondering again about the failure of the radio operators to make contact with the Americans who had the transmitter, whoever they were.

As we rode, we descended from the mountains into hill country that made for easier riding. We still saw many caves, and occasionally a patch of land level enough to be used as a rice paddy. Some of the patches were flooded, and after we'd sloshed through one of these we came to a bit of high ground where we stopped to rest.

Sitting next to Scotty, I asked him, "Can you tell me why she wants to go into Peking instead of around it?"

"There is someone there she wants to see, lad."

"Oh? Boyfriend?"

Scotty laughed. "Far from it. The man is a Communist named Sing Yet-soo and he is a former admirer of hers. Three or four years ago she was a Nationalist and had a job in the government. When Sing made a play for her, she snubbed him and he had members of her family killed in retaliation. That is probably why her sister was left with the Mongols—to keep her safe. The Dragon Lady has been waiting patiently for a chance to avenge her family, and now she sees it."

''So she really is not a Nationalist anymore?''

''No, lad. She should never have been in the government. She couldn't function in a bureaucracy, I'm sure you can see that. Whenever she saw corruption—and there was much of it to see—she spoke up. When she didn't like what the Americans were doing, she did the same. Of course that just wouldn't work and eventually, since she didn't get on with them, she simply quit and went her own way. Now she fights for herself and her people, *against* the Communists, but not *for* the Nationalists. I think that is a mistake, and I have told her so. I stayed a Nationalist even though I saw so much that was wrong. That's what brought us to a parting of the ways.''

Now, of course, I understood why this amazing woman wanted us to stay out of her mission to Peking.

We mounted again, and hadn't been riding long when Charlie dropped back to say that we were about a mile from the wall.

One mile from the Great Wall! As I write this, I recall having read that the Great Wall of China is the only manmade object visible to the naked eye from the moon. I didn't know that at the time, of course. But what I would soon be seeing by the clear light of the moon was to me a schoolboy's dream.

As I rode, I tried ticking off the days, though I couldn't be sure anymore that I knew which one it was. I knew we'd made our drop into Manchuria on May 9 and as nearly as I could calculate, a little more than two weeks had gone by since then. That would make it either the twenty-fourth or the twenty-fifth. I supposed that none of the people who'd sent us had expected us to last this long—but then how could I know? There was so much I didn't know. How could anyone have predicted that this was where the expedition would take us? Who could predict how it would end?

Scouts were riding up to report and then going off again, and I could feel a kind of buzz around me, as though the others also thought of reaching the wall as a milestone.

We rode to the top of a rise and there it was.

12

The wall went off in both directions, over hills and valleys, for as far as I could see. A minute after we'd sighted it, we broke into a gallop. We were out in the open, where we could be spotted from a long way off, so we had no time to waste. As we got closer, I could begin to make out some details. It was maybe three stories high and wide enough on top to be used as a road. Every couple of hundred yards, a watchtower rose one story above the wall itself.

"It's fifteen hundred miles long, lad," Scotty told me, "and it begins at the sea."

I asked him, "Is there anyone in those towers?"

"Let's hope not, lad!"

We pounded toward a spot about fifty yards from one of the towers, where we reined in. From there I could see that the construction was of earth and boulders, which in one spot had simply crumbled apart. Several of the Dragon Lady's men had managed to roll away some of the bigger stones from what I could now clearly see was a breach in the wall.

Dismounting and leading our horses carefully, we picked our way through the opening. As I led my mount through, I looked up and around me with an eerie feeling. I was looking up at a wall that ran fifteen hundred miles and was God knows how many hundreds of years old!

But there was little time to be marveling over how old it was. As soon as we were all through, we had mounted again and were on our way. The Communists might not be in every tower, but we had to suppose they'd be sending out patrols.

As we left the wall behind, I had to turn back for one more look, wondering as I did so whether I'd ever see such a spectacle again. After about five miles we halted, and the Dragon Lady brought us several bundles that her men had been carrying. She said, "This is the clothing for the six of us who go into Peking, so that we will look the same as the population. When we get to the outskirts of the city, the others will take our horses. They will circle around Peking to the south and then go east. We shall meet them on the North China Plain."

While I wondered exactly where on the North China Plain we would meet—though I was sure she'd arrange that—she told us that the plain, in contrast to where we'd come from, was heavily populated and would be the most dangerous part of our journey. Besides Gunny and me—she referred to me as Khan—she would be taking the Mongol lieutenant and two of his men with her while the others, led by Charlie, made their circuit of Peking.

The Dragon Lady told Gunny and me, as she handed us the clothes we were to wear, "The hats you will pull down so that your hair and your faces will not show. You decidedly do *not* look Chinese," she added with a smile.

"But with our size—" I began.

''There are all sizes of Chinese. Some who live in the north are tall, as tall as you. Not only the Mongols, but people from all over China come to Peking. It is a very big city. It will be all right, if you keep your hats low. We shall enter in daylight.''

''In daylight?'' It slipped out, even though I'd resolved to keep my mouth shut.

''Yes, in daylight. But there is a holiday,'' she went on, ''and Peking will be empty. The people will go to the Great Wall to hear Mao Zedong make a speech. But I am told that the man I seek will remain in Peking because he has much work to do. He works very hard. He is a very ambitious man.''

The moment came to split up. We shook hands and said our good-byes. I hugged Nancy, and she said, ''You be careful.'' Then they were gone.

There were now ten in our party, including the four who would take our horses with them to wait at our rendezvous. The clothes we put on were standard Communist dress: high-necked tunic jackets, wide baggy trousers and huge hats, worn low as the Dragon Lady had instructed. Light was appearing in the east as we rode over rolling hills toward the city. Soon we came to a rise from which we could see it in the distance. Then we dismounted and turned our horses over to the four, and they rode off.

On foot now, we went in single file at a steady pace, each carrying a basket of gear. I wish that I could describe the city of Peking as it looked to us, but the truth is that I had my broad-brimmed hat so low that I saw nothing but a narrow circle of ground, with no more than a glimpse of the buildings we were approaching. I've read that the outskirts of the city have since filled up with schools and housing for workers. But this was 1952, before the Communist government had done much building, and the population was only two and a half million rather than the nearly eight million it is today.

As we got closer, more and more people came into my range of vision, all of them headed out of the city. Many were carrying flags and banners; some were playing flutelike instruments; a few were on bicycles. No one paid any attention to us. The baskets we carried looked innocent enough from the outside, though they actually held weapons and bandoliers under a layer of kaoliang and maize. They were large enough, in fact, to hold the hunting bows and arrows the Mongols had brought with them.

The numbers of people became first a wave and then a flood of humanity, all in high spirits because of the holiday. In the midst of all this the Dragon Lady spotted a group of bicycles and one tricycle with a cargo platform, which she somehow managed to commandeer. In a moment we had fastened our baskets to the tricycle platform and were pedaling into Peking. I still kept my hat so far down and my head so low that I saw little except the wheels in front of me. Out of a corner of my eye, as we moved from the outskirts toward the inner city, I could see that the bases of the buildings were becoming grander and more elaborate. Once again I was scared and at the same time oddly exhilarated by the notion that with all those thousands of Communists out looking for us, we were cycling straight into their capital.

I saw an imposing stone wall to my left and I sneaked a glimpse of a huge stone lion in front of a wall, confirming my impression that we were now in an older, grander part of the city. The wheels ahead of me finally came to a stop before an old stone building, where we pulled the bikes off to one side and waited with them while the Dragon Lady and the lieutenant knocked at the front door. An old woman opened it and the Dragon Lady motioned for us to enter—quickly, as always.

In a darkened room we were greeted by six other people, each one of whom the Dragon Lady embraced, smiling, and to whom she then introduced us. Our baskets had been retrieved by the two Mongols, and we now each took out our weapons and put them all into a single basket. Meanwhile the Dragon Lady was speaking rapidly and quietly with two of the older people in the house, while the Mongols posted themselves at the windows to watch the street.

The Dragon Lady now told Gunny and me that her "friend" was in the city, and that she knew where to find him. "So we shall go," she said.

The Mongols secured the loaded basket to the tricycle, we got onto our bikes again and rode until we came to a wall. Here, after we had parked the bikes, we took our weapons from the basket and concealed them inside the baggy pants and tunics we wore. This was not difficult, since the Russian guns were so light and small— only about three feet long, or the same length as the Mongols' hunting bows.

Cautiously, we began walking along the wall. After we'd gone about three hundred yards, we came to an arched opening that might have been eight feet high. First the Dragon Lady motioned the two Mongols to go through; she followed and then she beckoned to us. We made our way past four buildings; then we came to a fifth and went in. It was an immense structure that might have been a shrine or a museum, with many statues and carvings of marble and jade.

As we entered, the Dragon Lady hurried to a window on the far side of the building. She peered through it and then waved Gunny and me over to her. She said, pointing to a building directly across the way, ''My 'friend' is there. We shall wait.''

We sat and watched, not talking, for what seemed like hours. Then, all at once, the Dragon Lady's entire body came to an alert, and in the same instant I saw two men emerge from the building we had under observation and head straight toward us.

The Dragon Lady signaled to one of the Mongols, who handed her his bow and an arrow. She fitted the arrow to the bow and moved toward the nearby door while the Mongol lieutenant, with bow and arrow likewise ready, stationed himself on the other side of the door. The Dragon Lady motioned us into a small room off the main chamber while she and the lieutenant waited, partially hidden by the statues that guarded the entrance.

The two men were talking as they strode into the building and past the statues where the Dragon Lady and the lieutenant had concealed themselves. They passed into an adjoining room, and the Dragon Lady and

the Mongol lieutenant immediately stationed themselves on either side of the door leading into it. Within
a few moments the two men reappeared, still engrossed
in conversation, and the Dragon Lady spat out a curse
as they passed. They looked up simultaneously; one
froze in his tracks, and the other wheeled, intending to
flee. Instead he caught an arrow in the throat.

The two Mongols, Gunny and I now ran out to seize
and gag the other man. His face had a look of utter terror and hopelessness; shaking with fear, he sagged as
though about to collapse, until a blow from the Dragon
Lady's open hand straightened him again. "Khan and
Gunny do not have to watch what will happen," she said,
never once taking her eyes off the man. "This is something I must do." Then, when we didn't move, she said,
"I do not wish you to see me like this."

Gunny clutched my arm. "Come on, Khan, let's
wait," he said, and I followed him into another room.
We could hear the stifled sound of the man's voice, and
then a scuffling noise. Gunny nudged me and pointed
to the window. Looking out, I saw four men headed our
way, and raced for the other room. What I saw there
stopped me short.

The body of the Dragon Lady's "friend" hung naked from the outstretched arms of a statue—all except
for the head, which had been placed neatly in the cupped
hands of another statue.

While I blurted, "There's someone coming!" I saw
that the body had been castrated. The marble floor was
slippery with blood. I turned away and saw the Dragon
Lady and the Mongols making for the entrance. They

took up positions just inside it and Gunny and I joined them.

We could hear voices outside, where the men had stopped to talk about what I could only suppose was the life-or-death decision of whether or not to go in. One man hesitated and then withdrew, while the other three entered. The Mongols were at them instantly—a hand clapped over the face of each, one man and one knife at the throat of each. The only noise any of them made was a sort of strangled gurgle.

While the Mongols were dragging the three bodies across the bloody marble of the floor to a smaller room, two more men came in through the door. Without batting an eyelash, the Dragon Lady spoke to them, and whatever she said was funny enough that one of them laughed. As if on cue, she and the lieutenant went to work with their knives; quickly and quietly, the two had been finished off, and more blood was spreading on the surface of the marble floor.

At a shout from one of the Mongols, the Dragon Lady held up her hand. "Guards are coming," she said. "In here, quickly." She and the Mongols had already taken up their positions at the entrance, with their knives out. I took mine from my belt; I saw that Gunny had his ready too. Outside we could hear the guards talking. There were five of them and the same tactics served us as before.

Gunny said, "We better get the hell out of here," and with the Dragon Lady in the lead, we headed for the exit. I did a quick calculation. We'd come to Peking for one

killing and we'd ended up with twelve. I asked, pointing to the corpses, "What do we do with those?"

"We leave them," she said. "We shall go and meet
Charlie now." And she led us to the spot where we'd left
the bikes, which for some reason she now decided to
abandon. We stuffed our weapons back into the basket
and set out on foot. A couple of times I reached up to pull
my hat down low, although there was no one else around
to see me.

After passing between two buildings, we came to a
road, which led to a square enclosed by massive buildings. Here again, the place was empty of people. But as
we crossed it I heard a sound—and that sound led to one
of the most bizarre events of the entire adventure in
China. What I heard was a kind of screech from the
direction of a building on the far side of the square. As
we walked, I saw alongside the building what I soon
made out as a row of about half a dozen cages.

Without thinking, without asking, I went closer, until I could see that the cages were hardly more than three
feet square and three feet high and made of strong wood.
And I now realized that the screeching sounds were
made not by animals but by human beings—men down
on all fours in a space too small to let them stand!

Even though I didn't want to see any more, I couldn't
help going closer. What I saw were men in rags, so filthy that you could hardly see the color of their skin. Yet
not only were they human beings; I now saw unmistak-
ably that they were white! "White" is hardly an accurate word, since they were so dirty; gray would be more

like it. Still I was certain that their features were Caucasian.

One of these men was reaching an emaciated gray arm through the bars and pawing the ground in front of him. Then I realized that food had been dropped on the ground—just out of his reach. He raised his head to stare at me—a creature close to starvation, with a gaunt, bearded face. But what struck me most was his blue eyes and his long, matted hair, which had once been blond. Our two stares met and locked. Finally he managed a word—drawn out and hesitant, as if he hadn't used it in a very long time. But there was no question that the word was "American."

American. A chill ran all through my body, and I began to shake. Crouching down, I reached out toward his arm. His bony hand, with almost no flesh on it, plucked at my arm, desperately but with no strength whatever.

"American?" I repeated, feeling stupid, but not knowing what to say. "You're American?"

He opened his mouth, but whatever he was trying to say came out as a sort of croak.

"I'm American too," I said, pointing to myself with my free hand while he still held onto the other.

Then, in the same drawn-out croak, he said other words, which I am certain were, "Loo ... ten ... ant ... com ... mand ... er ... U ... nited ... States ... Na ... vy."

At that I pretty nearly went crazy. Leaping to my feet, I started tearing at the bars with my hands. The wood frame of the cage and the bars themselves, which seemed each to measure two by two inches, were hard as iron. I pulled out my knife and started to hack at it, shaking the cage with one hand as I slashed with the other. Then two figures came at me from the other side of the cages, shouting and waving what I guess must have been sticks or clubs. They wore high-necked tunics and red arm-bands. In my furious excitement I ignored them, and went on slashing at the bars. Before they quite got to me, a couple of arrows whizzed in my direction. Then the Dragon Lady was tugging at my arm, and the prisoners in the other cages had begun screaming. ''We must go, Khan!'' she kept saying. ''We must *go*!''—while I went on with my slashing.

I remember hearing her give a shout in a language I didn't understand. Then came a blow on the back of my head that knocked me unconscious.

I woke to find myself tied to the platform of the tri-cycle, with the Mongol lieutenant pedaling, while the rest rode ahead on bicycles. For some time my aching head kept me from thinking clearly of anything. But then the men in the cages came back to me.

Were they all American? I couldn't be sure, but it seemed likely. And I knew that one of them was. 'Loo... ten... ant... com... mand... er... U... nited... States... Na... vy.'' I couldn't get the sound of that out of my mind then and I still can't, to this day.

While all this came running back into my mind, we had reached the outskirts of the city. There we left the bikes and headed south on foot, carrying the basket with the weapons. Even then I was moving as though in a trance. How did those men get there? Were they pris-oners of war taken in Korea? But prisoners of war, as any boot is taught, are supposed to be treated according to the Geneva Convention.

One thing I had learned: the Chinese were brutal to their enemies. The Dragon Lady had shown little mercy to her captives. She had decapitated two men and castrated one of them. Mercy appeared to be a luxury nobody in this place and at this time could afford.

I kept going over and over what I could have done to help that caged American. The little capsule in its plastic case leaped to mind, a thought that startled me into realizing that I'd lost track of it somewhere and left it in one of the many changes of clothes while I was cold, sick or unconscious. What had I done to help those men in the cages, except maybe raise a little glimmer of hope—which was probably worse than nothing?

Another thing I'd never be able to get out of my head was how many men I'd gunned down, or knifed or blown up. Sure, I had reasons—but those reasons didn't change what I'd done, or keep me from remembering.

As we moved along, I wondered whether Gunny was thinking the same kind of thoughts, blaming himself in the way I was. He had kept silent all this while, and when I looked over to him he would not meet my eyes.

As we left the city, we began to encounter hordes of people returning from the holiday celebration. More times than I could count, I tugged my hat down over my eyes again. I have no idea how far we had trudged when we reached the top of a small hill and caught sight of the four Mongols with the horses.

Soon we had mounted and were heading south toward the main group, going from a walk to a gallop. We were all glad to put some distance between us and Peking, knowing what we'd left behind us. No one was gladder than I was, now that I had a picture of what had been done to a captured American. When I gave the question a little more thought, I realized that no one would suffer more on being captured than the Dragon Lady. I shuddered every time I thought of it.

13

Crossing the plain, we began to see walled villages with the dark rich green of fields and trees around them. Great numbers of people were hard at work, paying us only casual notice as we galloped past.

Finally we came in sight of our main group. The re-union with them didn't last long; soon the order came to split up into two groups. "We are too many, too no-ticeable," the Dragon Lady told Scotty. "You and Charlie will take one group. I shall take another."

Gunny, Audy, Nancy and I were to go with her; we'd take some of her people and half the Mongols, to make up a force of fifty. Scotty and Charlie were to form an equal force out of the other twenty Mongols and the rest of the Dragon Lady's people. She explained to Scotty and Charlie where we'd meet again, outlining what she thought was the best route to follow.

Looking over my shoulder as we took off, I could see the others disappear into the haze and I had to wonder whether I'd see them again. After a few miles, there were new orders. "We shall be passing many people," the Dragon Lady said. "We shall travel in single file, keep-ing twenty yards between. Do not pay any special no-tice to the people you pass. Act as if you were one of them. If anyone questions you, don't answer. Just keep your head down. I or one of the others will answer for you.''

Though this was the country with the largest population in the world, we hadn't seen very many people thus far. But the more of them we met now, the greater the chance that something could go wrong and interfere with our chances of reaching the coast. We were proceeding slowly, and although I could understand why we didn't dare act like fugitives on the run, the pretending to be casual, with the hat kept low over my face, was beginning to be a strain. I couldn't help thinking about what would happen if anyone got a close look at the blond, blue-eyed boy from Massachusetts underneath the disguise. I tried to hypnotize myself into staying calm by concentrating on the steps of my horse.

People and wagons were all around us now. The rice paddies appeared more frequently and often we would cross a bridge over one of the streams that watered them. Suddenly we were being led off toward a village with a high stone wall around it. When we reached the gate, the Dragon Lady spoke to an old man who was acting as a sort of gatekeeper and he motioned for us to go in. As we filed through, what struck me was the number of people swarming inside those walls. After we had dismounted, the Dragon Lady spoke with a villager and then said to Gunny and me, ''Go with him. You will change clothes, then we shall have to leave. Quickly.''

In answer to a question from Gunny, she explained, ''You are wearing *Communist* clothes. I don't like to wear those. Do you?''

"No sir!" Gunny said. "I mean, no ma'am!"

Her face eased into a grin. "Five minutes."

Following the villager into a hut, Gunny and I were given clothes in the Mongolian style, though less heavy than the ones we'd seen in the north. We got into them quickly. Outside we found the Dragon Lady, who had also changed her clothes, already mounted and waiting for us. "Why have you taken so long?" she asked good-naturedly, and we had been so tense until then that we all laughed.

Once we were on the road again, I noticed that the people who passed would glance at us and then look away quickly. The Dragon Lady told us that all the Chinese, whether Communist or non-Communist, were afraid of the Mongols, and I could believe that it must be so.

By now we were continually crossing bridges, many of them spanning canals with dikes on each side. The plain was so low that without the dikes it would have been flooded. After we had been traveling for a while, we came to a halt. Up ahead, a group of Communist soldiers appeared to have gotten out of a truck and rounded up a group of about fifty people. When the Dragon Lady started around the truck, a soldier who looked like an officer shouted something to her. She answered and waited calmly as he approached, with a kind of leer on his face. After another exchange, he reached out to touch her arm, and now his grin was really ugly. She pulled back her arm as she answered him, and in the same moment the Mongol lieutenant pulled up alongside her at an angle that allowed me to see what happened next, though I was twenty yards away. The Mongol riveted the soldier with his powerful stare, whose effect I knew about from my own experience. I watched the soldier's hand fall away from the Dragon Lady's arm as he took a step back. Then, calling out something harsh, as though to save face, he waved us on. We passed the soldiers one by one, looking straight ahead. I was so anxious that it wasn't until we'd gone a hundred yards that I risked a peek over my shoulder to make sure we'd all been allowed to pass.

Some time later, the Dragon Lady dropped back alongside me to say that we would soon be stopping at a village and that she thought we would leave the horses there. When I asked why, she said, "They make us too noticeable. But there is a chance we can keep them. We shall see later."

"Do you know people there?" I asked. She said she did, and I asked, "How is it you know everybody everywhere? You seem so young to have met so many people!"

She shrugged, and I said, "How old *are* you?"

She gave me a stare that ended in a smile. "I told you. Very old and wise."

"Okay," I said. "But let me ask you something else. In Peking—those prisoners—"

"Yes. Those prisoners were American, and we could understand the way you felt. But you were putting all of us in danger. So—" She gestured with her head toward the Mongol lieutenant. "*He* hit you. I told him to do it."

I nodded, but I must have looked as unhappy as I felt, because she now went on, "You must understand that he has vowed to protect you with his life, to make sure you reach the water and then go to an American ship. He made a promise, Khan, and he will keep it.''

She pointed to the right. "We must go that way, across the fields there. The village is not far now.'' We left the road, and were soon moving at a fast pace between rice fields, where people were at work. The stone wall of the village came into view, and then we were reining up at the entrance. While we dismounted, a group of people came out to meet us. After the Dragon Lady had spoken with them briefly, several of them took our horses and we went in on foot. Once again I was struck by the density of the population. The whole area was small but with hundreds of people packed into it.

"Are the villages always this crowded?'' I asked her.

"Yes, all very crowded,'' she replied. At a word from her the Mongol lieutenant spoke to his men, and in a moment they had fanned out and were mingling with the villagers. A figure now came toward us who had the look of a head man if I ever saw one. After a few words with the Dragon Lady, who pointed to Gunny and me as she answered him, the man strode up and made us welcome. Our little party—the Dragon Lady, Nancy, Gunny, Audy and I—followed him to the far side of the village, where he led us to a house that I suppose was his. It had just three rooms, and in one of them at least fifteen people sat in a circle. They had been eating, but now they all got to their feet and bowed to us. We bowed back, and then the head man motioned for us to sit down with them. We were given rice and maize, which we ate without speaking while the chief and the Dragon Lady talked quietly.

When the food was gone, the people all bowed their heads and began a kind of mumble. I looked over at Gunny and saw that he was just as puzzled as I—until the Dragon Lady caught my eye and then bowed her own head. I realized then that the mumbling was a prayer. As Gunny and I sat there with our heads bowed, nobody had more to pray for than we did.

After that, the Chinese people began chatting among themselves. One young fellow, who must have been about my own age, insisted on talking to me. The Dragon Lady, noticing, slid closer and explained, "He wants to know if you are American."

"What will you tell him?"

"What do you want me to tell him?"

"Do you trust him?"

"He is my cousin, and I trust him."

She turned and addressed the young man, who was still looking at Gunny and me as though we were the main attraction in a museum. He went on talking with the Dragon Lady but every now and then he would begin looking at us again.

Soon I could hardly hold my head up, and I asked Gunny if he was as tired as I was.

"More so," he said.

I turned to the Dragon Lady, with a motion to let her see how sleepy I was. "You come with me," she said, and walked us all to another room where there were several mats on the floor. "You sleep here," she said.

"Don't say another word," Gunny told her, and in an instant he had flopped down on a mat.

I looked at Nancy, thinking she would be sent to another room to sleep. But she declared, "I sleep here."

"How about you?" I asked the Dragon Lady.

"I shall sleep here, too."

Audy said with a laugh. "And I'll sleep here *too*!"

I suppose the Dragon Lady was still amused by my modesty. But what was really on my mind just then was how five of us would find floor space in a room that must have been no more than six by four feet. I didn't wait to learn how it could be done; I was so exhausted that I was no sooner on a mat than I was sound asleep.

I woke in the dark, to a faint flicker of light from the fire in the next room. Nancy and Audy were still asleep, but I found Gunny and the Dragon Lady sitting by the fire in the other room, eating rice and talking.

They looked up as I came in, and I asked what time it was.

"The middle of the night," the Dragon Lady said.

"What are you two talking about?" I asked them, and Gunny said, "Business." I thought he looked a little uncomfortable.

"What kind of business could that be?" I said. "In the middle of the night?"

"Well, mainly what's going to happen in the future."

I said, "What future is that? Is there anything to make you think there even is a future for guys like you and me?"

The Dragon Lady said, "You should not think that way."

"I'll tell you what I think," I burst out. "I think my future ended back in that tunnel. Back there, I had no thought of ever getting out alive. From then on, every minute I've lived has been a bonus—one minute more that I didn't dare expect."

Gunny nodded, looking somber. But then he said, "Well, dammit, you did get out of there. That's what counts now."

"No," I said. "What counts is that when I was in that tunnel, I wrote myself off as dead. Something came over me that made me lose all fear. It wasn't that I suddenly became a hero, or felt like Superman—nothing like that. It's just that every minute, every day I get now is extra. So I have *not* been making any long-range plans for any future!"

I was a little surprised at hearing myself say all this, and I halfway wondered whether I really meant it. But it was true that for days now I hadn't once seen myself back in America. The place known as the future was nothing but a blank screen with nobody looking at it.

Gunny said, "For Christ's sake, smarten up, kid. You're gonna get out of here—that is, unless you go on thinking like that!"

"Gunny is right, Khan," the Dragon Lady said. "You must not think that way. We all care for you too much."

I shook my head and then I shrugged. "If there is a future for me, I won't throw it away." Then I said, "But you never did say what the business was that *you* were talking about."

He laughed, and then said, "Seriously—"

"Seriously?" I grinned at him. "You don't know what the word is. But don't get me wrong, Gunny. I think you're one hell of a guy." Once again, what I was saying surprised me—but this time I knew I meant every word of it. "Back in the States, if you were a senior NCO and I was a snuff, you might have treated me like shit. All I know is that here, you've never pulled rank on me. A lot of people would have." I stopped, feeling a little embarrassed by all that I felt. The experiences we'd shared had brought us closer than anything else ever could have. Those experiences weren't over yet, and who knew where they would finally take us?

Gunny said, "Well, Rick, I'm pulling rank on you right now. Rack out. We got a long way to go tomorrow and we got to be off early. I'm going back to sleep." And he got to his feet and headed back to his mat.

"What about that business?" I said again.

"I'll tell you. Only not now. Now let's get some sleep."

In no time I'd dropped off again, and when I woke next it was daylight. Nancy appeared with plates of food for Gunny and Audy and me, and we'd just begun eating when the Dragon Lady came in. I knew this meant there wasn't much time to finish our meal. As soon as we had, we went with her into the room where the Mongol lieutenant was sitting with two of his men. They left after she'd talked with them briefly, and then she said to us, "We shall take the horses. We do not yet have to leave them."

Just then there was a commotion outside the door. We heard Audy's voice, and he came in in a rush, bringing Kim with him.

While the Dragon Lady spoke excitedly with her sister, Audy explained, "She came with some important news." The two of them talked for some time, and it seemed to me that I had never seen the Dragon Lady as she was now—almost rigid with anger.

"It seems that some of the people we killed in Peking were high government officials," she told us finally. "Very high government officials." She paused. Then she said to me, "Do you remember the man who came to the door with three others, the one who did not enter with them?"

Yes, I remembered. I'd seen how one man hesitated and then walked off—the decision that had saved his life.

She said, glaring at me, "That man was Mao."

"Mao?" I repeated. "Mao *Zedong*?"

"Yes!" She was almost spitting with rage.

I said, "I never really looked at him."

"And neither did I!" She was almost shrieking. "But if I had, I would have given *anything*—I would even have spared Sing Yet-soo—to put an arrow into him! *Anything!* And now I shall never be so close again!"

I couldn't think of anything to say.

Getting back her self-control, she went on, "As you can imagine, they are furious in Peking. They are sending out troops over all the area to look for us. But luckily they do not know which way we went. So those troops must go in every direction." She seemed to take some satisfaction in giving them that much trouble.

"But we're still in the middle of it," Gunny said.

"Yes," the Dragon Lady told him. "That is why we must head south. We must now split up."

"We're already split up," I reminded her.

"Not split enough," she said. "We must now form at least *six* groups. We shall head toward Loshan, where I have friends, and cross the Grand Canal. We shall pass many, many people, so we must be careful. Until we meet at Loshan, our six groups will be near each other. But I must warn you: we may have to change our direction at any time. So the groups will be close enough that we can speak with each other every day."

I asked, "What about Scotty and his people?"

Before answering, the Dragon Lady spoke to the Mongol lieutenant, who nodded and went out. Then she turned to Gunny and me. "The lieutenant will send two men to warn Scotty and tell him to detour to meet us at Loshan. If we can all reach that place safely, we shall have a choice of routes to follow. But I must warn you," she said again, and her face and voice were as grave as I'd ever seen them. "We can trust no one. The Communists are determined to capture us. Their spies are everywhere. They have offered a large reward to anyone who captures us. The trip to Loshan will be very dangerous."

"They can't outfox the fox," I said, trying to sound as though I believed it.

She did not smile at being called a fox, but answered with a shrug, "We shall see. Once we reach Loshan, our chances will improve."

"Let's say we get to Loshan," I began. "And let's say we make it from there to the coast. How are we going to contact the Americans?"

"We must find a transmitter. I think we shall do that without much difficulty."

I had one more question: "What happens to Kim?"

After a word to her young sister, with both of them glancing at me, the Dragon Lady said, "She goes with us." Then as though anticipating what I was thinking about the danger, she went on, "When I was her age, I wanted the same thing—not to be left out."

Kim said something now, and the Dragon Lady translated: "She has something to give you—something that belonged to our parents. She wants you to have it." While I stared, Kim put into my hand a set of rosary beads, made of greenish jade, with a hand-carved ivory cross.

"They're beautiful!" I said, putting my arms around Kim. She reached up and kissed me on the cheek, and when I saw tears welling in her eyes I had to turn away or I would have been crying too. I saw the Dragon Lady watching with a soft look that made her a totally different person from the one she had been only a few minutes before. Now I put one arm around Kim and the other around the Dragon Lady, and hugged them both at once.

But in a moment the thought of the commander came back into the Dragon Lady's face, and I heard it in her voice: "Now we shall divide into groups. It would be best for you Americans to go separately. So if one is caught, the other will have a chance to get to the sea."

It was a sobering idea, and I hated having to think of it. I said, looking at Gunny, "We're the only two left."

"Yeah," he said. "But she's right, Rick." He turned to the Dragon Lady. "Okay, so we split."

"Khan, Nancy, Kim, the lieutenant and one other Mongol will go with me. Audy and Gunny will go with three Mongols. Do not worry, Gunny. You will be in good hands."

"I'm not worried about *me*," he said, staring in my direction. "Take care of the girls, and don't go gung-ho on us. Play it safe."

"Right," I said. "I'll take care of them. And no gung-ho."

Then the Dragon Lady began outlining our trip. "From here we travel south. We do not divide into groups until we reach the meeting of the Grand Canal and the Hwang Ho."

I asked how long it would take us to reach Loshan, and she said, "Perhaps two days, perhaps a week." She turned abruptly and shouted an order to someone, who disappeared and came back with a leather bag. From it the Dragon Lady pulled out two sets of binoculars—one for Gunny and one for me. The first set she'd given me had been lost in the fighting.

Gunny already had his up and was scanning the distance.

"A good thing that," Audy said. "With the land so flat, you can see a long way. Spot a Commie from miles off."

"There is also another enemy out there," the Dragon Lady said. "This is the season of floods."

Audy confirmed this: "The whole bloody area can go under water."

"But also the floods might work for us," she said. "Now we go. They are searching for us every minute."

Outside all of our people were waiting. A number of villagers were standing by. When the Dragon Lady said something to them, Audy explained, "She's telling them we are heading east."

"But aren't we heading south?"

"Quiet there, mate," he warned. We mounted, and we did start by heading east. When we were a mile or so from the village, two scouts dropped back as rear guards. After we had passed a few more villages, we took a route through the rice paddies that veered slightly to the south. There was a halt when we reached a kind of basin, where we waited for the scouts to appear.

"It is all right," the Dragon Lady told us finally. "We are not being followed." She appeared to read my thoughts about the friendly villagers. "There are spies and informers—eyes and ears everywhere. We cannot be too careful. Soon there may be planes looking for us. Now we must get back on the road and mingle with other people. You two must keep your hats down low."

After riding due south for less than half a mile, we came to a road that was simply a river of people—so many of them that we had to ride alongside. After a while we dismounted and walked our horses, with the Dragon Lady in the lead. I was right behind her; then came Kim, Nancy and the others, strung out in a long line, our weapons hidden in baskets that had been secured to the backs of the horses.

Before long we began to see Communist soldiers standing by the road, keeping a close watch on the people going in both directions. The farther we went, the more of them there were, and the closer together what seemed to be checkpoints. But the guards were only watching, not stopping anyone.

Out of the corner of my eye I saw Nancy working her way up to me. "More Communists as we go south," she whispered.

"I can see," I told her, doing my best to keep my head down. "You must get back in line." I smiled from underneath the hat, and could see her smile as she dropped behind me.

Over the next few miles there must have been a hundred soldiers stationed along the road. They made me feel like a hunted animal. While I tried to sneak past, unarmed, right under their noses, my heart pounded so hard that I halfway believed they would hear it.

It was midmorning by now, and the flow of people along the road was thicker than ever. I was surprised to see one of the Mongols mount his horse and leave the road, heading off toward a rice paddy. Seeing that we were near a checkpoint, I lowered my head. Then I heard a commotion, and up ahead I could just make out that the Mongol was being stopped by three soldiers, who had begun interrogating him. As I got closer I could hear the threat in their voices. But the Mongol went on sitting astride his horse with his hands folded, not saying a word. I didn't know whether they thought he couldn't understand them, or were afraid of him or just baffled. But finally, looking annoyed, they waved him on.

My spirits had risen briefly at seeing the giant outwit the soldiers, but now they fell again at the thought of how noticeable the Mongols were; it seemed to me that the Communists had to connect them with our raids. How many Mongols could there be in China at the moment who were giving trouble to the authorities?

As we rode, I noticed that the soil was darker and richer than before. This was river-bottom country, with canals everywhere, all of them held in their channels by high dikes. Toward early afternoon a light rain started to fall. At the same time, the weather was so much warmer that I took off all my extra clothes, keeping on a long-sleeved shirt to hide the color of my skin. I'd smeared dirt on my hands, neck and face. But what mainly helped me at times when soldiers were within a couple of feet of me, was simply the unbelievable numbers of people crowded along the roads—literally thousands of them. It must have been that after a while anyone trying to watch would be hypnotized by the sight of so many people passing.

Again and again I made out the walls of a village off to the side of the road with hundreds of people at work in the fields around it. The rain became heavier and it felt so good that I would have loved to throw my head back and let it wash the grime and sweat from my face. But of course I didn't do any such thing.

The checkpoints now seemed farther apart, and after a while the Dragon Lady dropped back to tell Nancy and me, "After the next checkpoint, we shall leave the road. There is a village nearby where we can stop and rest for a time." She veered off the road a little later and after

riding less than a quarter of a mile we were in the midst
of a huge, soggy rice field. Keeping clear of the green
rows while we sloshed through water, we made our way
across it and uphill onto a plain. After a mile or so we
came in sight of a village. Before we got to the wall sur-
rounding it, the Dragon Lady signaled us to stop while
she rode on ahead. Hundreds of men, women and children were working in the fields, and they gave us a curious glance now and then while we waited, not moving.
It must have been nearly an hour before she returned and
signaled for us to enter. During those final few hundred
yards the wind was blowing and it began raining harder,
so I was all the happier at the thought of shelter.

The houses of the village, as those in the others we'd
seen, were small and primitive—and just as packed with
people. I wondered how they could live jammed together that way. Some of the Mongols took our horses
and we went in on foot—Gunny and I still keeping our
hats pulled low. After what the Dragon Lady had told
us about spies, we could hardly feel relaxed. The Mongols, always a little remote and wary, stayed outside the
village with the horses, and didn't mingle at all with the
people of the village, while we were led into a low-
ceilinged hut and given food.

From the beginning, though, there had been some
uneasiness in the air. After a few moments I saw that the
Dragon Lady and Audy were both agitated and soon she
was saying that we must leave.

I asked what was the matter.

Audy answered my question. "The Communists have been really butchering people. It's no good here. The villagers are too bloody upset."

So we went out into the downpour. Just as we were mounted and about to start off, three figures on horseback appeared in the distance, heading straight for us. They were all riding like madmen. As they got closer, I could see that one of them was a white man. When he leaped from his horse, he turned out to be at least as big as the Mongol lieutenant—maybe six feet six, and weighing as much as 250 pounds.

Two smaller figures, wearing robes that covered them from head to toe, sat on their horses while the big man walked toward us. He was black-haired, with dark eyes. "And are you just going to sit there and stare all the day?" he asked, with a grin that showed a lot of very white teeth. I guessed from his accent that he must be an Irishman—not Boston Irish but the real thing. An M-1 rifle was slung over his shoulder, and he carried two knives on his belt.

The Dragon Lady dismounted to meet him, and several of the villagers came outside the walls again. As soon as they headed back inside, she was motioning for Gunny and me to follow her, and soon we were back in the same hut as before.

The black-haired giant looked around and grinned again. "O'Malley's the name, John O'Malley. And whose company do I have the pleasure of on this hell of a fine day?"

We introduced ourselves, and I went on wondering about his two small companions. They were still en-

gulfed in the robes they wore, though they looked as
though they must be soaked through. Finally, with a
glance at them, O'Malley said, ''We have a bit of a
problem.'' When the two figures finally shed those wet
outer clothes, I saw what it was. They were both women,
Caucasian, and dressed in the garb of nuns.

While they stood there quietly shivering, O'Malley
said, ''The Communists seem to have gone quite daft.
These two sisters are from a little church on the other
side of the Grand Canal, four miles to the south. A force
of Communist soldiers came up the road, shooting
everything and everyone in sight. They walked straight
into the church, firing. I was in the back with a priest
and the sisters. When the priest ran out into the sanc-
tuary, they shot him. I gathered up the two sisters here,
got them onto horses, and off we rode. As we were leaving, the soldiers were setting the church afire.''

A couple of the villagers now took the nuns aside and
gave them food. They were Belgian, O'Malley told us;
whether they didn't know English at all, or were under
some kind of vow of silence, or were just in a state of
shock, I never found out. For a moment the rest of us
simply stood there, no one saying anything, until I
thought to ask O'Malley where he had come from.

It was a second or two, while he looked at me as though
it was none of my business, before he answered,
''Burma.''

''That is a very long way,'' the Dragon Lady said.
''What is your destination?''

O'Malley glared at her for a second. Then he said, "You're a tiny thing. If you stood sideways, I might not even see you."

Though he sounded genial, it was a brush-off and the Dragon Lady knew it. "But I am *not* standing sideways," she retorted. "I am asking your destination."

He let out a big laugh. "No, you're not standing sideways, and I *can* see you. Very well. I am heading for Indochina."

"Are you lost, perhaps?" she asked. "You are a very great distance out of your way."

He said, laughing even louder, "I came up here to go to *church*!" Then he added, "No, I have to meet some friends first. Then we will go south again. To help my countrymen in the fighting in Indochina."

The Dragon Lady stared. "I did not know the *Irish* were fighting in Indochina!"

This time he nearly exploded with laughter. "Sure, and you'd be deaf not to hear the Irish in my voice. But I was in the French foreign legion for fifteen years, and now I'm heading for where the fighting is."

"And what about *them*?" I nodded toward the nuns. They now sat in a corner eating rice, looking nowhere but down into their bowls.

"Oh, I'll manage. We're only three, and we should be able to slip through. The soldiers are busy looking for someone else." He seemed to be thinking, and his stare moved from the Dragon Lady to each one of us.

"It wouldn't be yourselves, I suppose?" he said then.

The Dragon Lady answered with another question. "Have you seen many Communist soldiers?"

"Many? The whole road is a nest of them!"

Audy was now looking alarmed. "What road did you say you were on?"

"I didn't," O'Malley said, still parrying. Again he seemed to be thinking before he replied, "Just south of Tungping."

"That's the very same bloody road Scotty would be on," Audy said.

"If you have a friend on that road," O'Malley told him, "he'll be overrun."

The Dragon Lady now said, "Our schedule must be changed."

"Then you'd best hurry!" O'Malley told her. "You've a long way to go, and the mud will be so deep that horses will be of no use."

"Perhaps Scotty and his people will not be stopped," the Dragon Lady said quickly. "We passed many Communist soldiers and we were not taken. Scotty may not have been so lucky. But if he has been taken, we must try to help him. With surprise and the weather, even a small strike force, one of our size, could perhaps succeed. If necessary, we must be ready to try."

Audy, Gunny and I all readily agreed—though I couldn't help adding to myself, "But how?"

Then O'Malley said, with a look at us, "I may as well go too."

"You have the sisters to care for," the Dragon Lady reminded him.

"Ah, then, if I'm killed," the big Irishman said, "you must agree to look after the sisters."

"Agreed," the Dragon Lady said.

O'Malley gave his flashing grin, shook hands with all of us, and then reached into his pocket like a magician about to perform a trick. What he brought out was an old, battered tin flask. Unscrewing the top, he held it up and called out, "A toast for the battle to come!" After a healthy swig he said "Ahhh," and passed the flask to Gunny.

"Whiskey?" Gunny asked.

"Homemade."

"It's been a long time," Gunny said, and took a mouthful. He swallowed, gasped, and held out the flask to Audy, who declined it. Then he offered it to me.

Although my experience with drinking was close to nil, I filled my mouth with the fiery stuff. That was my first mistake. Trying to swallow it all was my second. I choked, gagged and spat all over the place, trying to catch my breath while the whiskey made its way through my insides, burning all the way.

"Have another, son," O'Malley said, while Gunny tried to keep a straight face. "Half of that one went on the floor."

When the laughter died down, the Dragon Lady got back to business with a question to O'Malley. "Tell us about the condition of the terrain between here and Tungping."

"Mud, as I said. Getting worse all the time. We hardly made it ourselves. I was sure our horses would break a leg. Now it will be impossible; you'll not be riding there."

"How can we make any time without horses?" Gunny asked.

"I made it all the way from Burma without one," O'Malley told him.

Gunny said, taking on the challenge, "Well, hell, we came all the way from Manchuria, and half of that was on foot!"

"Ah, saints preserve us, so you *are* the ones the Communists are after!" O'Malley declared.

I said to Gunny, "You sure know how to keep a secret!"

"Never mind, lad," O'Malley told me. "It's hard to keep that kind of secret. There are only a few of us foreigners in China, and when you hear about a group of them causing trouble, it's not too hard to figure out who it might be. Believe me, your secret is safe with me!"

The Dragon Lady had been talking with several of the villagers, who now brought out some skins. "Get your weapons," she said, "and wrap them in these to keep them dry."

We went outside to follow her instructions, and found a gale blowing. Huts were swaying; here and there a roof had been torn off, and the rain seemed to be driving at a forty-five-degree angle to the ground. Following the Mongols outside the village walls to where the horses were, we retrieved our weapons from the baskets and took them back to the hut. We found the nuns kneeling in prayer. Almost without thinking, I put down my machine gun and bandoliers and knelt down myself.

"The Lord is my shepherd, I shall not want..." I hardly knew where the words came from, but there they were. When I looked around, the Dragon Lady, Gunny, Audy, Nancy and Kim were all kneeling too.

I had always believed in God, and right now the time had come when it was comforting just to ask for a little outside help.

We got up and no one said anything for a moment or two. Then, as if there had been a signal, we were all moving. I slung the bandoliers and the binoculars over my shoulder again, checked my weapon, and wrapped it in the skins I'd been given.

The Dragon Lady was saying, "Nancy, I should like you to take Kim, the two sisters and some of our men to a place where we shall meet you. It will be difficult, for you will not be able to travel on the roads; you will have to cross the plain, which is like a marsh in this weather. You will have to take great care."

She paused and looked for a second at Nancy. "If we are late," she said, "—if we do not come to the place by the right time, then the Mongols will lead you back to the mountains. You must not wait longer than the time I shall tell you."

"No!" Nancy said. It was as though the word leaped out of her. "We wait. We do not leave without you."

"Nancy!" the Dragon Lady answered sternly. "You will not wait one minute past the time I tell you. Every minute is a danger to the people with you. You must promise!"

Tears broke from the girl's eyes and rolled down her face. She stared at the Dragon Lady and then at me. I walked over to her, put my hands on her fragile shoulders, and said gently, "We're going to be there, don't worry. But you must promise."

She went on looking at the two of us. At last she said, "I promise," and added, "Please be there!"

I could hardly keep the tears out of my own eyes. While I turned and walked away, the Dragon Lady put an arm around Nancy and walked with her, telling her in Chinese exactly where and when we were to meet. And then, once again, it was time to go.

In a couple of minutes we stood outside the village wall, in the pelting rain, watching while Nancy and her group veered off to the right and vanished into the storm. Then we had to concentrate on our own journey. The mud gave us trouble almost from the first step. At best it didn't quite reach our ankles; at worst, we were sucked in up to the knees, all the time struggling to keep upright in the face of the wind. Adding to our exhaustion was the fact that it was now getting dark. Soon the mud was an intimate addition to our clothes, and it kept working its way through to the skin. I'd wrapped my machine gun as carefully as possible, but I worried about how I was going to check it before firing, if I ever had to.

Darkness came fast and we slogged on, bunched close together so as not to lose each other. There was almost no visibility. Even in all that rain, I was sweating like a pig. Whenever I stopped for a drink of water, I got a dose of mud along with it. Finally the Dragon Lady held up her hand for a stop and we gathered into a single group. There were about thirty of us now. She told us that the Grand Canal was just ahead. "Scotty had to cross the canal here," she told us, "where it meets the Hwang Ho. So we shall cross. We shall take the road he took, and we shall catch his group very soon, I hope."

We resumed our plodding for about half a mile. Then we were at the canal, and again she was signaling a stop. She and the Mongol lieutenant went off to make a reconnaissance, leaving the rest of us there to rest. I looked over at O'Malley, who was so quiet that he might have been in a trance. Gunny, noticing it too, shook him and said, "Hey Irish, snap out of it!"

But O'Malley only said, "Things are not going right. When they are, I'll be the first to tell you. But now they're not."

Gunny asked what he was talking about, and after another couple of moments his eyes seemed to focus.

"Now," I said, "tell us what the hell you were talking about."

"Talking? Was I talking? What did I say?" O'Malley asked.

"A lot of bullshit," Gunny told him.

"So I was. So I was, I suppose," O'Malley said. None of us was satisfied with that, but we all settled down to wait for the Dragon Lady. About ten minutes later she was back.

"There is a big bridge up ahead," she told us, "But it is guarded. So we shall walk under it."

Gunny asked how we were going to do that—by walking on water? I was glad he had begun asking the dumb questions.

"Yes," she answered with a laugh. "You will see. There is a footbridge along the abutments, at the level of the water. We shall walk on that."

What she called a footbridge was hardly even that. It had no rail, it was narrow and slippery, and in places it was actually under the water of the canal, which was turbulent with flooding from the storm. But there was nothing to do except follow her, watching our footing as we moved in single file along those swaying planks, with nothing to hold onto except the pilings of the bridge. These were spaced about ten feet apart, and what made things worse was the way the planks kept moving away from the pilings and then drifting back with the movement of the water. That meant having to dash from one piling to the next while the planks were up against it, and then squatting down on the boards to hold on as it moved away again—then another dash, another squat. The footbridge was held together with rope, but didn't seem to be attached to the main bridge. I don't know what kept it suspended.

When I finally set foot on land, the Dragon Lady was waiting, moving each one of us along while she watched to see that everyone had made it. We waited while she took a final count. It appeared that no one was missing.

Then we were moving through the mud again for another half hour, until we came to a road. The storm had left it deserted. After the packed roads we'd traveled in daylight, the emptiness seemed strange. There was a delay while the Dragon Lady sent out scouts. The road, once we started forward again, was so muddy that it was very little better than trudging across the plain had been.

Some figures up ahead meant another halt, and this time the Dragon Lady ordered us to get down. Staying at a half crouch in mud and water left our clothes and skin in worse condition than ever, but we hid until it was clear that the people coming were our own scouts. The

Dragon Lady talked with them for a while and then came over to report.

"The Communists have camped about a quarter of a mile ahead. In a field just across from them they have shot about two hundred people."

I suppose the same thought went through all our minds. Audy was the one who voiced it: "What about Scotty and Charlie?"

"The scouts do not know. We shall move up as close as we can and see what we can find out."

We trudged forward through the mud, and again the signal came to halt. I said, "Why not hit them now, while they're asleep?"

"No," she replied. "We shall wait for the scouts to come back again." And she told us to check our weapons.

Glad for a chance to do this, I unwrapped my machine gun, and found that it wasn't quite as filthy as I'd feared. I did the best I could to clean it in that weather, squeezed out the water from the skins and rewrapped it.

Half an hour must have passed before the scouts returned once again with their report. Now she told us, "We are thirty yards from the bodies of the prisoners they killed. The Communists are right across the road. We shall get into their camp to see if any prisoners are alive. If there are not—" She paused. "Then that will mean that Scotty and Charlie escaped, or else they are out in the field . . . with the other bodies."

14

O'Malley was the one who finally broke the silence.

"I've got a plan," he said. "But it depends on the weather."

While Gunny and I looked at him in surprise—we'd gotten used to expecting nobody but the Dragon Lady to offer any plans—she said, "I would like to hear it. But with any plan, we must finish off all the Communists and get away quickly. And there must be no survivors who might send out a message."

O'Malley began, "You may think I'm daft. But first hear me out. You know how afraid they are of ghosts." Gunny was giving him a hard look. But the Dragon Lady put up her hand to give O'Malley a chance. "If we could spook them," he went on, "scare the hell out of them, and then have people hit them from the rear..."

While Audy made a gesture toward his head that showed what he thought, the Dragon Lady was saying, "It might work."

O'Malley then explained his plan in detail. He wanted some of us to rise from the midst of the field where the bodies were, as though we were ghosts, and walk straight into the Communist camp. Covered with mud, we'd certainly look like corpses just risen from out there. But the rain would have to have stopped, giving some visibility, before it would work.

"Yes," the Dragon Lady agreed, "they do frighten easily. And that would perhaps distract them long enough for us to attack and finish every one of them off. Remember: No one must be left alive to send out any warnings."

Since she thought it had a chance to work, all at once it became our plan. She got everyone together and then divided us into five groups. Four would attack from the sides of the camp and the fifth would play the challenging and dangerous role of the dead who had been raised. The Dragon Lady, Gunny, Audy, O'Malley, the lieutenant and I, along with several others, made up this group. The Dragon Lady was to fire the first shot to signal the attack.

We moved out, with the wind and rain driving as hard as ever. Crouching low, wading through mud and water, we sloshed into the field, where I tried not to look at the corpses. Covered with mud until they were partly submerged, many revealed neither sex nor age, except for the very young ones. The size of the children made them unmistakable; those tiny bodies made me so angry that as at no other time, I actually wanted to kill the soldiers who had been responsible. And if O'Malley's crazy plan worked, my chance to do it might come.

When we'd moved about ten yards in from the road, our group spread out and we lay down in the mud and water, waiting for dawn and a break in the weather. The dawn we were sure of; the weather we could only pray for.

After we'd waited for what seemed to be hours, light finally appeared in the east. As I looked around me, the first thing I could see was the outline of the body nearest me. I closed my eyes, not wanting to look. Opening them again, I realized that the wind and rain had both died down, as though approving of our scheme.

While I slowly turned my head to peer across the road at the Communist camp, the Dragon Lady came crawling toward me through the mud. Speaking softly, she told me that Scotty and Charlie were prisoners. For a second I was relieved just to hear that they were alive. Then I began to remember the kind of thing that was done here to prisoners of whatever side. Still lying motionless, she whispered, "We must continue with our plan."

The forms of the Communist sentries were now becoming visible only yards away. There would have been no way to hide there if the fields hadn't been strewn with corpses. As I tried to erase the image of them from my mind, I heard voices. Lying there afraid to move, with our weapons wrapped, we were never more powerless than at that moment.

The pounding of my heart brought a new wave of terror as I heard the voices growing louder. What now came into view was a group of what appeared to be farmers, perhaps thirty or forty of them, all ragged and muddy, with their hands bound behind their backs, being herded in our direction by Communist soldiers. I scanned the group for any sight of Scotty or Charlie, but didn't see either of them. A soldier who seemed to be an officer was shouting orders to the others. Obviously this was the field of execution.

With a sudden, deliberate and yet fluid motion, the Dragon Lady stood up. Holding her weapon behind her, she gave a low moan. Then the rest of us, our weapons hidden, rose likewise and moved slowly toward the road, moaning as we went. Through the morning mist, I saw that I was part of a skirmish line, an assault carried out by ghosts—and that we had scared the hell out of those soldiers. As they panicked and ran screaming, a few of them dropped their weapons. The prisoners were every bit as frightened, and their flight added to the confusion. The terror was catching; soldiers pouring out of their tents were in a panic even before they saw us.

From the size of the bivouac and the number of men I'd seen running, I guessed there were about a hundred soldiers. Thus far, not one had turned to look at us. Then an officer appeared to have grasped the situation. From a distance of about twenty-five yards, he began to bark orders, drawing his pistol meanwhile.

From the speed of her response, it was clear that the Dragon Lady had been watching for this moment. Tossing away the wrappings from her weapon, she let loose a burst of gunfire that knocked him off his feet.

At that the rest of us began firing. In the slaughter that followed, we had not only surprise and superstition on our side, but also confusion as the farmers started running for freedom. Now the four other groups of our force caught the Communists in a crossfire that finished them in a few minutes.

Audy was the first to reach Scotty and Charlie; he was untying them when I got there. I could see that they were alive and in fair shape, though Scotty had been slashed badly and Charlie had a deep, ugly wound in his scalp.

"For a while, lads," Scotty told us, "you had me pretty frightened too. I really thought the dead had come to life."

O'Malley, coming up behind me, roared at that. We explained, as we introduced him to Scotty, that it had been his idea. Now Gunny and I helped Scotty to his feet.

"Can you make it?" I asked.

"Aye. I've been worse. I've also been better." He turned to O'Malley. "And thanks for your help."

"I'd do it any time," he replied. "But now I believe we're going in different directions. So I'll be saying good-bye." And he shook hands all round.

"If you have trouble, try to get word to us," the Dragon Lady said. "You know our direction."

"You're a remarkable woman," he told her, "and I thank you for your offer. But John O'Malley has been looking after himself for quite a while now. Got to be moving on."

After one more round of good-byes, O'Malley was off down the road, alone and on foot, a stranger in a dangerous country. I've thought many times since about how China had its way of converting the likes of O'Malley, Audy, Scotty, maybe even myself. To what? Different customs, a different way of life, a new way of seeing the important things? I'm still not sure.

When he was about twenty-five yards from us, O'Malley halted, turned, waved and shouted, "God bless you all!"

As we waved back, I couldn't help saying softly, "God bless you too, John O'Malley!"

Then the Dragon Lady was assembling us once more. Once we had picked up as many of the slain Communists' weapons as we could carry, we were off. We saw no one—the weather had taken care of that. The road was muddy, but easier going than the land around it would have been. From it we had a broad view of the field where the slaughter had taken place. I stood there sickened yet hypnotized until Gunny slapped me on the shoulder to get me moving.

Seeing that Charlie needed help, I pulled up alongside him and lifted his arm around my own shoulders so that we could walk together. Though Charlie was still a little dazed, Scotty seemed to be in good shape. We'd lost only one man in rescuing the two of them. As I looked around at our group, faces splattered, hair matted, clothes caked with mud, I could understand how O'Malley's trick had succeeded.

We were marching into a fresh wind. Before us I could see the canal. Then the Dragon Lady signaled a halt. She conferred for at least fifteen minutes with a scout who had just returned—which meant, I could be pretty sure, that a new plan was being hatched. By now I'd lost track of the number of changes of plan, and I wasn't surprised to hear her announce, "We have a boat but we shall not go to the Grand Canal. We shall go on the Hwang Ho instead—and it will take us to Laichow Bay. That is near Weihai."

"And Weihai," I exclaimed, "is where we get the boat to Seoul!"

She nodded and all at once what had been a kind of dream seemed close—a thing that was possible, that could really happen. And knowing that brought a new kind of uneasiness. What had kept me going up to now was *lack* of hope—not giving a damn. I didn't want to change that, all of a sudden; it would make a nervous wreck of me.

I tried not to think of all this, to force my mind in other directions as we trudged on. The sun had come out and the wind was drying the mud that still covered most of me. When I began to brush it from my clothes, the Dragon Lady cautioned, "Don't clean up too well. You should look like a farmer or a Mongol."

After twenty minutes or so we met two more of the Dragon Lady's scouts. They told her the Hwang Ho was only a mile away, and that there was a boat waiting for us. "The owner of the boat is a friend of mine," she said, "and he will take us to Laichow Bay. Also he has a radio."

A radio meant contact with Americans—another sign of how close we were. Once again I tried not to think about what it meant. The Dragon Lady ordered us to leave the road and to form into two columns, one on either side of the road. We moved like this for so long that I lost all sense of time. Finally, as we descended a slight hill, two large expanses of water lay before us: the canal on one side, the Hwang Ho on the other. Several junks were tied up at piers on the river, and the Dragon Lady headed for one of these with her usual sureness, as if it were something she did every day of her life. People at work on the piers or repairing boats in the water glanced at us, but didn't seem concerned.

Following her cue, we went aboard. She pointed to a cabin, told us to go inside, and then leaped back onto the pier. Inside the cabin, which was dark and stuffy, we found three men, to whom I nodded, not knowing what else to do. They nodded back with no sign that they were either startled or worried at seeing us. Audy explained presently that there were to be two boats and that the Dragon Lady was dividing up our people between them.

Soon the Mongol lieutenant was aboard, along with the others assigned to our junk. I could hear the crew preparing to cast off, with still no sign of the Dragon Lady. I was beginning to be nervous and at seeing from the cabin porthole that the lines were cast off, my heart started to pound. Then out of nowhere, she came into the cabin. She had been on board, up front, the whole time. She told us now, "You must stay away from windows and doorways, out of sight. Before long, if all goes well, we shall be at Laichow Bay."

In a couple of minutes we were under sail, out on the river and moving swiftly with the current. The Dragon Lady motioned for Gunny and me to follow her. "We shall try the radio," she explained as she led us into a smaller cabin just behind the other.

"What is your call sign—your call letters?" she asked.

Gunny and I stared at each other, looking blank. "Christ, I don't know," he said.

"Do you remember if Lieutenant Damon said anything about a frequency?" I asked him.

"No, dammit! We were none of us briefed about any such thing. Now what a time to think about it!"

The Dragon Lady spoke to the captain, who started fiddling with the transmitter, tuning in on various frequencies. We could hear the static and voices fading in and out. Then, after some time, we heard an American voice.

"Eagle One to all eagles. Return to nest. Return to nest. Acknowledge. Over."

"Jeez, Gunny!" I said.

Sounding as excited as I was, he said, "How do you work this?"

"Press it to talk," the Dragon Lady said. "Release it to listen."

Pressing the button with his thumb, Gunny said, "Eagle One, Eagle One. Can you hear me? Can you hear me?" He released the button and waited. There was no answer. He pressed the button and spoke into the mike again. "Eagle One, I'm an American. Can you hear me? Come in! For God's sake! I don't have a call sign! I'm an American. Come in!"

Again he released the button, we waited, and again there was nothing.

"Dammit!" Gunny barked. "Why don't they answer?"

"They do not know who you are," the Dragon Lady said quietly. "And they do not want to give their position away. Neither do we. So we must stop now, so as not to give it away."

Scotty had walked into the room, and when we told him what had been happening, he said, "You need some sort of code word, lads, so your own people will know who you are."

"Code," I said. "Wait a minute! When we landed in Manchuria, what was the password the lieutenant used with Yen?"

Gunny looked at me, trying to remember. Meanwhile the boat captain had been fiddling with the radio. Frantic, I said, "What's he doing? He'll lose them!"

"He has to remain in contact with his friends," the Dragon Lady told me. "They are watching the Communists for us."

"But hell," I insisted, "we'll *lose* them!" But behind the angry annoyance, my mind was searching for the password. I paced up and down, groping; then I shouted, "Quick! Sand! *Quicksand*!"

The operator went on fiddling with the radio.

"I remembered the password!" I shouted. "So let's send it, let's see what happens!"

But when the Dragon Lady looked up, it was with bad news. "The Communists have gunboats at the mouth of the river, in Laichow Bay. We must go ashore."

"Can't we try the password once?"

She spoke to the captain, then told us firmly, "No. Not now. They are too close, they might pick up our position. We shall have to wait."

"But where will we get another radio?"

"As soon as we leave, the captain will call someone— someone on shore who has a radio. We can try to send the message from there."

I asked how long it would take us to reach Weihai.

"A few days—if all goes well," she said. Then she stared at me and asked, as though out of nowhere, "Have you decided now what you will do?"

It took me a second or two to realize what she meant. Then I remembered that I had said I wanted to stay. I hadn't thought about it in any systematic way but not that we were so close to actually being at the sea, I knew where my wishes were aimed.

"I think I'm going to go," I said. "I'll miss you, and I'll miss Nancy and Kim. But at least I'll see them once more."

The Dragon Lady replied softly, "You will not see Nancy and Kim again."

"What do you mean? Why not?" Suddenly I was upset, and surprised at the emotion that surged through me.

"They have started back to Inner Mongolia, where they will be safer. Our journey has become dangerous, with so many people. So I had to send them back." She looked at me, and I saw her eyes go soft, as they rarely did. "Please do not feel you were deceived. I know you cared for them. But it had to be done, and quickly. It is better this way."

I said soberly, "I know you did what you thought was right."

Just then we felt the boat bump gently alongside the pier. I welcomed the interruption. The thought of not seeing Nancy or Kim had brought me closer to what I dreaded even more—the thought of not seeing *her* again either.

Out on deck the captain gave us baskets to hide our weapons in. The day was warm and pleasant, the water was bright in the sunshine. We were all smeared and caked with mud—a total mess. Without hesitating, I took a flying leap and landed in the water.

"Come on in," I yelled, and in a minute they had joined me—Gunny, Scotty, the Dragon Lady, even Charlie—for a leisurely bath before we waded ashore. Our skins and our clothes were now a couple of shades lighter. Feeling the water run from my sopping hair on my face, I asked Gunny if he had a comb.

"Got something on the line?" he teased, and I gave him a shove that sent him back into the river. While we were still splashing and shoving each other, the Dragon Lady was assembling her people from the second boat. We would be bidding good-bye to most of them before they began the long trek back to Mongolia. In no time they were on their way, leaving only a small group of us to head for the sea: the Dragon Lady, Gunny and I, Scotty, Audy, Charlie, the Mongol lieutenant and three of his men.

Staring at the backs of the departing group, I felt a tense sadness. This was the end of something. I didn't know what might be beginning, but the long journey with them was over.

Then almost at once, we were also moving on.

The ocean of mud left by the storm was already draining and beginning to dry out. Now there would be only an occasional slight dip in the terrain. Altogether it was as flat as anything I'd ever seen. After we'd gone a mile or so, a village came into view and we headed toward it. The place seemed strangely solitary. Not many people were working the land around it and inside the walls I saw no more than fifty people, with perhaps half a dozen huts. We were led by a villager to one of these. Audy told us, after listening to what he was telling the Dragon Lady, that this was the shack with the radio.

Though I was eager to try it, the Dragon Lady said, "No, we shall eat first. The villagers suggest caution because the Communists are near. If we have to flee, I should like to do it with full stomachs."

While we ate, Scotty told us what had happened to him. He and the others had been passing some soldiers on the road when suddenly they found themselves in a fire fight, for no reason that they could see. "They had the jump on us," he said. "Some of our people got away; most were cut down. They overpowered Charlie and me and wanted to shoot him on the spot. But I told them he was too important, their superiors would be angry." He smiled. "I believe they thought *we* were *you*." He looked at Gunny and me. "Good thing we weren't, lads, or you wouldn't have come to rescue us."

When the meal had ended, the radio was brought from its hiding place somewhere within the hut. The Dragon Lady began tuning carefully, and while we listened an American voice broke through.

"It would be good if we had some sort of call sign," she said.

I urged, "Try Quicksand."

"But that was only a password and countersign," Scotty told me. "Something to use in the field. Not the same thing at all."

"All the same," I persisted, "what have we got to lose?"

The Dragon Lady pressed the button to transmit and spoke into the mike. "Quicksand, this is Quicksand. Come in."

We waited. All we heard was a crackle of static. We waited again. Still nothing but the crackle.

Scotty said, "Let me try. Maybe the accent is scaring them off." While he picked up the mike, the villager who had come in with us spoke to the Dragon Lady, and she explained, "He is afraid that if we transmit for too long, they will know our location. Then the whole village may be in danger.''

"Maybe they're not hearing us," I said, feeling depressed.

Audy put a hand on my shoulder. "It's the right frequency. They're just not answering."

The Dragon Lady went on conferring with the villager—asking him, Scotty explained, about another transmitter somewhere out on the road. "In an hour we can try again," she said. If that failed, she went on, we had two choices. One was to go to the coast, to Laiyang, where we might find someone with a portable transmitter we could use. Then we could travel south along the coast, sending messages as we went.

"That'll be bloody dangerous," Audy interjected. "We'll be trapped with our backs to the water, with nowhere to go if we're found out." And Scotty agreed.

The Dragon Lady nodded silently. Then she said, "The other choice is to head back to Mongolia."

We all groaned. Then I said, "You people have got to get back there whether we get out or not. And how many times can you roll the dice without crapping out?" I said it as much to myself as to anyone else.

The Dragon Lady looked mystified, and Gunny started to chuckle. "It means rolling the dice many times and being lucky, and then finally not being lucky," he explained.

"Oh," she said earnestly. "I shall remember that"— and we all laughed.

But Gunny had turned sober again. "Suppose we go to the coast," he said. "What are our chances?"

The Dragon Lady said, "They will depend on whether we can make radio contact and get help before we are found. If they find us first, we shall not have much room to move, and there will not be many of us to fight . . ." Her voice trailed off. Then she brightened. "We roll the dice," she said. "But we shall be lucky."

"I never won anything in my life," I told her, trying a feeble joke. "But I'm willing to bet on you."

All business again, she said, "We must have some sort of code, a signal for the radio. Something so that the Americans will need to talk to us. Something . . ."

We all sat puzzling over the problem until Scotty jumped to his feet. "The message Roberts had on him! Do you remember how it went?"

While I tried, still drawing a blank, Gunny slapped his hands together. "Get that radio working!" he shouted.

The villager ran up the antenna again and Gunny said, "I'm going to send this message, and then we run like hell for the coast!" He picked up the mike.

"Command post," he said, "this is Quicksand. Roberts. Roberts. Six ships sunk. Will not return. They feel the same as most of us. But hung his name on anyway. Sing a song to Jenny next. Quicksand, Quicksand, can you hear me? Over."

The son of a bitch had remembered every word!

While we listened, Gunny repeated the message, this time pacing his words, taking care to pronounce each syllable. Again there was no answer.

After he'd tried one more time, still with no response, Scotty said, "They're bringing the brass in on this one. Give them five minutes. Then try again."

The villager was beginning to look concerned and the wait seemed to go on forever before Gunny said, "Let's have a go at it."

And this time the answer came!

"Quicksand. Quicksand. This is Spec One. Do you read me? Over."

I slapped Gunny on his back. He ignored me. "Spec One, this is Quicksand. Affirmative, we read you. Over."

"Quicksand, this is Spec One. What is your approximate location? Over."

Gunny stared at all of us for a second. Then he spoke into the mike again. "Spec One. This is Quicksand. We are near onion. We are near onion. Over."

"We read you. Can you stand by? I say again, Can you stand by?"

"Negative, we cannot stand by," Gunny answered. "I say again, we cannot stand by. We are moving. Will call you tomorrow morning. Tomorrow morning. Do you read us, Spec One? Over."

"We read you, Quicksand, loud and clear. We have your approximate location. We will wait for your call tomorrow morning. Over."

"This is Quicksand. Affirmative. Tomorrow morning. Out."

Ecstatic, we broke into a cheer. "I kept it short," Gunny explained, "because I figured we were being monitored. Give 'em time, and they could triangulate our position."

"Tell me one thing, Gunny," I said. "What in hell is *onion*?"

"Hold on a minute and I'll tell you," he said. "I remember when I was in Korea, I was looking at a map of China. I saw this place, L-i-e-n-y-u-n, and I pointed to it and asked one of my buddies how it was pronounced. Lienyun. Sounded to me just like *onion*. Throwing that at them, I figured we'd be close, but not *too* close."

I said, "Too close to what?"

The Dragon Lady said, quick as always, "He means that the Americans will not be the only ones plotting our location. We cannot even be sure those are real Americans we spoke to. They could be defectors, in the pay of the Communists. What is good is that we are not really close to Lienyun. Not close enough to be there by tomorrow morning."

"You're some shrewd son of a bitch," I told Gunny admiringly.

He said, pretending to be hurt, "Took you a while to find out! But now we've got to be cutting out of here. They'll be looking for us."

While we got ourselves ready, the Dragon Lady was having a lively conversation with the villager. After the rest of us had gotten our gear together and gone outside, she and Audy came out carrying a large basket. When I asked what was in it, she said, "The transmitter. The owner has made us a gift of it. But it is better for him too not to have it any longer." While I peered inside the basket at the portable radio with its hand-powered generator, I saw Charlie waiting with an expression that made me uneasy.

"Now I must say good-bye," he told us. "My injury is not all healed. You will be traveling fast. I will only slow you down. Instead I will prepare for our trip back to Mongolia. That way, I can do more good.''

Charlie's words gave me another jolt. I thought of Nancy and Kim. Every time I left someone now, it was for the last time. I went over and gave Charlie a bear hug, and once again I had to turn away and walk away so as not to be seen with tears in my eyes. I had been through more with him in a few weeks than I would in a lifetime with most people. While the others made their farewells, I realized that what I felt about Charlie I also felt about everyone else in this strange, exotic crew. When—*if*—Gunny and I ever got out of here, I knew I'd be leaving a sort of family behind.

We marched off at top speed. From our full strength of a hundred, now we were down to just nine—the Dragon Lady, Scotty, Audy, the four Mongols, Gunny and I. The afternoon was warm, and as our clothes dried out completely, I began to feel parched; but we traveled without stopping for a drink. I thought how strange it was—drowning in water one day, thirsting for it the next; one day nothing but mud, the next day nothing but dust.

We cut across country, keeping to narrow footpaths, avoiding main roads. We now saw few people. Fatigue was already creeping up on me, and Scotty had told us it would take two days to reach Lienyun—*if* we didn't run into any trouble. It was a relief when, with darkness approaching, the Dragon Lady signaled a stop. But it was only to tell us that we would not get there in time unless we traveled faster. Now, she said, we were going to run.

She turned and broke into a trot. We all followed and to my surprise, though my legs had been bothering me, with the change of pace they actually began to feel better. But it wasn't long before I was sweating heavily and feeling limp. We jogged for at least an hour before the next stop came. I sank to my knees, sucking in deep breaths, feeling drained of strength, breath and water. "Don't drink too much," she cautioned. "Just moisten your lips and take a sip. We shall rest five minutes. Then we run again."

The five minutes passed quickly. I saw that Gunny was exhausted too; so was everyone. But once again when the Dragon Lady was on her feet we all managed to follow somehow.

As I ran, my mind slipped into a kind of trance. I recalled incidents from my childhood, the sports I'd taken part in, the training for this mission, all the running we'd done then. And now an odd thing happened. With my mind wandering off, I'd ceased to keep an eye on the Dragon Lady and wasn't ready when she stopped short. There I was, charging into her like a runaway buffalo, knocking her down and falling over her.

We'd all been in such close quarters for so long that the physical contact in itself was nothing new. What happened now was that I realized in a way I hadn't before that she was a woman. Slowly I began pulling myself off her and at the same time helping her up, with my hands underneath her shoulders. I had never been quite that close to her before, or touched her body in quite that way. Our eyes met and stayed locked in the same steady gaze.

I heard Scotty saying, "Why don't we all take a breather?"

Her shoulders felt strong and wiry yet delicate under my grasp. "Are you all right?" I finally asked.

"Yes," she answered. "Are you?" I'd never heard quite that sound in her voice before.

"Yes, I'm all right."

"Soon you will be going home," she whispered.

"Yes," I said. "I guess so. It won't be easy." Then I leaned down and kissed her gently on the lips. I hadn't had much experience as a ladies' man, and God knows I hadn't planned this. We just stood and looked at each other again until she dropped her hands from my shoulders and we pulled apart.

After a minute she had the old amused look. "Shall we run all night, or shall we rest?" she said.

"I think we should follow Scotty's recommendation."

"Then let's tell them." We walked over to where Scotty, Gunny and Audy were sitting. The Mongols, as usual, had moved off by themselves. By now it was dark. I took out a skin bag of water, and we each had a long swig. We hadn't sat there long before the Dragon Lady was asking whether we had the strength to go on running through the night. There were hills ahead of us, she said. Also, we could not run during the day without arousing suspicion.

Though no one was eager to run again, we all agreed that we had to do it. This time, as I ran, my thoughts were all of the Dragon Lady and the way she'd looked and sounded. I wondered how I could want to leave whatever it was that *she* was to me. I asked myself what there was at home. My emotions were so confused that I all but broke out laughing at the thought of us nine, taking such incredible chances to reach the sea—for the sake of somebody who couldn't even be sure he wanted to go!

But also, as we ran, I loosened up and began to appreciate the task we'd undertaken. There was a moon now and I could see the terrain getting hillier. The ups and downs put a strain on my wind as well as my legs. The next time the Dragon Lady signaled a stop, I took a sip of water that went down the wrong way. I started coughing and for some moments I couldn't stop. The Mongol lieutenant came over, looking worried, and put a hand on my shoulder. He said something to Audy, who explained, "He's offered to carry you."

"No thanks," I told him as soon as I could speak. "Tell him I'm okay." I was embarrassed, all the more because there was no doubt in my mind that he could have done it. The Mongols were carrying the food, water, radio and weapons, but in all our running they never broke stride or asked for a rest.

As we resumed our run, I found myself worrying about the next message we sent. Each time we transmitted, the Communists would be one step closer to locating us. We took one more break just before sunup. With the first light of dawn I felt a little safer; all through the night, in the back of my mind there had been the fear that we might stumble onto an encampment of soldiers. With light showing in the east, the Dragon Lady quickened the pace for one last sprint before the cover of darkness was gone.

Once the sun came up, my aches turned into pains. I wondered about Scotty, Gunny and Audy, all of them a good deal older than I was. When it was full daylight, we paused on the side of a hill near a clump of trees. I saw the Dragon Lady standing there, her hair blown by the breeze, the rags she wore outlining the shape of her body. I was looking at her in an entirely new way now and I told myself I'd better stop it.

While the rest of us slumped to the ground, grateful for the rest, the Mongols stationed themselves a little apart from the line of trees. One of them had taken my binoculars for the first watch. After a silence, the Dragon Lady turned to Gunny and me. "When you first sent the message, you used a name—"

"Quicksand," I said.

"No, no. It was a man's name."

"Roberts," Gunny said.

"Yes, yes, that's it. Roberts. Who is he?"

"He was a CIA agent from the States. Or anyhow that's what I think he was."

She thought for a moment. "So they think you are this agent, this Roberts, calling."

"Well, if they do, they're in for some surprise," I said. The more I thought about this, the less I liked it. But I was too exhausted to brood for long. In a minute or two I was sound asleep.

The voices of Gunny, Audy and Scotty woke me. My legs ached. When I asked how long I'd been asleep, Scotty answered, "A couple of hours."

The Dragon Lady had been off talking to the Mongol lieutenant. Now she was beside me.

"How far to onion, or whatever it is?" I asked.

She said, "We could reach it by tomorrow morning."

"Only we told them *this* morning," I pointed out.

"They will wait."

"Because they think we're Roberts?"

She did not answer. Anyhow, we had enough other things to worry about—such as the message we were going to transmit right now.

Soon the radio picked up the American voice: "Quicksand, Quicksand, this is Spec One. Do you read? Over."

Scotty flipped the switch to send. "Spec One, this is Quicksand. Read you loud and clear. Over."

"Quicksand, have you reached destination? I say again, have you reached destination? Over."

"Spec One, this is Quicksand. We need another day. I say again, another day to reach destination. Over."

"Affirmative, Quicksand. Will look for you same time tomorrow. Be as quick as you can. The business is over. Be as quick as you can. Over."

Scotty flipped the switch again. "Spec One, this is Quicksand. We have a man ready for the world. We need shipment. We need shipment. Do you read? Over."

The voice came: "Loud and clear, Quicksand. One package for shipment. One package for shipment. Over."

"Spec One, will be at destination tomorrow morning. Need shipment quickly. Cannot wait. Need instructions. Over."

"Hold on that last interrogatory, Quicksand. Can you call back after dark? Say again, can you call back tonight? We will have orders. Over."

"Wilco, Spec One. Will call back after dark. Out."

Scotty snapped off the radio and turned to us with elation in his face. We all began to cheer, hug and pound each other on the back.

Then for a second or two the Dragon Lady clung to me.

I said, softly now, "I may really be leaving soon."

"Are you happy?" she asked.

"I don't know," I said. "Part of me wants the trip to start all over again. I know that's selfish but it's true."

"Yes, I know," she said. We strolled away from the others, full of things we wanted to say but couldn't and after a moment we reluctantly returned.

"The package ready for shipment," Audy announced.

"The *battered* package ready for shipment would be more like it," I told him. "Or rather, *two* battered packages." I looked toward Gunny, waiting for the laughter to begin. Instead there was an embarrassed silence.

Then Gunny said, "No, Rick, I'm not going."

"What?"

"That's right, Rick. I'm not going back."

Looking around, I could see that the others already knew. What I couldn't take in, what I couldn't handle just then, was that everybody had known but me. "Since when is all this?" I blurted out.

There was another pause. Then Gunny said, "Rick, I'm no traitor, you know that. And I'm no coward."

"But you don't want to go home."

"That's right. I never had a home, Rick, except the Corps. And after what happened to us, and what I've seen here, I'm staying."

"But in less than a year you'll have twenty, and you can retire!"

"Ricky, you've seen the way the government treated us. They couldn't care less. They'd find a way to screw me out of my pension too."

"Gunny, that wasn't the *government*!" I was beginning to yell.

Then Gunny was yelling too. "Wake up, kid. The government is supposed to know what its forces are up to. If it doesn't even do that—then God help us all! And even if I did get the pension," he went on in a tone that was quieter but grimmer, "could I retire on two hundred a month? I'm thirty-six years old, and I've been in the Marine Corps for nineteen of those—more than half my life. What am I supposed to do with myself now? I'd been in two wars, and still that bastard CO in Korea was all set to have me court-martialed. I can do without that bullshit!"

"And here you'll be in the middle of a war that goes on all the time," I said.

"So that's what I know how to do anyhow. I got nothing back in the States, no friends, no family, no job. So I'm staying."

I asked, "Then why did you keep it a secret from me?"

"I wasn't going to change *your* mind about going back. Once we got close to the water, I knew you'd have to change it again."

"I don't know how you can be so sure."

"You've got your whole life ahead of you, kid. You've got family. Also, you've got to go back and tell the story of what we did."

I looked around me, angry with everybody. "First you sneak Nancy and Kim away," I said, glaring at the Dragon Lady. "And now this."

It shook me to see her look at me the way she did then—as though I'd actually hurt her. I'd never seen this steely woman so near to crying. She said, "I didn't want them here because I was afraid you would decide to stay. That was part. Part was that I was also afraid for them, that they would not be safe."

Now I was unhappy with everything, including myself. But I said, "I understand," and then, "I'm sorry."

She shook her head as though she didn't think I understood at all. Tears rolled down her cheeks. "You fought here with us, Khan. You are a brave man. But now you must go home. Let me say to you what my father told me once. He was a wise man and he told me, 'Life is a beautiful miracle and it is given only once. The choice you make can never be made a second time. Enjoy what you have chosen. Never look back. Look forward and live the miracle.'"

It took several minutes for what she had been saying to sink in. Finally I said, "I'll always remember what you told me." And I've never forgotten.

Then she said something else I've never forgotten.

"Khan, although you have fought bravely here, your fight is not over. You may have another war to fight when you are at home."

When I asked what she meant, it was Scotty who answered, "Your group was sent over on a mission. It seems clear to me, lad, that you were never supposed to go back. Now, after you've done what you've done, seen what you've seen—now there may be people who will not *want* you back, not want you to tell your story.''

He was saying things that I'd been afraid to think through.

Gunny joined in then, ''Because maybe no one is supposed to know about our mission. Maybe they don't want anyone around to tell about it. Remember, it's most likely *Roberts* they're expecting to pick up. They may be in for one hell of a surprise, don't forget.''

By then I couldn't think of anything to say.

''We shall speak about this again later,'' the Dragon Lady said, and soon we were hitting the road again— walking fast now rather than running, passing many people at work in the rice paddies. All the while, my mind was racing. Gunny would stay in China—alive and by choice. The bodies of Damon, Craig, Holden and White would all remain. Sally and Yen had died, but at least on the soil of their own country. I thought of them and of all the bodies I'd left behind—scores of them, the Chinese and the Russians I'd killed. Could I justify all that killing, even in a country where killing was a way of life?

I found the Dragon Lady walking beside me, looking up at me. I wondered whether I'd been talking to myself. She asked, ''Are you all right?''

I smiled and said yes. I reached out to take her hand, and held it for a while before I let it go, thinking again about whether I really wanted to go back. The Dragon Lady had probably been right about sending Nancy and Kim away. I'd come to feel very close to them both, partly because they were young like me. And they might have influenced me to stay if they'd been with us now.

But no, I'd made up my mind; the thing was decided, for a lot of good reasons. Well then, why did I seem to keep forgetting what those reasons were?

The day had become hot and sticky, and when we came to a stream I was happy to jump in for a quick wash. But the Dragon Lady had warned that we were in a dangerous area and would have to keep on moving. Everywhere people were working in the rice fields. Though we skirted them wherever we could, while holding a direct route to Lienyun, we often wound up sloshing through the wet fields as a shortcut. Though wading slowed us down and was hard on the legs, after a while, once again, I could feel my legs loosening up.

As the day ended, we went even faster. Clouds partly covered the moon but there was enough light for us to see where we were going. As I adapted to the pace, it began to seem almost comfortable. At the same time I was becoming rather lightheaded, and it didn't seem long before we were stopping for a rest.

Once we were on the move again, I felt a strange tension growing among us. Like a scene in a Grade B movie, it seemed quiet—too quiet. And that I didn't like it. The small group drew in closer together, at the risk of losing its scouts—the Mongols, carrying our gear, now close to us instead of moving in isolation.

Near the top of a hill we stopped. While the Mongols fanned out again as security, we set up the radio. Establishing contact this time was not so easy. I had almost fallen asleep when I heard, "Quicksand, Quicksand, this is Spec One. This is Spec One. Do you read? Over."

What made this so crucial an exchange was not having any code; instructions for the pickup would have to be given in the open. Spec One's information was as guarded as possible: Pier Number Four at first light tomorrow, with no mention of Lienyun itself.

Almost immediately one of the Mongols came in, and after a frantic exchange with the Dragon Lady he raced off again into the darkness. He had learned, she told us, that a large group of people, perhaps fifty or more, were coming toward us. Whether they were soldiers or not, she did not yet know.

While the Mongols patrolled, the five of us who were left took out our weapons and waited, staying low. When the Mongols finally emerged from the darkness, they brought with them two men who looked distraught. They had come, the Dragon Lady explained, from a village about a mile off, where Communist soldiers were torturing and killing people—especially children. "We have a decision to make," she said.

"Decision?" I hefted my machine gun and said, "Let's go."

The Mongols sped into the darkness and we followed, running. Almost immediately I began to sweat. My heart was pounding. How much longer could our luck hold out?

We could hear the crackle of gunfire, muffled at first by a fold of the hills. As we got closer, a glow appeared in the sky; racing between two hills, we found the village on fire, and now we could hear both the shots and the screams of people in pain.

The Dragon Lady signaled a halt. "We cannot run in blindly," she said. "We must see what is happening." As we dropped to our knees and positioned our binoculars, the Mongols appeared on the slope and spoke quickly to her. "They are killing everyone," she told us. "They have gotten the children together and put them in the school."

We spread out; then, at her arm signal, we sprinted in a skirmish line toward the village. My thoughts as we careened down the hill were more confused than they had ever been—and yet it was all so simple. We were close to the sea. If we got through this, I was thinking, this would be the last combat for me. If we didn't, it would still be my last combat.

I brought my machine gun to the ready as I ran.

15

At the edge of the village, bodies were strewn about. No one had seen us yet, and the Dragon Lady and I crouched together, out of sight of the others among the buildings. Four soldiers stepped around a hut that was perhaps twenty yards away, spotted us and pointed. When I raised my weapon they merely stared—and then, for reasons I'll never understand, they burst out laughing. For an instant I froze; but in what would otherwise have been a fatal moment, the Dragon Lady fired a burst that knocked down the four of them before they could get off a shot.

The firing was ricocheting all around us. I fired back in the direction it seemed to be coming from, and we ducked between two huts. But soon it was apparent that the soldiers weren't shooting at anything in particular. They might almost have been drunk, and they were in as much danger of hitting each other as they were likely to hit us, because there were so many more of them. While I watched, in fact, that was actually what happened, as the rain of bullets continued and the Dragon Lady went on firing.

Now I could see Gunny across the road, firing from behind some sort of cover, while the Dragon Lady was leading the way to the school. Running, we kept low, using the huts for cover, and waved for Gunny to join us. We stopped firing as we moved through the village, and the soldiers' shots tapered off as well. Thinking of the soldiers who had laughed, I wondered whether everyone hadn't gone crazy.

"The school," the Dragon Lady said, pointing to a large building, and we headed for it. Gunny and Scotty had caught up with us. Gunny kicked in the door, and the Dragon Lady and I went inside.

Years later, the scene would come to me as one of the worst of my bad dreams. In a far corner, half a dozen kids huddled together crying. Almost a hundred others had been butchered. I was all the more shaken because of the Dragon Lady's reaction. Her hold on her machine gun tightened until I could see it quiver. Then she turned and would have run out—except that I reached out and stopped her, just as Scotty pushed through the doorway and had his first glimpse of the slaughterhouse.

Looking around, we counted five living, whimpering children—the oldest possibly three years old, the others hardly more than infants. Why they had been spared, there was no telling. The others ranged in age all the way from babies to teenagers. The walls were sprayed and splotched with what looked like red paint but wasn't; it was blood. I turned away myself and the Dragon Lady said, "We must see if any of them are still alive." Then Gunny, Scotty and I began going from one child to another, picking up one body and then laying it down again next to the others. Halfway through, Scotty had to go outside; I could barely control my own stomach, and as soon as I got outside I heaved my guts. The final count was ninety-eight bodies.

What had become of the soldiers wasn't clear. Meanwhile, the Dragon Lady told us to consolidate and get to high ground before a counterattack took place. Scotty and I each lifted two of the surviving children, and Gunny grabbed the fifth. We got out quickly, making our way to a ridge beyond the town from which we looked down over the burning houses. Suddenly the Dragon Lady asked, "Where is Audy?" While the rest of us stared, she was saying, "You wait here!" and had taken off down the hill. Realizing that it was too late for any word of protest, I quickly put the two children on the ground and started after her. "Be right back!" I called out.

The four Mongols, who had covered our withdrawal and were now making their way uphill, likewise turned and followed as we tried to retrace our steps among the huts, but without finding any trace of Audy. Then the Dragon Lady sent the Mongols to comb the outlying areas, while she and I waited in the doorway of a hut. I wondered how long we could wait, not knowing how many soldiers were left alive or where they might have gone. It seemed that the town had been deserted, though, until a squad of soldiers dashed by. We were concealed and held our fire. Then the Mongol lieutenant came striding toward us with Audy over his shoulder, two of his men following. They paused among the huts to reconnoiter before making a dash across the open space that separated them from us. All this happened very fast. I saw that Audy's back was covered with blood, and then the Dragon Lady was signaling to the Mongols to keep on moving.

After I'd gestured to the lieutenant that I'd carry Audy for a while, and been waved off, I ran back with the Dragon Lady toward the high ground. The lieutenant was close behind us while two of the Mongols again covered our withdrawal. I asked the Dragon Lady where the other Mongol was and she replied, "Do not worry about him. He will get away."

We had no sooner reached Gunny, Scotty and the five children than the Dragon Lady ordered us to pick up the children and be on our way.

Keeping to the line of the ridge, we moved off even though the fourth Mongol had still not appeared. With Audy hanging like a sack over the lieutenant's shoulder, there was still no telling whether he was more than barely alive. One of the kids I was carrying had fallen asleep. The other had discovered my ear and was busy playing with it. There was a sudden halt as the Dragon Lady discovered that the radio had been left behind. While two of the Mongol lieutenant's men went back for it, we had a chance to lay Audy on the ground and see how he was. I was relieved that there was no blood coming from his nose, mouth or ears, though he'd been hit twice in the back and had lost a lot of blood. As Gunny and I were leaning over him, he opened his eyes briefly and looked as though he might be trying to say something; but all he could do was cough.

"Easy buddy, easy," Gunny said, and Audy managed a smile. His breathing was hard, with a rasp. We all looked at each other with the same worried question, and then Scotty said, "Let me look after him for a while. You three go and get some rest."

The Dragon Lady, putting one hand on my back and one on Gunny's, led us off into the darkness. We'd sat there for a while, none of us saying anything, before I finally asked the Dragon Lady, "What was going on with those soldiers that made them so crazy?"

"Like a bunch of zombies," Gunny said, and I agreed. Only zombies could have done what they did in that schoolhouse. Thinking all over again about the frightful bloodbath we'd seen there, I couldn't handle it anymore. Trying to control myself only made it worse. I threw myself face down, landed my forehead on my machine gun and lay there shaking.

I could feel Gunny and the Dragon Lady both leaning over me, and Gunny was saying, just as he had to Audy a little while before, "Easy, buddy, take it easy."

Once I'd gotten a grip on myself, I felt a bit ashamed. Why the hell was I feeling so sorry for myself when we had those five children to worry about? "The kids," I said. "Is anybody looking after them?"

"They're all sleeping," Gunny said, and for some reason I started to cry again.

"We shall have to take them somewhere that is safe," the Dragon Lady said. "You know that now we cannot reach our destination by morning."

"Who cares?" I yelled. "I don't give a damn when we get there!" Then a kind of stupor came over me, and for a while no one said anything. "But about those soldiers," I asked finally. "No one normal would act that way."

"They were not normal," the Dragon Lady said. "They were machines. Before a battle they are given a drug in their food or their drink or else they smoke it, so that when they fight they do not know what they are doing. It makes them unafraid."

There was silence again until Scotty walked over to us. He took a deep breath and said, "Audy is not doing well. I've stopped the bleeding, but he had already lost a good deal. The bullets went straight through him. I tried to close everything up as best I could. But..." He took another breath. "I had to push things back into place..." He dropped his head, looking exhausted. When the Dragon Lady asked if we could help, he only shook his head and went back to watch over his old friend.

Then came the bellow that was the Mongols' signal, and in a couple of minutes the lieutenant and his men were back, bringing the basket with the radio in it. With that worry disposed of, our main concerns now were Audy and the children, and after that the question of the delay in our schedule.

·In answer to the first, the Dragon Lady said, "There is a village near called Kenyu, where I have friends. We can leave Audy and the children there to be cared for. But we shall not be able to reach Lienyun by the morning."

"Will we make it by tomorrow night?" I asked, and when she said yes, I was suddenly struck by an idea: we could radio to ask for a twenty-four-hour delay, which meant we'd have twelve hours' leeway—time to look things over instead of just walking in.

Gunny asked, "Will they wait another twenty-four hours?"

"I think so," the Dragon Lady said. "It is a good idea, Khan. We shall do it. Now we must get started."

We picked up our burdens and took off at a fast trot in the moonlight. Soon, from a ridge, we could spot the village. The lieutenant put Audy down gently; we did the same with the kids, who were drunk with sleep, and the Dragon Lady and two Mongols went down to negotiate. Before long everything had been cleared, and with a reminder from the Dragon Lady that we must slip in and out quickly, we had entered the town and were following her into a hut. A group of women were already waiting there to take the children, and in another room others immediately started tending Audy.

After one long look at the man and the children I'd never see again, I made my way with the others back to the high ground. The pace became more exhausting as the ground got hillier and steeper. Nobody was talking. I kept thinking about Audy and about the third Mongol. It now seemed clear that he would not meet us— which meant that he must be either dead or captured. After a while we stopped to bivouac and set up the radio. While I sat with my back propped against a rock, resting, Gunny came over and joined me. I said, "You know, I'm going to miss you, you son of a bitch."

I could see his grin in the moonlight but his voice when he spoke was serious. "Same here, kid. I never really had a friend in my life before. But you, Ricky—you're a friend. I figure if you have one friend in your whole life, then you're ahead of the game. If I ever have a kid, I hope he'll be like you."

I was so touched that I could only growl a little. And I knew he was just as uncomfortable with so much emotion. "So now, kid," he said, "I'm going to find myself a place to sack out. See you in the morning." He got up and walked off a little way.

The Mongols were out there somewhere in the darkness, and Scotty—who could fall asleep faster than anybody I ever met—was around on the other side of the rocks. I slid down and stretched out on the ground right where I was. In a couple of minutes, just as I was beginning to doze off, I realized that the Dragon Lady was sitting next to me.

"Now it is very peaceful," she said. "And soon, Ricky, you will be gone."

"Ricky?" I said, a little scared at hearing her call me that. "No more Khan?"

She had propped her head on her hand, and she lay there looking at me in the moonlight. "You are not Khan the warrior now. You are Ricky."

I said, "Maybe some day I can come back." I didn't quite know what I was saying, but I meant every word when I whispered, "I'll never meet anyone like you."

She put up her hand and touched my face. "You do not have to tell me anything," she said. Her face was close now, and I leaned over and kissed her.

Then I put my hand on her hair.

Then I ran my hand down her back.

Then I pressed her slim little body against mine. I could feel every inch of her, from her face down to her toes, responding.

We were together when I woke. She was still asleep— the first time I had ever seen her sleeping. I didn't want to wake her but neither did I want to be seen with her like this. When I tried disentangling my arm from her, she woke.

She gave me a smile, raised her hand and ran it over my face. Then abruptly she sat up. "We must get on the radio."

We found Gunny and Scotty already fiddling with it. Had they seen us together? One look at their faces was all I needed to know that they had. But there were no remarks from anybody.

Scotty said, "Shall we try?"—and at a nod from the Dragon Lady he began fiddling with the transmitter again.

"Spec One, Spec One, this is Quicksand, this is Quicksand. Do you read us? Over."

He had to repeat it twice more—while we all got more and more jittery—before the answer came.

"We have a delay," Scotty told them. "We cannot make destination on time. I repeat, we have a delay. Do you read?"

"Loud and clear," the answer came back. "Interrogatory. What is the cause of the delay?"

Scotty ignored the interrogatory. "We have a twenty-four-hour delay. We need twenty-four hours. Over."

"We will give you twenty-four hours. No longer. Say again. Twenty-four hours, but no longer."

"Loud and clear," Scotty replied. "Rendezvous in twenty-four hours. Out."

The Dragon Lady told us now that it would take only two or three hours to reach Lienyun. "We shall wait so that we arrive in darkness."

"What the hell are we going to do all day?" Gunny asked.

The Dragon Lady smiled. "Rest."

And that is what we did. We lay around all day in the warm sun, with the Mongols patrolling, as seemed to be their nature, until the shadows began to lengthen. That was our signal to be on our way—to whom or whatever it was that would be waiting.

The last thing we did was to hide the radio among the rocks. It was an unnecessary weight now that we didn't need it anymore. Then we were off and in less than three hours we came in sight of the South China Sea. It glistened in the moonlight as we made our way down to the beach, where we huddled together on the sand while the Dragon Lady sketched out the area. The fourth pier, our place of rendezvous, was perhaps half a mile away.

The four of us were to approach it through the water, armed with knives, while the Mongols wrapped the rest of our weapons and carried them overland to meet us. It was less likely that they would be stopped, and they would be nearby to act as a support once we'd boarded the boat.

After we'd left the weapons and bandoliers with them, there was a brief rehearsal and then we headed into the water, holding our footing as long as we could and then swimming parallel to the beach. Soon we could make out the piers in the darkness. The moon disappeared behind the clouds and that was a good sign. While the Dragon Lady swam in an arc to find the right pier and then the boat, I followed with a slow breaststroke. Finally, treading water, she pointed to a large, two-masted junk among the pilings.

The whole ocean seemed to be at our backs as we closed in. I could make out a figure walking along the deck; then it disappeared through a hatchway. We found a ladder near the stern. The Dragon Lady signaled silence with a finger to her lips; then, with her knife's blade clenched between her teeth, she positioned herself to climb aboard. I lunged, intending to go ahead of her, and clamped my hand above hers on the ladder. Though she shook her head, I insisted and finally she moved aside for me. With both hands on the ladder, I listened a moment or two and then carefully and quietly pulled myself up out of the water, moving slowly to avoid the least splash. Moments later, with my head at deck level, I could take in the entire boat from one end to the other.

Though the moon was out, luckily our side of the boat was in shadow. Seeing no one, I hoisted myself onto the deck and darted for the cabin door. Glancing back, I saw the Dragon Lady's head appear; I waved her aboard, and she glided toward me like a cat, with Scotty and Gunny behind her.

As we positioned ourselves on both sides of the cabin hatchway and I reached for the knob, we heard a man's laughter inside, and then the sound of a second and a third voice. We stepped back into the shadows, and I whispered, "The weapons!"

The Dragon Lady vanished into the darkness; then she was back with the three Mongols and our guns. Armed with those, we moved back to the hatchway.

She whispered, "We go on the count of three. Do not shoot unless it is necessary."

She held up one finger. With my machine gun gripped firmly in my left hand, I unsheathed my knife with my right and held it at the ready. Two fingers. Then three.

Gunny threw open the hatch, slamming it against the bulkhead, and we bolted through, down two steps and into the cabin's interior before fanning out while the Mongols covered our rear. My wildest imaginings could not have prepared me for the shock that would come in an instant.

A few feet away three men sat at a table, with filled glasses before them. Caught by total surprise, they sat frozen in place for several seconds while we stared at them and they stared back at us. It was a deadly silence. Then Gunny broke the quiet, "Holy Mother of God!" He spoke for me as well because I saw the terrible truth.

Of the three Americans or whatever they were, I recognized one at once. A rage came over me—over all of us—that I've lived with ever since. A calculated breaking of faith by our own people had caused the deaths of our comrades. We were trained, sent on a mission, and abandoned—purposely.

The man turned white. Then he blurted, "You're— how in hell . . . ?"

"You know him?" Scotty asked.

"We know him."

"Watch this," said Gunny quickly. "Spec One, this is Quicksand. Do you read? Over."

"You worthless bastards!" snarled one of the others. Then quickly assuming an air of command, he spoke to me, "Stand at attention. Where's Roberts?"

But my eyes never left those of the one man I knew had betrayed us. "We know him." I was in a cold fury. "Just like we knew that bastard Roberts. This is the other one who trained us. And threw us to the wolves."

It was all in the open now and both sides knew it. The countless nights I've lain awake thinking about what happened next have all ended in a question: Could it have been different? Conditioning by teamwork and unrelenting fighting over the last three weeks had accounted for our survival. Killing the enemy was the important goal if you survived. And here was the enemy.

Suddenly it happened, so quickly that our response together was reflexive. Out of the corner of my eye I saw the third man lunge for a weapon leaning against a nearby bulkhead, and that triggered the two others to do likewise. Diving across the table, I drove my knife into the body of the man who had trained and betrayed us. The blade entered where the chest merges with the throat and when I pulled it out, he was dead. Quickly I turned to see that Gunny and Scotty had made quick work of the two others while the Dragon Lady and the Mongols looked on. No shots were fired: it was silent work with cold steel, done according to the law we'd lived under in China: Kill or be killed.

As I looked at the bodies, the reality of what we'd done for revenge and survival hit me. We had killed three Americans.

I felt Gunny's hand on my shoulder, trying to steady me as he said firmly, "Three Americans, Ricky, but not *our people*." In a frenzy, I shook his hand off. I turned over the table, I punched at bulkheads, all the while screaming at the top of my lungs. Gunny, Scotty and the Dragon Lady had to wrestle me down. The Mongols who had come rushing in, now stood over me with expressionless faces. At a word from the Dragon Lady, they and then Scotty left the cabin. In a few minutes I

could feel the boat underway. Calmed by exhaustion, I
tried to get my thinking clear again.

Finally I asked, "Where are we going?"

"Out to sea," the Dragon Lady said.

I stared at the bodies on the floor. "You see what we
did." I said it to no one in particular.

Gunny said, "We killed three bastards. They were
playing games with us, and the last one they played, they
lost."

I sat there stupefied, wondering what we could do
now. "We can't just go out to sea," I said. "Between the
Communists and the Americans, we'll get cut to pieces."

The Dragon Lady answered, "We must get out, away
from here. Then we can use the radio. We shall keep
moving, to make it harder for anyone to find us."

"They'll find us," Gunny said.

"Yes," she agreed. "They will find us. But now
search through those men's pockets. Perhaps you will
find something to help with the radio."

It was a while before I could bring myself to go and
help Gunny. When I did, I found in the pockets of the
man who'd trained us a wallet containing an ID card
with a photograph. It read, UNITED STATES GOV-
ERNMENT, CENTRAL INTELLIGENCE AGEN-
CY. The name on it was James Strong. Again the bewilderment. Why would an American intelligence agent
carry ID papers? What was going on?

While I stared at it, Gunny was saying, "Tell me, kid,
do you still want to go back?"

The question stung like a whip. "I've got to find out,"
I said. "Do they think *we're* traitors? I've got to find
out."

Gunny gazed at me. "You don't think you'll get a straight answer, do you?" While I stared back, he said, "Rick, you're not going to be able to get them. I can smell it now."

Pointing a finger at him, I said slowly, "We'll see about that. And I'll tell you one thing more: they're going to know I'm back, they're not just going to write me off!"

Gunny's face changed. He nodded slowly. "I know what you mean. And you're right." He turned to the Dragon Lady. "The question is, can he get back? Can we stay close enough to shore to broadcast and beach the junk if something happens—and then run like hell back across China?"

"Yes," she answered. "We can."

"Well," he told her, "it's a long shot. But we don't have much choice." He looked at me hard. "She said a few days ago that once you made up your mind, you wouldn't change it."

"That's right," I said. "I did choose to go back. And by all that's holy, that's what I am going to do. Whether they like it or not."

The Dragon Lady said there was something she must do and hurried from the cabin. That left the two of us with the corpses.

"Better search these other two and get it over with," Gunny said. It wasn't a pleasant assignment, and my own search turned up nothing. But then Gunny was shouting, "Look at this!"

He held up a card.

Turning it to the light, I read out loud, "United States Foreign Service. Aleksei Kutuzov."

I was just saying, "What would that be, German?" when the Dragon Lady came back into the cabin. She said quickly that it was a Russian name.

While we both stared, she added, "Perhaps he is one who works for both sides."

To this day, I have no clearer idea than I had then about who trained us or where their orders came from.

"Whoever they are," I said then, "the question is, what the hell are we going to do with them?"

Gunny said without hesitation, "Feed 'em to the fishes. Like any other garbage."

The Dragon Lady concurred. She shouted a command through the hatchway, and in a few moments the two Mongols had come in and were dragging the bodies out. "We shall feed them to the fishes," she said. "To the fishes who swim down deep!"

Gunny said, "Okay, now we send a message." We headed for the radio room where in a couple of moments we were joined by Scotty and the Dragon Lady. "Well, here goes," Gunny announced. "Either we make contact real quick or we start running like hell back to Mongolia."

He pressed the button to send. "This is Quicksand, this is Quicksand. We are Americans. This is urgent, I will not say again. If I don't get acknowledgment, we'll defect, we go straight to the Commies. We'll go straight to Mao if we have to. Will tell everything. Everything. Acknowledge loud and clear—or God help you and everyone. We're standing by. Over."

We waited. The radio operator was obviously calling in the communications officer. In a couple of minutes we had an answer.

"Quicksand, who are you, mister? We're in dark here. Need specifics. Give more identification. Over."

Gunny replied, "This is Quicksand. We are Americans waiting for a pickup off the mainland. Strong and Roberts are gone. That is all I can tell you. Say Wilco or we return to mainland . . . and God help us all. Give me a call sign. Over."

The answer came. "Quicksand, interrogatory. Can you tell us the star of *The Outlaw*? Say again, who is the star of *The Outlaw*? Over."

Gunny looked at me, puzzled. "Jane Russell," I told him, and he transmitted it.

The reply came back at once. "This is Eagles Nest, Quicksand. Correct on interrogatory. Need coordinates. Say again, your location. Over."

Gunny looked at me. "If we give a location from the charts, we're dead ducks." He hesitated. "I'll try onion," he told me. "Strong understood that one. Let's hope these guys will too."

He sent the message: "Eagles Nest, this is Quicksand. We are two miles east of onion. Repeat, we are two miles due east of onion. Over."

Christ, I said to myself, how many times before the Communists know we're at Lienyun? But Eagles Nest, apparently not understanding right away, asked us to stand by. While we did, I wondered about Eagles Nest. Wasn't this the command post for those same bastards, Roberts and Strong?

We waited, getting more and more nervous. Then the answer came. "Quicksand, this is Eagles Nest. We have your approximate location as two miles due east of onion. Hope we understand you. Can you head due east from your present location? Over.''

"This is Quicksand. Wilco. Due east. How long to pickup? Over.''

"Less than two hours," was the answer. Then Eagles Nest said, "We hope you're authentic. If you're not, the devil take you.''

Gunny was running with sweat as he spoke, but what he said was simply, "Likewise. No sweat. Out.'' Then he put down the mike. "Well, it's done.''

"What happens now?'' With all the doubts I had about Eagles Nest, I couldn't help shaking at the thought that I would soon be on my own.

It was Scotty who answered. "We're taking the small boat to shore. You're staying aboard this one. The currents will take you east without power; you can't risk running a motor. Then, lad, you're on your own.''

The leavetaking I hadn't dared imagine was quick. It was also emotional and my tears flowed freely: Gunny throwing his arms around me, then Scotty embracing me, the Mongol guards clasping my arms and their lieutenant with his right hand on my left shoulder, repeating the only English word he knew, a word he'd first heard after I fought him: "Friend.'' Seeing how shaken I was, Scotty cut in to lead me to the wheel. "It's a calm sea, lad. You shouldn't have much trouble.'' Then he climbed down into the small boat, which now rode free in the water. The Mongols were already waiting, steadying the boat by grasping the ladder.

Before he finally climbed down, Gunny handed me a folded piece of paper. "Keep it with you,'' he said. "It's for you to read—you and the people who pick you up.''

Then he turned and jumped into the small boat, without looking back.

I felt the Dragon Lady's arms around my waist. Turning to receive her head against my chest, I realized what I'd already forgotten, how tiny she was. Leaning down, I put my arms around her, lifted her until her face was even with mine, and kissed her on the lips. "I love you."

"I love *you*."

She climbed down the ladder, quickly. Through the darkness, I watched them cast off and then wave. After a while they were barely visible. Then there was nothing.

Alone, I found myself clutching the rail, as though for support. Then I reached up to finger the rosary beads I'd worn about my neck ever since Kim gave them to me. I wept long and hard. I watched the water as the boat cut cleanly through it. A sudden chill seized me; rushing to the cabin, I retrieved my machine gun and took it with me to the bow.

Remembering the note Gunny had given me, I reached into the pocket of my tattered pants, unfolded and read it.

Dear Rick,
First, I hope you understand why I'm staying—because I found what I wanted, just like Scotty did. But the important thing is that I have found out from the Dragon Lady a way to check and make sure that you are safely back in the States. Sometimes when you pick up the telephone and it's a salesman, just listen. Then you can tell him to bug off. Through friends, we can check

*and see if they are leaving you alone. If at anytime
something happens to you, we will take matters into our
own hands even if it means going to the Communists. I
don't think the bastards will want that, so they better lay
off you.*

*Don't think every telephone call you get is going to be
from her friends. It won't. You won't even know, neither will the bastards.*

So long and God bless you. We all love you.

> *Gunnery Sgt. Robert Masters, USMC*
> *Special Force Group One, China.*

The moon had gone behind clouds, it was dark, and
there was no one now to see me shivering in my wet
clothes, lost and crying. What had I lost? What was I
gaining? What lay ahead? A thousand miles in twenty-
two violent days through the heart of China with death
stalking us every step of the way to the southeastern coast
and now waiting for a rendezvous with my people. *My*
people? Hadn't I just left *my* people? Your *other* people,
a voice seemed to say to me. Why was I crying? Because
I had been involved in so much killing? You'll just have
to live with that. Can I? You'll have to. I'm afraid now.
Afraid of what? Of what they'll do to me. You've got another responsibility now. I know that. But there's
something else. Like what? I've learned something.
What? I don't know how to say it: a sort of discovery.
Mine. But I'm not sure what it is. What *is* it? I'm not
sure. Try. I can't. Yes you can, name it. I'm not very
good with words, I'm seventeen, I . . . *Name* it. It's just
that I've learned so much in the last three weeks.
Enough to last a lifetime. In a way it has been a lifetime.

Before words like *brotherhood*, *compassion*, *love*, were only words. Now I think I know what they mean. Not bad. What's the matter with that? But not just because the Dragon Lady and I . . . I know. It's more than that: there are Kim and Nancy and the baby I rescued. Anybody else? Gunny, Scotty, Audy, Charlie and John O'Malley. And many others. So what's the matter with that? I can't stop crying. Why bother? It can be good sometimes. You know, all these things I have trouble finding the words for, I learned from a strange people. I had come as a stranger and was made welcome. You are very fortunate: for that reason if for no other. Let not thy heart be troubled. The ancient comforting words. Touching the rosary. Sobbing softly now. Remember the miracle. I could almost hear her speak those words by which I would live. A sudden breeze chilled me, and then as quickly as it came, it died. Then there was no sound but the waves against the side of the boat as the current carried me to my mission's end.

I DON'T KNOW HOW LONG IT WAS before a powerful thrust upward broke the surface less than fifty yards off. Moments later, along the starboard side, I could make out the conning tower of a submarine.

Clutching my machine gun, I watched for the next several minutes as a small, dark shape bobbed its way toward me; and when it appeared alongside, I saw it was a manned rubber raft. Then through the darkness I heard a crisp American command: "Ahoy topside. Show yourself."

ABOARD THE SUBMARINE no one said a word, and I was hustled into a cabin. I saw a clean bed and a sink—everything spotless and in order. After a minute there was a rap on the hatch, and three men came in. One of them was an officer. I smiled at them. Nobody smiled back.

The officer asked, "Who are you?"

"I am PFC Lawrence Gardella, Special Force Group One, United States Marine Corps."

It's no wonder he stared at me, I suppose—ragged and bruised, with a string of green jade rosary beads around my neck.

"And just where did you come from?"

I'd been ready for that. "I'm sorry, sir," I told him. "I cannot say any more than that."

"Who else was with you?"

"I can't say that either, sir."

After staring for a second or two longer, he turned to one of the men with him. "Get this individual a bath and some chow. And some decent clothes."

Glaring at me now, he said, "I'll talk to you later." He wheeled and made his exit. The hatch closed behind him.

A couple of minutes later another sailor appeared.

"First a shower," he said. "Then some chow." He actually smiled; he seemed the friendliest of the lot. But I wasn't exactly getting a hero's welcome.

After my first shower in a month, I put on the clothes they'd left for me. They weren't a perfect fit but they were an improvement on what I'd been wearing. The same sailor was waiting to lead me back to the cabin, where I found a tray with soup, coffee and pudding on it. As soon as I'd finished everything, I slept—I don't know for how long. When I woke I couldn't remember where I was. As soon as I did, I stepped outside the cabin. Two sailors intercepted me. I said something about wanting to take a walk, and one of them said, pleasantly enough, "Sorry. This is a submarine, not an aircraft carrier."

"Okay then, how about some more chow?"

"Right away," he said. He seemed a nice enough guy. I went back into the cabin, sat down on the rack, started to doze and was almost asleep again when the food arrived: bacon and eggs, ham, pudding, coffee, milk and juice! I was halfway through when a couple of corpsmen in white coats walked in. One had a tray with some medical paraphernalia on it.

"Time for your shots," he said. "We don't know what you might be carrying."

I held out my arm for him to swab. They gave me the shots and were gone. The last thing I remember of my stay aboard the submarine is the sight of their white coats framed by the hatchway. From May 30, 1952, through the entire month of June, I was pretty much out of it, although I remember the voices I heard now and then. In particular, I remember a meeting with someone— someone very special. Before I put down what I remember of that, though, there are a few things I should tell you about the rest of my life.

16

My adventure in China lasted from May 9, 1952, when we were dropped in, until May 30, when I was picked up by the submarine—just three weeks. After three weeks of living so fully, it might seem that the rest of my life—twenty-eight years of it as I write this—has been dull by comparison. I think it's more accurate to say that I've lived two lives, almost as though I'd been two different people. My life since I left China has been enough like the lives of most people that a few pages are all I need to tell you about it.

On July 5, 1952, my mother came to visit me at the U. S. Naval Hospital in Annapolis, Maryland. She found me with my arms and legs bandaged, and was told that I had been hospitalized because of a severe allergic reaction to poison ivy in the field. This was, of course, not true. What those bandages covered, if they covered anything, were the various bruises, scrapes and scratches I'd acquired on the other side of the world.

About ten days after that visit, I was dismissed from the hospital. After another ten days, on July 24, I was honorably discharged from the Marine Corps. When my mother met me at South Station in Boston, she was clearly upset by the way I looked. And for a long time my refusal to talk about my experience in the Corps was both a mystery and a source of anxiety to her.

I didn't know what I was going to do with the rest of my life. I tried reenlisting as a marine and was rejected. I lived with my parents in Allston, about a mile from Harvard Stadium, and for months I kept to myself, drank a lot and worked at odd jobs now and then.

In the spring of 1953 I met Marie, who brought me back from the hell my life had become. I stopped drinking and found steady work. On November 21 of that year, when Marie was still only sixteen and I was one day short of my nineteenth birthday, we got married.

In 1955, the year I went into construction work, our first daughter, Susan Marie, was born. Our second, Janet Muriel, arrived three years later.

In 1958 I began moonlighting as a cab driver in Boston, working from five to midnight after an eight-to-four day in construction. I kept that up for years. I got my first assignment as a construction foreman in 1960, and by 1963 I was a general foreman—the youngest in our area, so far as I know.

Our grandson, Robert Edmund Storme, was born in 1974.

It was in 1977 that I found I had leukemia and decided to put the story of my China mission in writing. On May 31, 1979, just two weeks after the manuscript was sent to a publisher, I returned home from work to find my wife had been beaten, left bloody and dazed as though she'd been drugged. Nothing had been taken—none of Marie's jewelry and none of my collection of guns. The local police kept an eye on her all that summer.

On July 13, 1979, I had the encounter in Harvard Stadium with which this book begins.

Three weeks later, on August 7, our apartment was broken into and ransacked, though once again nothing was taken. In our bedroom we discovered several peculiar and frightening things. Marie's coat had been laid on our bed with the stuffing from a pillow inside the hood to suggest the shape of a human head, and with the right sleeve folded across the chest. My pistol had been placed where the hand would have been. The fabric of the coat had been ripped with a knife. And in a picture on the wall, a circle had been drawn around Marie's head.

Around this time Marie received a number of mysterious telephone calls.

I am as certain as I can be of anything, as I write this, that these incidents add up to deliberate terrorization with the purpose of scaring me out of having my story published. Just who was responsible, of course, I do not know.

Now let me go back twenty-eight years, to just after I left China.

17

On May 30, 1952, before I could finish the American meal I'd been served aboard the submarine, I was given a shot that left me drugged. I woke dazed and groggy. Again I didn't know where I was. When I tried to get up, I found that I was strapped to the bed, across my legs, waist, arms and chest. As my vision cleared, I saw the total whiteness of a hospital room. To this day, I don't know where that room was. It couldn't have been aboard the sub—the quarters were too spacious for that. Was I in the naval hospital at Annapolis or somewhere en route? Hospital rooms everywhere look pretty much alike. The two figures in white who were present were not the two corpsmen who had given me the shot.

One of them asked how I was feeling.

I said, "I've felt better. What's going on?"

"Take it easy," he said.

I noticed a pole with a bottle attached, and a tube from it leading to my arm. Never having seen such an apparatus before, I asked what the hell it was. The corpsman explained that I was being fed intravenously, because I'd been sick and in shock.

Then the second corpsman asked me a question: "How about the others?"

I looked at him. "What others?"

"Don't play games," he said disagreeably. "The others in your group."

I answered, "I'm not playing games. Find out for yourself."

While the men looked at each other, I began to wonder whether they were doctors at all. One of them came toward me with a syringe, and injected something into the tube leading to my arm. I remember that a kind of whistling went through my head. After that I lost track of things again.

Other things were happening as I drifted in and out of consciousness. Once I awoke and heard voices through a slightly opened door.

"How are they going to list the others?"

"Missing in action."

"The poor son of a bitch in there," the first voice said. "He should get a medal. Instead, he'll get nothing but a hard time."

"You think it's all true?"

"After what we've been giving him, it's got to be. It's a wonder he's even alive."

"That's for sure."

"The letter we found on him is probably what did it."

"Yeah. The blackmailing son of a bitch!"

I managed a hoarse yell, "They're not missing in action, they're dead! They're dead, you bastards!"

The two men came in, and I heard one of them mutter. Then I went under again.

I remember, another time, seeing three men standing over me while I tried to bring my eyes into focus and hearing one of them ask how I felt.

"A little bit groggy," I told them. "But okay."

"You've been through a lot," the same voice said. "Can you hear me? Can you understand me?"

I said, "Yeah."

"We want to send you somewhere. Somewhere in Asia."

I said, "Yeah, where?"

"Indochina."

"So I can be missing in action?" And they put me under again.

Then I remember waking in another hospital room. This time I wasn't strapped down. The sheets were crisp and smooth, and I was dressed in pajamas. I had a radio by my bed and there were flowers on the window sill. I swung my legs over the side of the bed and tried to sit up. Immediately I felt dizzy and my head began throbbing. A second later, the door opened and two civilians came in. One of them spoke softly. "You'd better get dressed. There's someone upstairs waiting to see you." He pointed to a corner of the room, where a set of marine tropicals was hanging.

I stood up slowly and carefully and managed to get into the uniform while the two men watched. I felt like an old man—weak and stiff and tired. The corridor into which I followed the two men was thronged with people in white. At least I really was in a hospital this time.

We got onto an elevator, and when its door opened we walked through a doorway and into a room with the shades drawn, with almost no light coming through. As my eyes became adjusted to the dark, I saw that several people were waiting.

A voice came from the far end of the room: "Son—"

Someone interrupted.

"John, leave this to me. Those ——have gotten us into this. Now let's see if I can get us out of it." The voice was snappy, and somehow it struck me as familiar.

"Son, we are . . . awfully sorry for what happened. Awfully sorry. May God help us all." The voice paused again, as though saying a prayer. "We know everything now, son. I didn't know before. I'm sorry I didn't."

"Didn't know?" I asked. "*Who* didn't—"

One of the others said, "Keep your voice down. Do you know who—"

The snappy voice with the familiar twang intervened again. "John, I told you to keep quiet!" Then, more calmly, "Son, there's nothing you or I can do about it now. It's too late. If you talk about what happened, what you did, you could start a war. You've got to keep your mouth shut."

As my eyes grew more accustomed to the semidarkness, I could see that the figure was short and blocky, and wore a square-cut, double-breasted jacket. As he moved, even in the dim light, there was a tiny glint of a reflection from his glasses.

The voice softened. "You deserve a lot but this country can't give it to you. It can't give you any medals, because all of this is going to be forgotten. None of it will be in the records. None of it will have happened. I'm not asking you to forgive *me*, I'm asking you to forgive our country. I found out about all this only by the grace of God. But I can make you a promise. This happened. It won't happen again. That's my promise. You have to make one in return."

"Yes, sir?"

"You must remain silent. Tell no one. I'm asking you to promise that for your country."

"Yes sir, I promise," I said. Then I asked, "Sir, what happens to me now?"

"You will be discharged for medical reasons. I understand you have a history of asthma."

"Sir, I have a favor to ask you," I began. Though what I really wanted to ask was to get back into the marines, I also knew there was no point in asking for that. So I said, "When I was picked up, I had on a set of rosary beads. They were very special. I'd like to have them back."

"John—" the short man said. He didn't have to say any more. He sounded very much the boss.

The man who had left the room was soon back. He handed something to the short man, who now walked toward me. The rosary beads were in his hand. I took them and thanked him.

Then one of the others drew up a shade, and there was no longer any doubt in my mind about who the speaker was.

"Son," he said, "I'd like to shake your hand."

The hand he held out was small but strong.

Before I let it go, I asked, "Sir, where am I and what day is it?"

"This is the U.S. Naval Hospital at Annapolis, Maryland, and it is June 28, 1952." Then, abruptly, President Harry S. Truman released my hand, wheeled about and walked smartly out of the room, with the others close behind him.

Two weeks later I walked out of the hospital, with the rosary beads in my hand.

Epilogue

Not all the questions you must have about the story I have told can be answered. For some of them, the reason is simply that I don't know the answer. For others, to give it would endanger the lives of others. But there are a few things that I can at least try to clear up, though they will raise further questions.

Why did I go back on the promise I made, never to tell the story? There are several reasons. One is that it was an old promise and the world has changed. I believe my experience has something to say to policymakers. And I now know that the government never really kept the promise that was made to that seventeen-year-old kid. My illness, my wife, my priest—all of them gave me the same message: that it was right to tell the truth about what I knew, regardless of how awful it might seem.

Where was President Truman on June 28, 1952? Could he have been talking to me in the hospital that day? A journalist who checked his schedule for that day found that he was in Washington and that no appointments were listed on his calendar. Annapolis, Maryland, is thirty-five miles from Washington, no more than an hour's drive away.

What do Marine Corps records say about me and the special force? That I never left the States, that the medical records of my stay in the naval hospital were destroyed by fire, and that there are no records that any of the men with me—Damon, Masters, Holden, White or Craig—was ever in the Corps.

What happened to my friends in China?

I'm happy to be able to say that as of the time I write this, Gunny, Charlie, Kim and the Mongol lieutenant are alive and well.

Audy is also alive, but has never really recovered from the wounds he suffered when we rescued the children from the village near Kenyu.

Nancy and Scotty are dead. Nancy was killed in a battle in 1954. Scotty, after surviving forty years of combat, died of natural causes in 1977.

God only knows where John O'Malley is.

I've also learned the Dragon Lady is alive, and has twin sons—*our* sons. They are big and blond, and as of the time I write this, they are twenty-seven years old. Some day before I die, I am going to see them.

May God give me strength, whatever happens.

PUBLISHER'S NOTE:

Lawrence Gardella died on Monday, February 16, 1981, as this book was going into production.

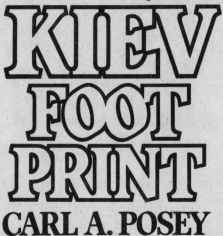

BULLETS OF PALESTINE

Howard Kaplan

A Kaplan novel is "an edge-of-the-chair, throat-grabbing page-turner! Accurate and terrifying."
—Gerald Green, writer, NBC's *Holocaust*

His name is Abu Nidal. A breakaway Palestinian known as the "terrorists' terrorist." An Israeli and a Palestinian join forces, despite the hatreds of their heritage, to eliminate this man. Will they ensnare Abu Nidal—or trap each other in a bloodbath of betrayal?

GOLD EAGLE